# Don't Stop Me

Eden Emory

*For those who like to call their MILFs daddy*

Don't Stop Me



*Cover design by Elle Mae*

*Edits by My Brother's Editor*

ISBN 979-8-9860203-9-6 (paperback)

ISBN 979-8-9860203-2-7 (ebook)

www.ellemaebooks.com

# Also by

**Eden Emory**

Club Pétale:

Don't Stop Me

Don't Leave Me (2023)

**Elle Mae**

Stand Alone:

Contract Bound: A Lesbian Vampire Romance

Winterfell Academy Series:

The Price of Silence: Winterfell Academy Book 1

The Price of Silence: Winterfell Academy Book 2

The Price of Silence: Winterfell Academy Book 3

The Price of Silence: Winterfell Academy Book 4

The Price of Silence: Winterfell Academy Book 5

Short and Smutty:

The Sweetest Sacrifice: An Erotic Demon Romance

Other World Series:

An Imposter in Warriors Clothing

A Coward In A Kings Crown

# Note

This is not your typical love story. This is a dark story with triggers such as blood, death, gore, BDSM, piercing, public sex, sex club, spitting, slight impact play, overstimulation, praise, degradation, cheating mention, drug usage and mention, dubious consent, coercion, sharing, and gun violence.

While they may get a happy ending these characters are flawed and far from perfect.

Themes: can make you come harder than he ever did , we shouldn't but like hell we will stop, sleeping with my boss , imma fuck you and your mom.

If this does not interest you please close the book now.

**For those who need resources:**

**National Suicide Prevention Lifeline**
988
https://suicidepreventionlifeline.org/

**National Domestic Violence Hotline**
1-800-799-7233
https://www.thehotline.org/

# Before you continue

This is not an accurate portrayal of the BDSM community, if you are curious and what to learn more please conduct your own research and do not rely on what you find in this book as accurate knowledge of the BDSM community, their etiquette, and their ways. Things in this book have been dramatized and are not an accurate reflection of reality or my personal thoughts and opinions on these matters.

# PROLOGUE

NYX

It's not every day that a nobody gets invited to New York's newest women-only BDSM club.

Yet the invitation to Club Pétale arrived in my email mere hours earlier with only two bright-pink words on a dark banner.

*Tonight 9 p.m.*

Club Pétale was known for its secrecy and had a thorough vetting process for all new and potential members. They had even given me the address only an hour before I was supposed to arrive.

I had been waiting in my shitty New York apartment, dressed in a skintight strapless black dress, kitten heels, and the required eye mask clutched in my hand while waiting impatiently for my confirmation text.

I wasn't *just* going there as a patron. I had a very specific goal in mind, and I was going to take advantage of the variety of services they offered. They may have been a club that held shows and allowed people the freedom to try and switch partners while they were there, but they also offered a type of matching for those who needed something a little *extra.*

And I just so happened to be one of those people who needed

a little more. On top of that, being matched was much less daunting than showing up to the house alone. At least I had someone waiting for me on the other side.

When I got it, I bolted out of the house.

"Are you sure this is it, miss?" the taxi driver asked, peering out at the well-lit multistory mansion that reached across the property in front of us.

To anyone else, it probably would have looked like some rich tech tycoon had moved out to the middle of nowhere and built the house of his dreams, complete with a sprawling stone walkway, beautifully trimmed hedges in the shapes of exotic animals, and trees that spanned stories tall and perfectly surrounded the house hiding it from prying eyes. But only a select few knew what really awaited us inside.

"Yes," I said, my voice clipped as nerves danced on my spine.

I gripped the hard mask with both hands. I had never had a chance to wear the beautiful contraption, not until now at least.

It was hard but lined with dyed black silk that felt cool to the touch. The edges of the mask and eye holes were bejeweled, and a beautiful sapphire sat right in the middle.

I had seen it once on a trip to my first ever high-class sex shop.

It had taken me months to get the nerve to walk in. Afraid that I would be seen by someone that I knew, but when I went in, I found myself unable to imagine how I ever stayed away in the first place.

And all of that... led to this moment right here.

"Thank you," I said after clearing my throat and casting a glance at the looming house in the distance. If I squinted, I could make out two large men in suits that guarded the front door.

With a deep sigh, I forced my stiff fingers to curl around the door handle and pushed myself out of the car. The small motion of simply walking forward had felt a thousand times harder as my mind raced through what was about to happen tonight.

I walked down the stone pathway, my heels clicking loudly

across the space. I had put on a coat before I left, but the chill of the spring night air still seeped into my bones.

As I reached the two men that awaited me, one of them cleared their throat and motioned to my face.

My cheeks flamed when I realized I had been so nervous that I had forgotten the most important part of the deal. With shaky hands, I tried to put the mask on but I found that my cold fingers would not cooperate.

"May I help?" asked a feminine voice behind me.

I jumped and turned to look at the new addition. To my utter horror, there were two of them, both already wearing masks.

The one who I guessed spoke was close to me, her hand stretched out. Her dark hair cascaded down her shoulders in dark contrast to her green silk dress. The girl behind her looked at me with an uninterested expression. Unlike her partner, she wore slacks with an unbuttoned shirt and a body chain underneath. Her dark hair was flipped out of her eyes and when I met her gaze, I flinched.

*I didn't belong here.*

"With your mask," she added after my hesitation and took a step closer.

I stood straight and handed it to her, not caring at the moment that my face was fully exposed to them. Even with the girl behind her glaring at me, I didn't see a need to fear them. Nor would I let my own weakness be so easily shown on my face.

Club Pétale said they strived for comfort, privacy, and freedom, which is how they came up with their rules. Every patron was supposed to follow them or risk being kicked out, or worse. It was no secret that behind these doors were probably the most influential people that roamed this city.

Why else would they have a need for such drastic measures? The NDAs alone were at least ten pages long, all their rules being a constant reminder and splash on every page you signed.

*Number one was masks, and I had already broken that one.*

"Please," I forced out.

She gave me a soft smile that caused me to breathe out a sigh of relief. I turned around, and she slid the mask onto my face before tying it.

"Is this okay?" she asked, pulling the strings a bit tighter.

"Perfect," I said.

The mask made the weight on my shoulders disappear. The mask was like an anchor, a comforting weight that tied me to the ground. There was still a buzz of nervousness flowing through me, but it now settled deep in my belly and turned into something like excitement.

"Good luck in there," she whispered and patted my back.

I turned to her with a smile and was about to say goodbye, but her partner interrupted me.

"*Jean*. We will be late for the show," she said and stepped forward to wrap her arm around the smaller girl's shoulder. The girl sent me a small, apologetic smile before letting her partner steer her into the house behind me.

The music from the inside was nothing more than a light background hum, but when the door opened, it spilled out into the night, jolting me from my trance.

I looked back to see just a glimpse of them disappearing through the doorway and then it was shut, leaving me standing alone in the cold air. Just like that, the wall was erected between me and the place again, but this time I had gotten a glimpse of what lay ahead, and there was no turning back.

*I wanted this. Needed this.*

Steeling myself, I walked up the steps to the door and nodded to the guard who moved to open the door.

The music blasted into the night once more, and this time, I was met with a warm breeze and the strong smell of floral perfume.

Inside there was a woman waiting in a skintight latex suit minus the mask. Her hair was pulled up into a high ponytail and there was an iPad in her hands, lighting up her face. She gave me a once over and a smile spread across her face.

"Name?" she asked.

"E-Elayne," I choked out, almost forgetting my own chosen name.

*Number two, fake names were a must.*

She nodded and turned back to her iPad.

I took my time to peer behind her and into the rest of the club.

*Club* was a loose term.

The inside *did* resemble a club. It was dark with dim lighting, and a soft glow from some of the neon lights littered the walls. There were some couches against the walls, and women were chatting and holding drinks. *That* part was very much a club, but the high ceilings, white walls with black dangling silk curtains, the hardwood floors that cracked under my feet all pointed to the fact that we were still in a house.

But even so, they managed to pull it together beautifully.

The atmosphere was comfortable and relaxing, and it caused my heart to pound in my chest.

I could only make out the few front rooms, but there were hallways leading to the back of the house as well that seemed to call to me. If I had been braver, I would have come here with no plan. Would have wandered the halls, exploring this new environment... but even what I was doing tonight was a form of cowardice.

*I just hoped it was worth it.*

"You're being paired tonight, is that right?" the woman asked, causing my attention to snap back to her. "Can you confirm your arrangement?"

"Yes," I said, though this part came out much easier. I knew what I was here for and if I backed out now, I may never get to experience this ever again. "Private room. Three-hour block with—"

"Ax?" the woman said, cutting me off. She looked up at me

with wide eyes and her face flushed when she realized what she had done. "Sorry. I just—I'm just surprised."

My own surprise unfurled in my chest, and I raised a brow at her.

"Is she not experienced?" I asked, suddenly feeling anxious about what I had put myself through. "I asked for an experienced partner, they said—"

"She is," the woman said quickly and typed on her iPad. "More experienced than most. She just never—"

Just then, a woman in nothing more than a tiny red bikini bottom and a black face mask in the shape of a bunny appeared.

"Ax has been waiting," the new woman said. "I have been sent to retrieve you."

The woman in latex shot her a look before meeting my gaze. It should have made me more nervous that this *Ax* person could evoke such a reaction out of people... but instead, it only made it all the more exciting.

I fished my phone from my pocket and handed it to the woman with the iPad.

*Rule number three, no phones.*

When she took it, I turned back to the girl with the bunny mask and nodded.

"Show me the way."

I waited outside the door to the room far longer than I should have.

My escort had long since left and I had just stood there, staring at the door as if it was going to magically open by itself, but alas, it stayed just as motionless as me.

There were people walking the halls behind me and entering the other private rooms. I heard them but didn't move my gaze from the door in front of me and the metal numbers that gleamed in the dull light.

*Room 63.*

With the last of my courage, I rolled my shoulders and grabbed the handle, and pushed the door open.

I was taken aback by how cozy the room was, even though I had requested it. It was small, with only room for a bed, a side table, and a small chest, and the door to what I presumed was the bathroom, but it was decorated in a way that kept the same seductiveness of the house.

A black duvet. Black curtains. The floor beneath my heels was a rich bloodred carpet that looked soft to the touch.

And in the middle of it all, taking off her suit jacket, was *Ax.*

I hadn't seen a picture of her at all during the time from my invite to now and a small part of me was worried that I would hate the person I was paired with... but she was *breathtaking.*

Her deep-blue silk button-down hugged her slim frame giving away just how toned she was underneath her clothes. As her lithe fingers folded her jacket, I caught a glimpse of dark tattoos that peeked above her collar and out from between where her sleeve and gloves met.

She wore tight-fitting slacks that made my mouth water and a sturdy belt that shone in the light of the room. She topped everything off with dress shoes.

The mask she wore was velvet and decorated with silver thread that was wound around the edges. The darkness of the mask brought out the honey color of her eyes.

Her tousled short brown hair *almost* matched the color of her eyes if not for the light-gray streaks that accompanied it.

*Fuck, she's hot.*

Even if I couldn't see her full face, I still got a good look at her full parted lips, her strong jaw, and her taut neck, which twisted to take me in as I entered. My eyes lingered on her before I stepped in and closed the door behind me.

"You're late," she noted, her eyes taking me in. There could have been a slight accent to her words, but I couldn't tell with such a clipped phrase.

My body heated as she devoured my frame, her eyes working their way up and down my body. But it wasn't scrutinizing, it was heated.

"It's my first time here," I said with a strange amount of confidence.

I should be cowering in front of her, should be nervous about what she was about to do to me. But there was something about *her*, about her aura, that made the room plunge into a comfortable warmth that felt akin to being dunked in a hot bath.

She was safe. She made *me* feel *safe.*

Her lips twitched, and she dropped her suit jacket on the chest before sitting down on the edge of the bed, the soft mattress bowing under her weight. Her legs parted and with one firm pat on her knee, I found myself walking toward her without even realizing it until I was almost to her.

When I was close enough, I held her gaze as I slowly lowered myself to the floor, my knees sinking into the soft carpet.

Her eyes widened and her mouth parted, surprised at my actions.

"Are you prepared, love?" she asked, her voice low.

The sultriness of her voice, combined with the slightly accented words, caused my skin to light on fire, desire coiling deep in my belly.

"Yes," I breathed and tried not to flinch as her hand came to cup my cheek.

Her hand, even through her glove, was warm, and I couldn't help but lean into it, butterflies dancing in my stomach as I did.

"No degradation, impact play, no piercing, no branding or marks of any kind—"

"Except from biting," I interrupted, unable to help myself.

In truth, I wanted all of that. I wanted to explore my limits and test every erotic service they offered... but not *tonight.* Tonight, I came here for a very specific reason.

Tingles shot through my legs, but no matter how much I wanted to move them, I kept still because even if they became numb or pained, there was one thing that I wanted far *more* than relief.

*It was her.*

Her eyes flashed and her lips quirked.

"You would do well not to interrupt me," she said, her hand trailing down my neck and to my bare shoulder.

I shivered as her soft touch sent shocks through me. Such a little movement but it held so much power. As if she was caressing me as if I was some prized possession or a *pet.*

"I'm sorry, Ax," I said quickly.

Her eyes flared at this.

"Sir," she corrected. "To you, in this room... I am sir."

I swallowed the lump in my throat. Arousal shot through me and my panties became uncomfortably damp.

"I'm sorry, sir," I said and looked down, feeling embarrassment rise in me.

Her hand gripped my chin and forced me to look up at her. She leaned in close, her delicious warm scent invading my senses.

"Don't be embarrassed, love. I am here to guide you through this," she said, and then surprised me by placing a kiss on my forehead.

Fire shot through me.

"I don't want to be a burd—"

"How many times have you come in one session?" she asked, interrupting me.

I stilled at her question and looked up at her. Her mouth was in a hard line.

"Session?" I echoed.

She nodded.

"By myself, I can usually get to four, but—"

"No more than that?" she asked, finishing for me.

I nodded.

"And with a partner?" she asked.

More embarrassment and shame filled me.

"Less than that," I answered in a whisper.

She nodded.

"You are aware that four would be unacceptable, aren't you?" she asked.

*Fuck.*

I nodded, feeling my pussy clench.

I knew going into this that this was going to be far out of my comfort zone, but I wanted this *so badly.* I wanted her to bring me to the edge over and *over* again until I couldn't think straight. Until I couldn't walk straight. I wanted to be thrust into a warm bath of pleasure only to resurface once I was totally and woefully satisfied.

Because no matter how many times I had made myself come, I always felt like I needed *more.*

"Say the words, kitten," she commanded and leaned back. The switch in pet name caused me to pause, especially with how much heat was behind it. She tugged at her glove, revealing heavily tattooed hands. Her knuckles spelling out a word I couldn't make sense of.

"Yes, *sir,*" I said.

She nodded.

"Safe word?" she asked and grabbed my wrist to pull me up.

"Pineapple," I said without hesitation.

She let out a full-blown smile.

"Perfect," she cooed and turned us only to make me sit on the bed.

She kneeled in front of me, much like I had for her, and her deft fingers found my heels and slowly took them off and placed them at the corner of the bed.

Her hands ran up the expanse of my smooth legs, her eyes following them until she came to the hem of my dress.

"If there is anything that I do that you don't like, say the safe word and we stop to reconvene," she said, her hands gliding across my dress and up my sides.

I was so entranced by the depths of her eyes that I almost forgot myself.

"Yes, sir," I whispered.

She leaned up, her lips brushing across mine. Her hands found the zipper on the back of my dress and she began to pull.

"I allow small touches, kisses, and the like" she murmured. "But for all intent and purposes I am no touch, do you understand?"

I swallowed the lump in my throat.

"Yes, sir."

She paused before letting out a breathy chuckle. Was my disappointment clear on my face?

Before I could say anything else her touch brushed across my bare back.

"May I kiss you?" she asked, her hands pausing.

"Please, sir," I choked out.

A wicked smile that caused my heart to stop spread across her face but before I could react any further, her soft lips were on mine and soon after, her tongue forced my mouth open.

I moaned into her as our tongues danced. Kissing her was as addicting as I had wished. She wasn't rough, but she was in control. She was overpowering everything, and I was so into the kiss and how it made my toes curl that I didn't even realize I was almost naked until I had to lift my hips for her to pull my dress up.

Then in an instant, I had been bared down to my underwear and only the mask that was tied on my face. But even then, I didn't feel ashamed or embarrassed, and whether that was the mask or the experienced hand of Ax, I couldn't yet tell.

"We will start simple," she said, pulling away, slightly out of breath. "Then onto bigger and bigger. You will tell me when you are ready."

I nodded and tried to go in for another kiss. She sent me a look.

"Yes, sir," I said quickly. She nodded and with a gentle hand, pushed me back onto the bed.

I sucked in a sharp breath when she tore my panties off and threw them over her shoulder. She placed a small yet sweltering kiss on my thigh.

"You tell me if I am too rough," she commanded and as if to prove her point, sank her teeth into my thigh.

I whimpered but spread my legs for her, nonetheless.

"As long as we stay in the perimeters, I welcome rough," I said, then cast my eyes down to her. Her honey eyes met mine though the lower half of her face was concealed by my mound. Her hot breath inches away from my aching clit. "*Sir.*"

Her eyes flashed.

"Is that a bit of a brat I hear in there, kitten?" she asked and leaned forward, her tongue running the length of my slit.

I let out a small, breathy moan and fisted my hands in the duvet.

"No, sir," I tried to keep my voice steady but when her tongue circled around my clit, I couldn't help but moan.

"You're so sensitive, love," she said, her voice filled with amusement. "Are you always like this?"

I wanted to say *no,* but the words were caught in my throat as her lips covered my clit and she began sucking. She pushed two fingers inside of me, and I cried out as I felt the sharp bursts of pleasure soar through me.

*Experienced indeed.*

Her touch felt like magic and *her mouth.* God, her mouth was positively sinful. Every touch, thrust, and suck felt like it was throwing me violently into an orgasm I hadn't even seen coming.

It hadn't been too long since I had forced myself to come again and again on the vibrator I kept in my nightstand... but *this... this was...*

"Fuck," I cried out as I clenched around her. My hands flew to her hair and my hips bucked in tandem with the thrusts of her fingers. I was going to come faster than I had before by anyone's hands or mouth.

A part of me was scared that she would stop. Was scared that she would disappoint me like the rest.

But she didn't.

She kept going until I was crying out and coming around her fingers. And then when she was done, she forced her fingers into my mouth to suck them clean.

She watched me with hungry eyes as I hungrily devoured my own release off her fingers, and then she popped them out and raised a brow at me.

"More?" she asked.

"I beg you, sir," I breathed and pushed up onto my forearms. "*More.*"

"*Little kitten,*" Ax sang. "You forgot your counts again."

I let out a weak moan and reached down to spread my pussy lips for her. My aching and swollen clit lit up as my fingers brushed across it.

"Eleven," I said and arched back into the pillows as the vibrator came in contact with my clit again.

"*Eleven?*" Ax teased. "Is that all you can handle?"

A chorus of *nos* came from my mouth, but it was cut short as she turned the vibrator setting up.

It was torturous being with Ax, in the best ways of course. I have never been with someone that so completely understood my body in the way that she had. The entire time she had been a comforting and calm force that brought me over the edge more times than I had ever been in my life, though for her, this was like child's play.

I didn't have it in me to feel embarrassed or ashamed by how easily she made me cave to her. All I could focus on were her soft taunts, her steady hands as they spread my legs.

It was a perfect first time with a pleasure domme. *She* was perfect.

A part of me wanted to delve more into the dark side of the things that were listed in her profile. The bondage, impact play, shock play, *knife* play... but I wouldn't get ahead of myself.

Not when she was taking care of me just fine.

I was so overstimulated at this point that I couldn't even speak as the orgasm ripped through me, only letting out weak sobs.

"Twelve," I sobbed, and for what felt like the first time in a long time, the vibrator was pulled from my swollen clit.

I let out a loud exhale, feeling my body turn into jelly and sink into the bed. I didn't have the strength to peer up at her.

Cold air hit my swollen pussy and I let out a cry. I pushed myself up on shaky arms to look at her between my legs, a devilish smirk on her lips.

"Your cunt is so beautiful like this," she said and leaned forward to kiss my clit. "I wish I could keep you here forever, love. Tie you to this bed. Make you come till the only name flowing out of your lips is *mine.*"

She bit down on my tight bud before climbing up on the bed and over my naked, sweaty frame. She hadn't so much as shed a single article of clothing besides the gloves, and as much as it pained me not to touch her, it made everything more erotic.

The feeling of the metal buckle of her belt sliding up my sensitive skin caused me to shiver, and I leaned up to capture her mouth but instead of the hot passionate kisses that we shared, she gave me a single peck.

"It is time to focus on our aftercare, or I am afraid we will not have adequate time for you to process this," she whispered, her eyes trailing to mine.

The warmth in my body froze, and slowly, I came back to myself.

Somewhere along the way, I had lost myself. Time was irrelevant, and so was the fact that I would be leaving this comforting space sooner than I would have liked.

*This was an arrangement. Nothing more, nothing less.*

My pride told me to skip the aftercare, but my mind knew that if I did, I would probably end up a crying mess.

The tears were already threatening to come out in my semi-disillusioned state.

"Can you hold me?" I asked, my voice weak.

She smiled and kissed my nose before twisting us so she could spoon me. I kept my eyes on the wall, even as I felt her tug at her clothes. Her strong arm wrapped around my waist and pulled me to her. I was so surprised by the sudden warm skin-to-skin contact of her chest on my back that I let out a small gasp.

She didn't say anything, so I relaxed against her, enjoying the warmth of her skin. If I had paid attention carefully, I would have felt the beat of her heart against my back, but mine was still beating rapidly in my chest and overpowering my senses.

She left a heated open-mouthed kiss on my back.

"You did very well for your first time," she said. I could feel the smile as she spoke against my skin and it caused my chest to flutter.

"I don't think I could have asked for a better partner," I said and reached down to intertwine my fingers with hers. She froze for a moment before chuckling.

"Don't flatter me, love," she said, though her tone had lost its teasing tone.

I swallowed thickly.

"The girls at the front seemed surprised you had a..." I paused, not knowing what to call myself.

"A client?" she supplied.

I nodded.

She left another kiss on the back of my neck.

"They talk too much," she muttered. "Maybe I need to find new staff."

Panic caused my throat to tighten, and I turned to look at her. I had long since gotten used to the masks that covered our faces, but now I wanted more than anything to see what lay beneath hers.

"I didn't mean—"

"I'm joking," she said, though her tone was forced. "How are you feeling? Do you need anything?"

I shook my head.

"Nothing..." I trailed off. "But is it too much to ask you about yourself?"

Her eyes trailed my face, and she was silent for a moment. The air between us thickened, and I found myself quickly becoming choked because of it.

The tension and electricity came back tenfold.

"If it is within reason," she said. "What is it you'd like to know?"

Nervous shivers played at my spine.

"You're very... experienced," I noted. Her eyes widened and there was a delightful twitch of her lips.

Her hands came to grab my hips and pull me closer to her before they looped around me and began rubbing my back. I positively melted at her touch.

"I am," she said. "Before the club opened, I had been in the *scene* for a while. Though they were right to say I don't normally take a client."

"Why me?" I couldn't help but ask.

"Why not?" she asked. "You're a beautiful woman, Elayne."

I pursed my lips to stop myself from correcting her and giving my full name.

She let out a light chuckle at my expense.

"When they told me what you were looking for... I found myself intrigued," she admitted. "Quite tame compared to my normal, but it became clear very quickly that... we work *well* together. It can be difficult to find someone you meld with."

Her lips pushed into a thin line and her eyes hardened.

"Thank you," I whispered, feeling as though we had already overstepped one of her boundaries.

"Go shower," she said in a soft tone. "I'll pour you some water while you are in there."

I nodded and moved to get up but her strong hand on my chin stopped me.

"Your words," she reminded.

"Yes, *sir.*"

# Ax

I didn't pretend to be a good person.

I had limits and I would put my family above all else, but my personal life was just that.

*Mine.*

Mine to do what I wish with and I always found it a bit more interesting to delve into the *darker* sides of society.

It had started innocently enough. When I was fresh out of college, I worked a normal job waiting tables, but I had been very particular with where I chose to work. I found the highest-class restaurant that would accept me and once I got the hang of it made some connections with the regulars... I just followed the money.

And wouldn't you know it, my next job was right in the middle of the most volatile and high-risk places I had ever been. But, boy, cozying up to men with guns and pockets lined with dirty money sure did have its perks.

After that, it was history. It took over fifteen years for me to be able to branch out on my own and start to do the things I had always dreamed of, but it was worth it.

And the extra cash after years of working in the dark wasn't too bad either.

"This is shit," I growled, crinkling the obviously fake money in my hand.

The paper was cheap and even though the picture on it looked immaculate, there would be no way something as disappointing as this would ever make it through a machine.

I threw the bill at the man across from me. His face had paled considerably and his hands gripped his suitcase for dear life. I should have known by the cheapness of his suit that his money would be subpar.

What the *fuck* was Jonson thinking sending this piece of shit to me? Did he want this to blow up in his face?

The lackey shifted in his seat, his eyes darting toward the window where outside was a somewhat busy New York side street. I had made sure to skip all the main streets and rush hours. The less I am seen with him, the better.

The limo was cramped and I could smell his sticky, gross sweat. I raised my brow at him and crossed my legs.

"Anything to say for yourself?" I asked.

His Adam's apple bobbed as he looked back at me then out the window again. With a loud sigh, I reached over and locked the door, causing him to jump.

I pulled out my phone and dialed Jonson's number. He picked up on the second ring.

"I will have your delivery boy gutted," I said and kept my eyes on said man as he scrambled to try and pull at his door.

"Not mine," Jonson said with a tone that caused my jaw to tic.

"You insult me," I said, eyeing the boy.

He looked to be in his midtwenties. I didn't like to kill young people, but he was testing my limits.

He fell to the floor of the limo, getting on his knees. His grubby, sweaty palms pulled at my slacks.

"Please," he begged. "They sent me here. I didn't have a choice, ma'am. Please—"

I shut him up by grabbing his cheeks with one hand and squeezing so hard the pitiful human let out a whimper.

"I handed you a diamond in the rough," Jonson said. "A little friend of ours said he would be of good use to you."

*A friend.*

Jonson was as dirty as they came. He had a comfy job in the FBI and had ties to every and all types of illegal activities you could think of. He liked to think he had power, but the power really came from the various people that contracted out his services. In turn, he kept his position and got a payout every now and then.

I had a few ideas where this fucker came from, but why the hell—

*Christ.*

"I understand," I said and hung up and shoved the boy away from me. "You're lucky."

I knocked three times on the window, and the divider that separated me and my driver rolled down. He turned to me, his scarred face shining in the light. His pale-blue eye narrowed in on the man on the floor then to me.

*Yvon.*

He had been with me for years. I had met him in the same dangerous environment I had wormed myself into but they had no problem carving up his face and leaving him half-blind and bleeding out in the kitchen. I took him in from there and never looked back.

He had been with me through all the ups and downs in my life and had never betrayed me. It was hard to find that type of loyalty in this business.

"Drop him off in Ryder's territory," I said and cast a glare at the boy. "Go into all Laundromats, mom-and-pop diners, *fuck*, hand that shit out on the street, and then disappear if you know what's good for you."

He gave me a panicked look then shot a look back to Yvon

who gave him a smile, showing off his broken teeth. The boy's panic-stricken look was almost laughable.

"You—you don't want it?" he choked out.

I shook my head.

"You should feel so lucky that I didn't want that money," I said and moved to leave. "If they ask who it's from, say it's from Ryder."

"Call me when you are ready," Yvon called.

I nodded and stepped out of the car. The air had a slight chill to it, but nothing unbearable. The cold actually helped calm the raging storm inside me.

Ryder was a small-time gang leader that had pumped the streets full of his weak drugs and forced each and every shop in the area to pay him an exorbitant fee to keep them "protected," though the only person who fucked with civilians was Ryder, none of the bigger players would dare.

We had standards, after all. And that included not fucking with civilians or getting them addicted to whatever dirty drug we came across.

It wasn't the first time he had tried to mess with my business, and it wouldn't be the last I fucked with his. Just that week, I had already tipped off multiple police in his area and led them to one of his *many* drug houses. I had no idea how long he had been around, but in recent years he had become a pain in my ass. I would have to reach out to some of my contacts and see what we could do to get him off the streets for good.

I walked down the familiar street, not even casting a look back at the car. Looking at my watch, I realized that I had spent far too long with that joker. If I didn't hurry, I might have missed the best part of my week.

I took a sharp right at the corner of the street, almost bumping shoulders with someone. I ignored their shouts and headed toward the bakery I knew was less than a block away.

I had known this bakery for years, and it was one of the few places that I had frequented that wasn't any closer to Club Pétale.

It had been the only thing I could afford at one point and the owners had been so nice to me that I made sure to repay it when I came into money.

Unlike Ryder, I didn't have to threaten people. They came to respect me, and when they earned my respect back, I would treat them like family. That included a fully paid-off store, and in return, they washed my money for me.

But that's not the reason I came today.

I slipped through the back door, nodding to the various employees that were in the back baking various pastries and getting ready for the day.

They were due to open in ten minutes and I needed to make sure I was in my place before the first customer came in.

Stalking toward the manager's office, I knocked twice, and the door swung open to show a smiling woman. Her age showed through her gray-streaked hair and loose skin, but there was a glow about her that made anyone in her vicinity do a double take.

"All ready for ya," she cooed and opened the door for me before sending me a wink.

I smiled at her and stepped through the door, sitting down on the creaky desk chair. The door shut behind me with a soft click and I scooted closer to the upgraded TV I purchased for the security cameras.

It was high definition and showed all parts of the bakery, but I made sure to double click on the camera with the view of the register and door. I sat forward as I saw a familiar petite figure outside the bakery windows.

My heart skipped a beat and when the elderly shop owner opened the door for her, I couldn't help but lean forward to take a closer look.

The black-haired, dark-brown-eyed woman that had been consuming my every waking moment stepped in and sent a beaming smile to the shop owner. Today her hair was pulled up into a messy bun with just a few strands framing her face and showing off the newly purple-dyed ends. She wore a baby-pink-colored sweater and jeans that hugged her form.

She held a tote bag in her hands, one that I hadn't seen before, and two cups of iced coffee. I watched her hand one to the shop owner and I had to force myself to stay seated.

This woman, *Elayne,* who had left the club promising to be back only never to return again, angered me and intrigued me all at once.

It had been pure luck that I found her again. I was here visiting when I saw a flash of black and lo and behold, it turns out my little *kitten* came here once a week to stock up on bread and have a chat with the shop owner.

Which happened to be right in the middle of my territory and a place I frequented. It was all too coincidental. Or maybe it had been a gift from the gods.

If they still existed after all this time. Maybe they had taken pity on me and decided to brighten up my life a bit.

*God knows I needed it.*

It was embarrassing that I had gone to such lengths to see her again, but I still had limits... which included not going into Club Pétale's system and pulling all her information so I could stalk her for real. It wasn't the stalking that I had a problem with, *obviously* I had been doing this for months by now... but I couldn't risk compromising our business.

We were in the business of secrets and private lives. The people who came there wanted to live out their wildest fantasies, and we let them. There was always something we asked of them as well though. Whether they were politicians, drug lords, art dealers, or even the FBI, they all knew that in return, they would be indebted to us and at some point, we would call on them.

So no, I couldn't cross that line. Not if it meant destroying the sanctuary we had built.

So I settled for Sundays at the bakery.

They leaned against the counter, chatting happily. Elayne mentioned her big win from work, something about signing on a new client. I leaned forward, trying to get any information about her company or anything that would give me any smidge of a detail that I could use to find her, but she kept it vague.

I had thought to corner her in the bakery once or twice. Maybe stage it as an accident, but every time I looked at her... there was something inside me that held me back. I tried not to think of the dread I felt when I made the move to open the door to walk out there, but each time my hand settled on the cool doorknob, I had been snapped back into my body, and for the life of me, I couldn't figure out how to move.

I wanted to feel her again. I wanted to hear her moans and taste her. I wanted her to call my name as I fucked her. I wanted to be the one talking to her about her job. Sharing a coffee with her... but I just couldn't.

She had started something inside me that had been buried after so many years... and it excited me as much as it scared me. A part of me didn't want to chance anything with her. She may have shown up at the club once, but this wasn't her normal life. *I* wasn't a normal part of her life.

And with a business like mine where things are settled with bullets to the head...

Like I said, I wasn't perfect, but I had my limits.

When Elayne left, I moved to leave too, only to run into the shop owner's husband. He gave me a toothy grin, he had long ago figured out what I had been doing in the room and took every moment he could to tease me about it.

I allowed him to. He reminded me of my own father in a way. His face was tanned and wrinkled from years of working in the sun, his hands were shaking but when they clapped my arm, they held a power to them.

"When are you going to stop hiding behind a screen?" he asked. "You know that you—"

"I won't be here next week," I said and shot a look toward the front of the shop. If I leaned forward, I might have been able to see the shop owner enjoying her coffee but I refrained, worried that Elayne may have still been lingering outside the shop.

If she had, I may just lose control for real this time and follow her home.

"Business trip?" he asked.

"A wedding," I replied and gave him a smile. "My niece."

His face lightened and he clapped my shoulder. "Congrats! Do you have a cake yet? I'm sure Judy would—"

"No no," I said quickly. "Don't worry about it. Too late of a notice and too many people."

His face fell slightly but he still nodded.

"Take care, Ax," he said. "Don't get too caught up in work. You are not as young as you used to be."

I tried not to outwardly flinch but he must have seen my distaste for his comment with how his lips twitched.

"I have people killed for a comment like that," I said in a light tone, though I was being completely serious.

He let out a booming laugh.

"Get out of here," he said through his guffaws. "And don't come back until you're ready to talk to her."

I rolled my eyes and left without another word, pulling out my phone as I walked and called Yvon. I prayed he'd get here before the tightness in my chest disappeared and I had the urge to chase after her.

After I told Yvon to come get me, I quickly dialed Asher's number. It rang far too long before he picked up.

"Sounds like you are avoiding me," I remarked before he could even mutter a hello.

There was a light chuckle from the other side of the phone.

"I've been busy," he said and let out a sigh. "What's up?"

"I can't call my son to just talk?" I asked. My chest tightening when he didn't answer right away. It had been distant between us for the last few months. He hadn't liked it when he learned of my latest business venture.

He had an idea of what I did. After all, it was hard to hide where the money came from when he literally grew up under my roof. But drugs, murder, and arms dealing didn't seem to bother him.

It was the BDSM club, of all things.

"You usually call me when you want something from me," he said. "Or lecture me about my life."

*He wasn't wrong.*

"The wedding is next week," I said. "I sent you an invite, but I wanted to remind you and... ask that you bring your girlfriend."

It was the only thing I got out of him during our last talk. I had been worried that he hadn't been taking care of himself, that he was off doing god knows what... but his response was that he was busy and with a *girlfriend,* no less.

There was another pause.

"The one you mentioned last time..." I trailed off.

*If you are still with her,* hung in the air unsaid, though we both knew what I was asking.

"Sure," he said. "I'll ask her. We are... more settled now. It would be good for us."

Shock ran through me.

"Perfect," I said. "I'll see you—"

My voice died when he abruptly hung up on me. I tried not to let it bother me, but it still stung.

*Hannah would have been so disappointed.*

I shook the depressing thoughts out of my head, and Yvon pulled up to the curb right in time.

*I had more pressing things to worry about.*

# NYX

There is one thing I never really understood about myself.

And it's why I *always* had to let toxic people back in my life.

First, it started off small. Like accepting a friend back after a big fight even though you knew they were spreading rumors about you behind your back.

Then, it got bigger.

Like giving a situationship one *too* many chances.

Then it turned into allowing my mother back into my life.

And now...

Now, I was face to face with my toxic ex-boyfriend in a situation I never would have expected.

"Asher," I warned and crossed my arms over my chest.

I felt uncomfortably bare in front of him. I had been caught off guard when he showed up at my house at seven a.m. on a Saturday. I was normally an early riser, so the time didn't bother me so much as the fact that he was *here* and interrupting my carefully crafted routine I had built for myself in the four months we had been broken up.

I only had a second to pull on a cardigan to cover up my thin tank top and shorts. It had been getting warm in New York, and I had taken the liberty of opening up my windows and allowing the fresh air inside before it got too hot.

And he had ruined my perfectly peaceful morning.

"Nyx," he said with a smile pulling at his lips.

He leaned in my doorway, his body towering over mine. His dark-brown hair had been trimmed on the side, keeping the middle long, which he had slicked back. He was dressed in clothing that was far too dressy for his casual wear.

The Asher I knew loved tight-fitting T-shirts, jeans, and tennis shoes... here the same man was with a white button-down, slacks, and dress shoes.

*It smelled like trouble.*

He looked good, better than before, but I knew no matter how dressed up he was, he was still an asshole underneath.

"I made it clear—"

He cut me off by shushing me and taking a step forward, the toe of his shoe passing over the threshold into my apartment.

"I need just a tiny favor, please, Nyx?" he asked, pouting.

I gritted my teeth and my grip tightened around the door's handle.

*I should slam this in his fucking face.*

Asher was... a playboy by all intents and purposes. He knew he was attractive and used it to get his way. I hadn't seen it at first but after four months and a sneaking suspicion his late-night "business meetings" had nothing to do with his work, let's just say I caught him in a rather compromising position when I decided to visit his work one day.

*At least his secretary has a good pair of tits on her.*

"Get the fuck out of here, Asher, before I scream," I growled. "Ms. Pruitt isn't a fan and you can bet she has been waiting to see you in the back of a cop car."

His face twisted and as if on cue, the familiar sound of a door unlocking sounded and I peered around Asher to see the familiar elderly lady open her door.

Ms. Pruitt had been here since the eighties and was the first to invite me over for a beer and a microwave pizza when I moved in and ever since, I reserved a weekend meal for her. She *loathed* Asher.

But to be fair, she loathed any handsome man that had too much pride.

She cocked a perfectly drawn-on brow at us and brought a lit cigarette to her lips.

"He bothering you, sweet cheeks?" she asked and exhaled, her smoke traveling across the small hallway.

Asher visibly frowned and his eyes narrowed in my direction.

"Just talking," he said, throwing a smile over his shoulder.

She glared at him. "You think I'm stupid, boy?" she asked and ran a hand through her white curly mane.

Asher turned back to me and leaned forward, his body heat and scent invading my space.

"Get rid of her," he commanded.

I rolled my eyes and moved to shut the door, but his strong grip stopped the door in its tracks.

"Asher, I'm serious—"

"Visit any *clubs* recently, Nyx?" he asked in a low voice.

My blood froze and my heart began pumping wildly in my chest. The world around us fell away and suddenly, it was just him and I.

His lips twitched.

"I don't—"

"You just signed Anneu, didn't you?" he asked.

I should be jarred that Asher knew so much about my work life even after we had been broken up for months.

Anneu was a client that I had been trying to get for almost an entire year. They were fresh and new, but boy did they know how to handle the youngest generation. Their success skyrocketed, and every company was aching to be a part of it.

The one I worked for included.

I was a design manager at a smaller firm and had recently signed them after many unsuccessful attempts and my boss had *finally* recognized my work and promised a big promotion at the end of this quarter.

And that promotion was the only thing between keeping me in this shitty place and actually affording the life of my dreams.

When I didn't answer, Asher continued.

"How would your company like to know they hired a sexual deviant and not the sweet innocent woman you pretended to be?" he asked.

I had to bite down on my cheek to stop from snapping at him.

For most places of work, I don't think his threat would have held any weight... but for my company *and* Anneu, they had a strict honor code and a brand to uphold.

It would *ruin* me if they found out I had gone to the club.

Before we broke up, I had introduced him to the BDSM world. He quickly took to ropes, spanking, and degradation... but he wasn't in it for the pleasure.

He was in it to take advantage of my state and hit me where it hurt, then turned around and cheated on me.

"You don't have any proof," I spat.

His eyes widened and he stood up straight, then pulled out his phone from his slacks. Before I knew it, an image of me in my skimpy dress and maskless face was thrust into my face. I remembered this moment.

It was the moment I was so nervous and in awe of the place that I stood there, *like a dumbass,* with my face uncovered outside a fucking sex club.

"How did you—"

"Not important," he said and pushed past me.

This time, I didn't have the will to stop him.

Ms. Pruitt gave me a look, but I gave her a smile and began to close my door.

"If he's not out in twenty, I'm breaking down that door myself," she called out just before I shut the door.

When the door clicked, I let out a sigh and steeled myself before turning around to face Asher.

"Do me a favor and I will delete the picture," he said, his eyes flitting down to the phone he was still holding in his hands. I hated the heat in his eyes as he looked over the photo.

"What is it?" I asked.

"A wedding," he said, finally tearing his eyes away from his phone.

"You are blackmailing me because you need a date?" I asked, my voice rising.

Asher crossed the room. I took a step back, hitting the door. He came to stand in front of me and leaned down, almost as if to kiss me, but he stopped short.

"I told my family I was settled down with a *nice* woman who I planned to commit to," he said and my heart lodged in his throat. "You are the only person that fits the bill and is *believable.* Though I wished you wouldn't have dyed your hair."

His finger twirled a lock of my black hair.

"Just tell them—"

His hand tugged on my hair, cutting me off.

"A week in Connecticut," he said. "You will meet my family first, *they insisted.* Then we will go to the wedding, put on a good show, then you are free to go fuck the rest of the goddamn city if you want to."

His insinuation hit me hard in the gut and white-hot anger flared through me. There was a lot I could overlook, but his insults hit deep. My mother, before the incident, had been a devout Christian and had pushed her purity cutter ideals on me. It had taken so long for me to break out of that and I didn't need *Asher* to come here and fuck that up for me.

"I have work," I said through gritted teeth. Asher gave me a look that told me he didn't believe a word that I said and the excuse would be enough for him.

*Fucking bastard.*

"Get dressed in that blue sundress, pack *appropriate* clothes, grab your computer, then get in the fucking car," he growled.

He reached behind me and jerked the door open, sending me flying into him. He pushed me off and left my apartment, leaving me in a cloud of my own shame and pity.

It didn't help that I could feel Ms. Pruitt's gaze on me.

*Damn it.*

After thirty minutes of packing, getting ready, and frantically trying to send a coherent email to my boss about time off, I finally met Asher down in the parking lot under the apartment building.

He scoffed when he saw my suitcase and motioned for me to put it in the back, though he didn't offer to help. I didn't expect much from him anymore though. When I had first entered into this relationship, I had high hopes. Asher had put on a good show when he showed up at my company's annual party. He put on a kind, charismatic front that reeled me in right away, and it took me far too long to see through it.

"Almost three hours," he said as I sat down in the passenger seat of his car.

I was never a car person, but I knew enough to understand that Asher was showing off his wealth. This was the third Porsche I have seen him drive and was relieved to see this one was all black exterior and interior instead of the god-awful red he had chosen last time.

The inside still smelled new and the leather seats squeaked as I shifted to buckle my seat belt.

"Good to see you upgraded," I commented, unable to help myself.

He let out an annoyed huff.

"Sugar to the tank requires some drastic measures," he said, sending me a look. "Thought I might as well upgrade after you gave me such a golden opportunity."

While I was dreading having to meet Asher's family, I was curious to see where the money stemmed from. He may work a well-paying job, but it was obvious that he came from money from the moment I saw him.

It was something in the way he moved, how he talked to you. Even when he was dressed in jeans and a T-shirt, they somehow looked like they had been perfectly tailored to him.

And after a while, I realized *he did* have his entire wardrobe tailored to his size.

But if Asher was *like this...* then it meant that his family couldn't be any better.

Asher was strangely quiet on the drive, choosing to let the soft pop music that was playing on the radio filter through the car instead of talking. It put me on edge. Because if Asher was quiet... it meant he was worrying about something.

I had only seen him like this one other time, maybe a week before we had broken up. I had found him sitting on my couch watching infomercials at two a.m. I had been awoken by the loud sounds from the TV, only to be scared shitless when I had seen Asher sitting there with a blank expression and his hands balled into fists.

I never was able to reach out to him during that time, and he tried to brush it off the next morning, but in that moment I started to see right through him.

"You're nervous for me to meet them," I said as he pulled off the freeway and into a town called Fairde.

The roads were wide but the town itself seemed small and mostly made out of run-down mom-and-pop shops. Large trees with small white flowers bloomed on all sides of us, making the place look absolutely magical. There was a calm and lightness to this town that seemed so far removed from the bustling city we had just come from.

Even with the situation at hand, I felt the worries and panic leave me. A week here didn't seem so bad anymore.

If I wasn't here with Asher, I might think this place was a dream come true. I would love to imagine myself walking down these roads, maybe with a dog, greeting the shopkeepers, then coming home to a sprawling house with a wraparound porch.

It was as simple as that.

I wanted a simple, easy life... even if my sex life tended to delve a bit darker than that.

"I'm not nervous," he scoffed. When I looked at him, the lie was obvious on his face. He had gone pale and his hands gripped so hard on the steering wheel that his knuckles turned white.

He turned down a windy road and we sat in silence for the last ten minutes it took to drive there. We stopped at a black metal gate that slowly opened for us as we pulled close.

Behind the blooming trees and gate was an incredibly gorgeous multistory home that looked like it literally came out of my dreams.

Ever since I was little, I had wanted a house like this. The large windows, white trim, and a delicate light-blue coat of paint on the outside. In front was a winding driveway and a fountain with cars already parked near it.

"You're fucking *filthy*," I gasped and looked toward Asher, who had a small smirk on his face. He obviously took that phrase with a double meaning.

"My *mother* is the one that makes the money," he confessed. For the first time that day, his voice lost its harshness.

"And your father?" I asked.

His eyes met mine for just a split second before he pulled into the driveway and parked the car.

"Don't have one," he said, then leaned close, his hand clasping on my upper thigh.

I wanted to feel disgusted by his touch, but in all honesty, I had missed the touch of another. It had been months since we broke up and months since I visited the club where I met a woman who turned my life upside down.

Since then, I hadn't dared to go back or to find another.

Chalk it up to my own insecurities, but I couldn't deal with possibly not seeing *her* again. All I could think about was the way her chuckle caused my insides to warm. The way her hands caressed my body.

*It was just sex,* I had tried to tell myself over and over again... but when I replayed back that night, I couldn't help but think that something else had been boiling beneath the surface from the moment I walked into that room.

The weight of Asher's hand on me began to feel heavier as though it was reminding me that no matter what, no one would live up to the expectations Ax had created.

"Should I stray away from that topic?" I asked, my voice weak.

He kept my gaze before shaking his head and letting out a huff of laughter and pulling away.

"She adopted me, Nyx," he said. "My mom is gay."

And without any other explanation, he left me in the car.

*Gay?*

I was pulled out of my shocked state when I heard Asher get my suitcase out and open my door.

Unbuckling my seat belt quickly, I stood and tried to grab my stuff from him but he held tight.

"We have an image to uphold, Nyx," he said. "Try not to be difficult."

Anger boiled through me and I was about to finally snap at him, but a noise caused us both to turn toward the house.

A woman wearing a loose T-shirt and jeans left the house and my heart skipped a beat when I got a better look at her.

Dark-black tattoos covered her arms, hands, and chest. She had light-brown hair that shone in the light with golden-honey eyes that matched.

I had dreamed about Ax. About what she would look like under that mask... but I never came close.

*I have to be fucking dreaming.*

"Ash," she called and waved us over.

Even from a distance her eyes ran over me, causing heat to explode inside me. My face flushed and I turned, hoping to hide myself.

"Be there in a minute!" he called and intertwined his fingers with mine.

His once warm touch now burned and I cursed myself for letting him talk me into this.

*But how the fuck did he know her?*

A sudden realization hit me so hard it felt like I had been doused in ice water.

*She couldn't have been the one to leak my photos to him, could she?*

"Whatever you do," Asher whispered in my ear as he pulled me toward the house. "Don't call her ma'am. She hates that. Just call her Axelle, or Ax."

*So much for it being a fucking dream.*

When we reached the front steps, I finally had the courage to look up at her and I was stunned. She looked far more beautiful than I ever imagined. Her full lips and jawline had given me some hint, but goddamn, those cheekbones and the way her wavy hair framed her face should have been fucking illegal.

Her eyes widened just a fraction but then she cleared her throat and a breathtaking smile spread across her face.

"Nice to meet you," she said, stretching out her hand. A rush of air left my lungs.

"Nice to meet you too," I said and extended my sweat-coated shaky palm to hers.

Her skin was just as warm as I remembered it and her grip just as strong.

"This is Nyx," Asher said, cutting through my haze. "My girlfriend of seven months and counting."

Her grip tightened and her jaw visibly ticced. She kept the forced smile on her face but dropped my hand like it burned her.

"Nyx," she said, her eyes roaming my frame. "So this has been the young woman that has been keeping my son in line."

There was a moment of silence before the ringing in my ears started.

*Son.*

*Her son...*

Horror so potent seeped into my bones and my stomach twisted so painfully it took all that I had not to keel over.

Asher was *her son.*

*Ax's son. The person who had...*

"Nyx," he said, shooting me a smile. "This is my mom, Axelle, but you can call her *Ax.*"

*Jesus fucking Christ, I was fucking cursed.*

# Ax

I didn't like the word "*workaholic.*"

It made it seem like an addiction, a compulsion disorder.

For some people it may very well be, but for me... I'd like to think it came from the need to provide. The need to break out of the cycle that kept my family in a choke hold for their entire lives and their children's lives as well.

But it was all in an effort to make sure that there was one day that I didn't have to work. One day where I could take the property in Fairde and retire there. Maybe I would go back to New York for the club, but I didn't want to ever go back there again if I had a choice.

*So why was it so damn hard for me to distance myself from it all?*

For *hours* I had been itching to go to my computer, or to check my mail on my phone.

I have worked out.

Prepped the chefs and staff before letting them go early.

Showered.

Dressed.

Fuck, I even made a pitcher of lemonade.

But I still found myself sitting on the couch of my living

room, the French doors open to the backyard and letting the breeze in. The sweet smell of the blossoms filled the room and it should have been easy to lean back into the couch and just... *stop.*

But I couldn't.

And fucking Asher was supposed to be here any moment but he had yet to show up.

Just as that thought entered my mind, I heard the sound of the gates opening and a car pulling in. I shot to my feet embarrassingly fast and speed walked to the front door.

My mind was whirling with thoughts. I wondered who he had brought. If she and he were happy.

I wondered if this would be the thing to mend our relationship. I had even promised myself that I would go easy on her knowing that I had given Asher's friends the third degree one too many times when he was younger.

But *this* was different. He was sharing a part of his life with me. It may have been a small part... but it was *something.*

When I walked outside, I saw them parking and Asher helped the noticeably petite feminine figure out of the car. I quickly tried to straighten my shirt and prepared a big smile for them.

"Ash!" I called and waved them over.

When they turned toward me, my heart dropped. My mind had to have been playing tricks on me.

Suddenly all of the excitement and nervousness of seeing Asher mixed with the hope of fixing our relationship fizzled into thin air and dread replaced it. Dread with powerful, unrelenting anger. Each step they took toward me felt like it was moving at a snail's pace, and the words coming out of Asher's mouth sounded like they were underwater.

I was thrown back into my younger body. The one full of anger at the world. The one that saw everything that happened to them as unfair. The one who hadn't yet lost everything that they have loved.

I had hurt people then and people had hurt me. It was a cycle and I thought that if I settled down, lived the life I was supposed to with the family that *I* wanted, that maybe the world would have forgiven my previous transgressions and I would *never* have to feel this way again.

But the universe had showed up on my doorstep with a big fat *fuck you* wrapped in a sinfully beautiful baby-blue sundress and perfectly kissable lips.

*Elayne.*

Or now, better known as *Nyx.*

The person who was currently holding my son's hand and looking like I had just punched her in the gut. The person who I had been watching from the bakery's camera for months with my son nowhere in sight.

*This was to punish me.*

All the instincts I had to run after her and force her back to my side came back like a tidal wave, and it took everything in me to stay planted on the ground. I wanted her, but I was furious. The universe had sent her here *with him* to show me just how much I had fucked up in my life.

I had gotten too comfortable. The darkness came too easily as of recent. I was getting sloppy and this was my big fucking reminder that I should have tracked her down from the very fucking beginning.

Nyx, goddess of light and daughter of chaos. Perfectly described the mindfuck that had just been delivered to me. It was far too easy to remember the way she writhed under me as my hands and tongue explored her body. Remember the way she tasted, the way she smelled, the sounds she made as she climaxed—

*Jesus Christ, get a hold of yourself, Ax.*

I was torn between an undeniable surge of rage that lit up inside me at the understanding that my son's girlfriend had come to Club Pétale to get fucked into submissive oblivion while she was *still* with Ash, and my own desire for her.

Seven months. Seven *fucking* months. Three of which I had been stalking her and imagining all the ways I could fuck her.

If there was one thing I knew, it was my son and he would *never* agree to associate with anyone in our scene. When he found out the type of business I was in, he had made it clear that he had never wanted to talk about it, never wanted to hear about it, and never wanted to see it. He had even gone as far as to ignore me for a whole six months when he found out.

So why *the fuck* had she gone there? And why the fuck didn't he know about it?

My own desire for her couldn't even be dampened by that realization because being with her... it had been everything. The way she submitted to me without any hesitation. The way she had reacted to my touch. It caused the obsessive beast in me to latch on so tightly that I couldn't even sleep without the sounds of her moans floating through my mind.

I had been disappointed when she didn't come back, but now I understand why. Everything from then was now all too clear and I felt... betrayed.

How could she do this? To me? To *Asher*?

"Cheryl won't arrive for another day," I said in a clipped tone and motioned for them to follow me through the house.

I tried my best to keep my gaze on Ash but I couldn't help but feel pulled to the little vixen he kept by his side.

"My cousin," Ash supplied to her, a smile stretching across his face.

She sent him a forced one and my anger roared to life.

*This was the woman he had said he settled down with?*

A part of me wanted to tell him. To spill everything I knew, but... how could I? How could I tell him that I had fucked the only girl he had ever brought home and the only girl he had dated for longer than three months?

Whatever it was she and I did together was *nothing compared* to what Ash had to be feeling for her.

He had been a quiet, reserved kid because of what happened to his mother. He had been young when she passed, but it left a mark.

On both of us.

I tried my best to raise him, but there was a hole where she should have been and I could see it more clearly after he hit puberty. He distanced himself from me, from everyone. So for him, this was a big thing... and I couldn't ruin it, no matter how much I wanted to.

I brought them through the main corridor, our shoes squeaking against the marble as we walked through the house. It felt odd bringing a stranger into this house with pictures of Ash and me splashed all over the walls and between the decorative paintings we had scoured the globe for.

Like Ash, I was a private person. This was not a space I allowed people in, even if it wasn't my main residence. I liked to keep my life private and having her here...

I shook my head and pushed through the house, bringing them to the large open French doors that looked out to the acres of land we owned. The land, littered with apple trees, had a hollowed-out middle and in the center would be the perfect place to hold Cheryl's wedding. The trees were still in bloom, the once wild grass had been mowed and now held over two hundred seats, a gazebo which would soon hold hundreds of roses, and a stone dance floor that I had made for her off to the side.

It was perfect, the wedding I had always dreamed that I would have. I imagined my wife and me dancing under the moonlight as the slowly dying flowers fell all around us, music flowing in the air.

But that would never happen. The world had made that clear.

Nyx gasped from behind me. I turned to look at her, my eyes narrowing. Her brown eyes widened, and she tried to take a step forward, but Ash held tight to her hand. My eyes followed the action and I glanced at Ash who had his lips pursed into a thin line.

"It's beautiful," she breathed, her eyes darting toward me. "I didn't realize that you would be having the wedding in your own backyard. It's such a beautiful space."

I *hated* the way her flushing face caused my stomach to clench. My desire was potent and all I could imagine was her bent over my knee as I pummeled that ass of hers until it was black and blue.

"Yes," I said and looked back to the white trees. "It was a lot of money."

Ash cleared his throat, bringing my attention back to him.

"Are you hungry, Mom?" he asked. "I was going to take her to Lucinda's."

Nyx had the audacity to look ashamed when he called me mom.

"I ate already," I lied with a smile. I had been too nervous to eat and there was no way I would be able to sit with them at a table. I needed to get a grip on myself. "I'll take your stuff to your old room, I'll have one of the staff hang your clothes."

"Just hers," he said and handed me the suitcase. "I didn't bring any. I'm sure the ones I left are fine."

I wanted to drop the suitcase on the ground as soon as those words left his mouth. The seemingly harmless chunk of plastic becoming something vile and disgusting. All the obsession and desire I had been feeling for her turned into something sour.

I hated that a thing that once brought so much life into me had been changed so horribly.

*Karma was a fucking bitch.*

"Enjoy yourselves," I said through gritted teeth and had to watch as my son led Nyx off with a hand far lower on her back than I felt comfortable with.

*I fucking hate this.*

I didn't hear them when they came back in.

I had taken to exercising my anger out, running on the treadmill until my legs felt like jelly, then sitting in the sauna until my mind went dizzy. The whole time I was trying to think of the best way to get out of this, or at least try to avoid them as much as possible.

The problem was that I wanted more than anything to spend time with Ash. He hadn't come to visit in many months and I wanted to try and repair the relationship I had broken all those years ago. I had thought this wedding would be a good chance. Getting the family together, celebrating something that was worth celebrating. Drinking until we couldn't walk straight and laughing until the sun rose... but how could I focus when all I could think of was bending his sweet little girlfriend over the nearest counter and making her weep for me like she once had?

*I'm sick in the head.*

I was so disgusted with myself that I had to brush my teeth in the gym bathroom to get the sour taste out of my mouth. When I pushed myself out of the bathroom, my hair soaked with sweat and in only a sports bra and gym shorts, I froze when I saw Ash and Nyx down the hall.

I stepped back into the enclave to the gym entrance and held my breath, my heart pounding in my chest. Their hushed voices flitted down the hallway and the image of Ash pushing her back against the wall flashed through my mind.

I couldn't help but peek around the corner. Anger exploded in me when I saw Ash grip Nyx's chin and force her to look at him. The movement was possessive and controlling, and I hated that it was him that was doing it and not *me.*

*What was he doing?*

Before he could say anything and before I could think anything else of it, I walked out. Their eyes snapped toward me and Ash removed his hand as quickly as he had put it there.

"You're back," I said and looked at the smartwatch on my wrist. "It's a bit late though."

Ash shrugged and buried his hands in his pockets. "Just wanted to show her around."

I nodded, trying to remain impartial as I felt the heat in Nyx's stare hit me head on. Though I couldn't tell if it was hate or desire in that moment.

"Join me for a drink?" I asked and ran a hand through my hair.

"Sure, but you better shower first," he said, his tone teasing. "You will start to smell soon."

My lips twisted into a smile.

"No matter how bad I smell, I will *never* smell as bad as that time after your football—"

"Don't," Ash said, a surprised chuckle coming out of his lips.

My heart burst when I heard it. It had been too long. A knot formed in my throat, making it hard to swallow.

I cleared my throat and gave him a forced smile, keeping up the act.

"Afraid I'll embarrass you, hmm?" I asked, then turned down the hall. "Meet me outside in twenty."

After I was showered and in a clean T-shirt and joggers, I made my way down to the first floor. Ash was waiting for me on the side of the house that overlooked the valley behind. It was out in the distance, barely visible, but we had long since used this as a place to watch the sunrise.

Even if our relationship had faded over time, there was no forgetting just how close we had been growing up.

I never had a plan to wait for a partner for a child. Even before Asher's mom, Hannah, came into my life, I had been planning on how to create a family for myself. I knew what I wanted, I had the money. There was nothing holding me back. So when Ash and his mom came into the picture... everything just clicked into place.

He was so similar to me in many ways, even if we were not blood related. The way he was quick to anger, the teasing cockiness to his voice, his drive for perfection. Though there were many things we differed on.

He may have had a drive for perfection, but he certainly acted as though he had all the time in the world. He had a job, but only after I had pestered him. He had a girlfriend, but this was the first time he was able to keep one for so long. His apartment was paid for by me, but even after everything, he seemed to lack the closeness to family that I had.

Though we had grown up in entirely different circumstances, so I couldn't blame him. My older sister and I had been forced to grow up fast. Our parents were immigrants and worked themselves to the bone to keep a roof over our heads, so we learned very quickly that money was everything.

But not Ash... because of my dirty money, he had always had a large home. The newest and best clothing. Trips to Rome, Singapore, and India for summer vacation. He never had to want for anything, that's how I wanted it, but I am afraid it made him too comfortable with the money.

And too blind to what it took to get it.

"Where's your girl?" I asked, walking over to the metal chairs and table.

He had changed into more comfortable clothing, a tank top and sweats, and looked out over the land. There was a garden off to the side that was in full bloom. Sweet floral scents filled the air and for a moment, even if Nyx was here, I was glad that I had this with him. He sat alone with a whiskey in hand, my own waiting for me on the table next to him.

"She's tired," he said, an edge to his tone.

*I am sure she is,* I internally scoffed. Tired of trying to keep up that double life she was leading. Tired of lying to her boyfriend of seven months. Tired of lying to *me.*

"How did you two meet?" I asked and sat down in the chair next to him. I tried not to make it too obvious that I was prying, but there was a burning need to figure out everything and anything that I had missed.

I had the resources to look into her, but I wanted to do this right, and for once, I regretted doing things the legal way. If I had hired someone to find out about her or even peeked at her file myself, maybe I would have found this out sooner. After all, how did she hide him? And how did she hide her interest from him?

There were so many questions, none of which were appropriate to ask.

The air was cooling, and we sat in comfortable silence. The sky was darkening already, and the stars were starting to peek out in the sky. We were far enough from the city that there was little light pollution, and it was perfect for stargazing.

"On an app," he said and took a swig of his drink. "Like most people nowadays."

I nodded and took a hearty sip of my own drink. The burn acting as both a grounding and punishment.

"Why didn't you bring her the last time we met?" I asked, raising a brow at him.

The last time we met was a week before I found that very same woman in my room.

He frowned.

"I didn't know if it would work out," he said, his eyes flashing toward mine. "You know how I am with girls."

I swallowed thickly.

"It must be serious if you are bringing her here," I said.

He sighed and looked up at the sky.

"I did tell Aunt Cyrille that I would," he said with a grimace. "As soon as you told her I was bringing Nyx, she called me and wouldn't stop talking until I *promised.*"

I cringed internally. I was more relaxed when it came to pushing my son into special expectations, and while I hoped for him to settle down, at the age of twenty-six, I didn't expect him to have any part of his life together. I knew that he and I had different expectations, and even though I was around his age when he came into my life, I knew we were not the same person.

Cyrille, my older sister... was different.

At age twenty-seven, she had three children and had been married for eight years. Her husband made good money, provided a life for them, and even helped out the club with our taxes. She had made choices for her life that reflected the dream life she wished she had. A big house, a full and happy family, and just enough money to live comfortably.

I was... hungrier than her.

As soon as I turned fourteen, I started working, and when I graduated from high school, I enrolled in the closest community college and worked my way through two years there. Then an additional two years at NYU before graduating from their business school, all while working under the careful gaze of the most dangerous men in this country. I took every opportunity that I got and stained my hands before I even knew the real meaning of life.

But I did it because I had a goal. I knew one day I wanted to be here, with my family. I wanted to provide and end the cycle that we were thrust into. And I did. I wasn't a good person, but I was proud of what I had accomplished.

"Are you happy?" I asked. I had lost my strength to continue drinking, and my abandoned whiskey sat on the table. The sourness I had brushed away earlier came back full force.

"I think so," he said.

The urge to tell him overcame me. I straightened my back, feeling a nervousness come over me. If I didn't do this now, while we were alone, there was no saying what would happen. And if my sister got a whiff of this—

I shuddered, thinking of what she would do.

That woman was a bloodhound when it came to secrets.

"Ash," I said, trying to keep the shake out of my voice. I could face anything, do anything, and not be fazed, but telling him something that would tear us apart forever was the scariest thing I had done to date. "This girl, Nyx—"

He let out a loud groan and shifted in his seat, the screeching of the metal against stone filling the silent air. I sat there frozen, watching as he fumed in his chair.

"I knew you were going to say something," he said, his tone hard. "Can't you just let me have this?"

"Ash," I chided, shocked at his sudden tone shift.

I had been a tough parent, I knew that. Growing up, I had wanted the best for him and for our image, so it required a hard hand. But that didn't mean that I was one to lecture him over nothing, and that was definitely not the way I was going to go with this.

"Don't *Ash* me," he said, his voice dripping with malice. "I did what you and Aunt Cyrille asked of me. I brought home a girl. One that is beautiful and fits your high standards, and you still *sneer—* "

"Ash," I hissed. "I have never pushed my standards onto your girlfriends. This isn't about that, it's about—"

"You hated her from the moment she walked in!" he exclaimed and stood abruptly, causing the chair to be thrown back to the ground. "Did you ever think that there was a reason why I never brought my girlfriends around you?"

His eyes were burning into me, and they caused a vile shame to waft through me.

*Say it,* my mind commanded. *Tell him you fucked the one girl he brought home. The one girl he thought important enough to stay with after so long. Tell him, ruin it, just like you ruin everything else.*

"Ash, I never meant to—"

"There are a lot of things you never meant to do, *Mom,*" he growled and let out a frustrated sigh. "I'm going to bed."

"Ash, wait," I said and stood. "Let's talk about this. I don't want to fight with you. Not like this and not now."

He rolled his eyes and walked toward the house, not listening to my pleas.

# Nyx

When Asher came back into the room, he was pissed. More pissed than when I told him at lunch he could go fuck himself.

It hadn't been the best move, but I was pissed as well. He can't just blackmail me and expect me to just go along with it. Especially after I found out who his mom was.

Staying here would be the end of me, and what I had done was going to be thrust into everyone's face. I was partly ashamed and embarrassed, even if I tried not to be. And on top of that, for my *job* to be on the line made the whole thing even worse.

He stormed into his room, his eyes landing on me immediately. I was in his bed, scrolling through my emails and praying to God that my boss had been kind enough to give me the week off, but he still hadn't checked his email yet.

It was a comfy bed, and his room was immaculate. No doubt because of the cleaners they hired. The Asher I know would *not* have had beautifully placed curtains, satin sheets, and a duvet cover that felt like pure magic. Even with his money, I doubted that he had a care as to what this room looked like.

But no matter, if I had to hide out in this room for the rest of my time here, at least I could be comfortable.

"What's up with you?" I asked with a raised brow.

He slammed the door behind him and started peeling off his clothes.

I scrambled up the bed and held the blanket close. When I was packing earlier, I only had a few minutes to decide on what clean pajamas to wear and my choices were limited, so I was left in shorts and a particularly thin top, far too little clothing for my liking.

Especially when I had to sleep in the same room as my ex, who was now getting naked.

"I don't know how you fucked it up but my mom already hates you," he growled and pulled down his pants, leaving him in only boxers. He walked over to my side of the bed and grabbed hold of my wrist to pull me to him.

Once upon a time, I may have found this anger in him hot. I would have wanted him to turn this into something more and use it to fuck the living shit out of me... but now it scared me. He wasn't the Asher I had known back then. There was something else behind those eyes, and I didn't know what he was capable of.

He had already tried to blackmail me, for god's sake.

"Don't," I hissed and tried to push him away, but he only used my struggles to push me back into the bed. His eyes were lit with rage and his grip on me began to hurt.

"You had *one job,*" he said in a low tone. "*One* job to impress my family so they will get off my back, so tell me, what the fuck did you do to piss her off?"

"I didn't do anything!" I cried, though I wonder if he, too, felt the lie.

Ax looked at me like I was nothing more than a disgusting whore because in her mind, that's what I was. Her own son had told her that we had been dating for seven *fucking* months, which would mean that I went to Club Pétale while I was with him.

It was a lie. Asher and I knew that, but *Ax* didn't. And she may never know if Asher's plan goes through.

He loosened his grip on me but didn't let me up.

"You better convince the rest of the family, or you can be sure that you won't have a fucking job when you get back, and you'll have to move in with that fucked-up mother of yours."

His words caused a panic to run through me.

When we had dated, I was open about my wish to have no contact with my mother. I had even divulged some things about my past that I hadn't before because he had seemed so understanding... how *dare* he use this as ammo?

"You're evil," I hissed, anger boiling under my skin. I wanted to claw at him, but I settled for a glare.

He smiled at me and stood up, looking down on me as if I was nothing more than a worm.

"You're lucky I'm not asking for anything more, though if you prove to be just as useless, I may just have to change my mind," he said without another glance back at me.

After many hours of trying to sleep next to a snoring Asher, I found myself slipping out of the room and down to the living area to catch a glimpse of what I couldn't when I was in between two of the greatest mistakes of my life.

The living room was almost pitch black, except for the light of the moon that shone through the French doors. The white trees beyond had turned grayish from the moonlight, and there were small balls of lights that I hadn't seen before intertwined with the seats and aisle.

Even in the darkness, it was stunning.

The house, as extravagant as it was, held some comforting feeling that Ax had exuded in the club. It was warm here and felt safe... until Ash reminded me of why I was *really* here.

It could have been a safe haven. A chance to rest before going back to the stressful life that I had been living. I tried to find comfort where I could, but that didn't mean my life was any less hard than it was.

I felt like him bringing me here and shoving this in my face was just another way that the world was getting back at me for my crimes lifetimes ago. I don't know what I had done in my lives previous to this, but *holy shit,* had I pissed off the universe.

"I hate him," I whispered to myself, feeling tears prick my eyes.

I meant it too. Hate was not a word to be used lightly, but I meant it. I *hated* him. Just as much as I hated my mother.

I jumped when a warm hand wrapped around the back of my neck. It took me all but two seconds to realize it was Ax's, but the momentary dream of her and I being alone again was shattered when she pushed me against the French doors.

The cool glass against my cheek felt like a slap to the face, but the way her hand gripped my hip and pushed it into the door caused heat to pool in my belly. She was close. So close I could feel the outline of her body brushing across my back.

Far too close for anything good to happen.

"What the *fuck* are you doing here?" she asked, her lips so close to my ear that I could smell the alcohol on her breath and feel the heat of it waft across my face. Her tone was harder than I had ever heard it and completely shattered the image I had of her before this.

She was not the soft domme that had shown me what my body was capable of. She was hard and sounded like she didn't give two fucks about what had gone down between us.

"I couldn't sleep," I confessed. "And I just wanted to—"

Her hand slid up the back of my neck and to the hair at the base of my skull before yanking my head back. A low groan left my lips, and my heart stopped in my chest.

Her hand on my hip tightened, pulling at my loose shirt and shorts. The action was so little, but the feeling of being at her mercy had already sent my body into overdrive. My nipples hardened, and I knew that if she hadn't seen them already from her position, she would notice soon.

"I mean, why are you *here* in *my* house with *my son,*" she growled.

I swallowed thickly. There were so many ways to answer that.

"It's not what you think—"

She pulled harder on my hair. This time the position became painful, but it became the last thing on my mind as I felt her lips brush across my neck, sending hot shivers down my spine only to pool in my belly.

Every touch from her did things to my body that should have made me ashamed. I couldn't even conceal my reactions at this point. It was indecent. *Wrong.* Especially when her *son* could walk in on us at any moment.

The worst part... is that a part of me *wanted* that. I was pissed at Asher, rightfully so. And while I didn't want to anger Ax, I wanted to get back at Asher. That, obviously, wasn't the only reason I would have let Ax fuck me into oblivion, but it would be the sweetest type of revenge.

*If only my job wasn't on the line.*

"You're saying you didn't spread your legs for me while you were dating my son?" she asked, her harsh tone sending shivers up my spine.

"No, I—"

"So he is lying to me?" she growled.

Panic gripped hold of me, causing me to freeze. "It's complicated, listen—"

"What's making it *complicated* is that I cannot tell my own son that his girlfriend spread her legs for me like a little *whore* only for her to come back and ruin everything for the both of us," she said, her breathing becoming erratic. "Is that why you are here, hmm? You have come to tempt me, further push the divide you caused between my son and me?"

White-hot shame flooded me at her words. I knew I wasn't in

the wrong here, but I couldn't possibly tell her or else Asher would leak that photo of me. But that's not what shamed me.

It was the way *little whore* flowed so smoothly out of her mouth and caused my pussy to clench. I loved when she gave me pet names, but *god* did I crave her anger.

"You're full of yourself," I said with a scoff. There was a jolt of excitement that ran through me when her hand shifted, her fingers brushing across my bare thigh. "Me being here has nothing to do with you, and I'm telling you I may be a lot of things, a *whore* even... but I am no cheat."

She paused, then slowly, her hand slipped under my shirt. I gasped when she made contact with my stomach.

"Such a dirty word from that sweet little mouth of yours, *kitten,*" she said in a husky voice.

I let out a whimper.

"I bet if I slip my hand in your shorts, your cunt is going to be wet for me," she said. "Shall I check and see?"

*Fuck.*

I nodded, unable to force the words out.

Ax let me go with a noise of disgust and put space between us. The absence of her heat hurt more than the shame that flooded through me.

She turned me around, her hand firm on my chin and forced me to look into her eyes.

"You don't deserve my son," she spat.

I glared at her, anger pushing away all the arousal she had caused inside of me.

"So then who do I deserve then, hmm?" I asked and fisted my hand in her shirt, pulling her closer to me. "Certainly not his *mommy.*"

Her nostrils flared.

"If I had any less shame, I would punish you for those words," she growled. "Bend you over a table, fuck you until you couldn't stand straight, hell I'd probably get my friends on it too so we could laugh about how much of a *whore* you are after we were finished, but I—unlike you—have some shame and am not foaming at the mouth trying to get fucked by anyone with two legs."

Her words turned me on and simultaneously hurt more than I'd like to admit. I wasn't the problem here. It was her and her fucking psycho son.

"Listen, *mommy,*" I said, putting extra emphasis on the word that seemed to get her so angry. "I don't want any of this, nor do I want your fucking son. Now either fuck me or let me go back to bed and sleep until this fucked-up wedding is over and I can go *home.*"

She leaned forward, her breath wafting across my lips. I parted without thinking, and she smirked.

"I wouldn't fuck someone like you ever again, even if you paid me," she growled. "Don't think I will choose a piece of ass over my son, and I can't wait until I tell him how much of a whore you really are."

"Do it," I dared. "Tell him how many times you fucked me. How many times that mouth of yours licked my pussy. Tell him that his own mother made me come more times than he ever—"

Her hand clamped down on my mouth.

"You *do* have some brat in there," she said. And then, the next moment, her hand slipped past my shorts to cup my bare pussy.

I let out a gasp as two of her fingers pushed through my wet folds. She circled my clit before plunging them inside of me. I moaned against her hand, the muffled sound shattering the silence in the room.

The once cold window became so hot it felt like it was being branded into my skin.

"Is this what you wanted?" she asked and used the heel of her palm to massage my clit as she began to fuck me with her fingers.

I spread my legs for her, my eyes almost rolling into the back of my head when she added a third finger, stretching me deliciously. I nodded and moaned when she slipped her fingers out of me, only to plunge them back in, but harder and deeper this time.

This wasn't the Ax I knew. This person was angry, and as she picked up the pace of her fingers, I learned that she was brutal too. Her movements were rough and hurried. The sound of the heel of her palm snapping into my clit echoed throughout the living room, and the wet sounds of her fingers thrusting into me over and over again plunged me closer and closer to the orgasm I had been longing for.

"You have me deprived," she hissed. "Sick and twisted in the head. Since I saw you in that fucking sundress, all I wanted to do was push you onto a table, pull that dress up, and lick that sweet cunt of yours until you were coming all over my face."

I moaned at the image of her doing exactly that as it flashed through my mind. I imagined her back in her button-down and slacks, pushing me down onto a table and burying her head between my legs. I wanted her to show me exactly what she had last time. Make me submit to her in ways I never dreamed of. But this time I wanted the anger. I wanted to push her until she was positively feral with rage.

I clenched around her and an evil smile spread across her lips. Without warning, she pulled her fingers out of me.

My cry could be heard cutting through the silence of the room.

"It's disgusting how much I want you," she said. "But I have never been one to tolerate brats."

*Not so fast.*

I don't know if it was the way she talked to me or all the shitty things that had happened today, but I got the courage to pry my fingers from her shirt and push them into my shorts.

She watched me with heat flaring in her eyes.

When I circled my swollen clit, I jerked against her hold. It would be easy to make myself come like this, with her watching me. Her strong scent had engulfed us and the remnants of her brutal touch lingered.

The thought of coming undone in front of her had been a

part of my late-night fantasies for the last few months and I didn't even think twice about rubbing hard circles on my clit.

"Are you really going to make yourself come, *whore?*" she asked, her voice still had an edge to it.

I whimpered and nodded before pushing one finger inside of me and using my thumb to circle my clit.

"Let me see," she commanded.

Without a moment of hesitation, her hand reached to the hem of my shorts and yanked them down. She sucked in a hard breath of air and her tongue came out to wet her lips.

"Do you want to taste?" I asked, breathless.

Her eyes snapped back to mine and the air between us became electric. For a moment, she looked as though she might drop to her knees right then and there, but that would have been too easy.

Her hand left my neck and she took a step back.

"No," she growled. "This has gone too far."

"Ax—"

She turned on her heel and disappeared down the hall, the muscles in her back bunching and her hands balled into fists.

I was left in the dark, with my hand still in my sopping-wet pussy and bared to the world. Shame, embarrassment, and anger flashed through me all at once.

*Fuck you.*

# Ax

I was fucking disgusting.

The water around me had long since turned cold, and I knew at any moment, my beloved older sister would be on my doorstep, and she would sniff out what was happening right away.

She would notice my tense muscles, the bags under my eyes, and most of all, she would see the absolute vixen on my son's arm.

*Nyx.*

She liked to act like she was an innocent girl. She had the whole look going for her. She was petite, barely wore makeup, wore those obscene *fucking* sundresses and walked around like she didn't know that everyone who was attracted to women was eye fucking her.

But inside... I knew the *real* her.

I knew the dirty and ugly parts that she didn't want to show anyone else. I saw her longing. I saw how she lost herself in the throes of pleasure riding wave after wave until the mattress was soaked.

I saw the fire inside her, even if she kept it at bay. I saw it tearing up her insides and threatening to explode. All she needed was a perfectly timed *push.*

*Like last night.*

"Fuck!" I growled and swiped my hand out, catching the many bottles of hair and body products, sending them clattering to the floor.

I had been in the shower for so long I had lost track of time. It could be eleven a.m. or p.m. and I wouldn't even have known the difference.

I had been tormented all night by images of her and how perfectly her lithe fingers fucked that dripping cunt of hers.

She was out of this world.

I'd had my fair share of women. Whether they were from the club or throughout my travels, I didn't have a problem with any of them. And none of them made me as crazy as she did.

But I waited like I was supposed to. I didn't give in to my urges to follow her home or force her back into the club. I was *good,* and *this* was how the world had repaid me.

*I don't want your son.*

"Then why are you with him?" I muttered and pitifully started to clean up my own mess.

After I had left the shower and dried off, I looked at my terribly worn-out face in the mirror, wishing that I had listened to my instincts and stayed away from her.

There was a light knock at my door, tearing me from my brooding.

"Mom," Asher called from the outside. "Aunt Cyrille is here. I'll take them out to the garden and have the chefs get some sandwiches started."

"I gave the cooks the weekend off," I called back. "To prepare for the wedding... can you manage?"

He paused outside, then in a low voice, he said something, but I couldn't make it out. There was another light shuffling and my chest tightened when I realized it was probably Nyx out there.

"We got it," he called, then I heard the sound of his feet against the floor outside.

I cursed.

Ash was a lot of things, but a cook was not one.

I rushed to dry my hair and put on something presentable. Today would be a light-pink button-down and slacks. It was my normal outfit when we had company, though I wasn't really paying attention to anything other than the thought of Nyx waiting for me.

And the threatening cloud of doom that hung over me when I realized that I would at some point have to tell Asher that I was knuckles deep in his girlfriend last night.

With a sigh, I pushed out of my room and walked the way to the garden, dreading every second. When I reached the familiar French doors, I took a deep breath before I looked through the window.

To my relief, Ash was with them, but Nyx was nowhere to be seen.

My sister and Cheryl were sitting in the seats across from him, both wearing flowery dresses. Cyrille had deep-mahogany hair that shone in the light, telling me she had just had an expensive dye job. Her blue eyes, so similar to our mom's shone with excitement and creased in the corners as she smiled.

She reminded me so much of a younger version of our mother that it stole the breath from my lungs.

Her daughter had inherited her looks, though her nose and thin lips had come from her father. Mother would have been overjoyed to see everyone here. She would have been the one to fuss about food and drinks, making sure everyone was taken care of.

Even times when she was so tired she could barely stand, she would come home and put together snacks for us as we studied, stating that if she didn't, there was no way that we would have the energy to keep up our studying.

*Food.*

As soon as I pushed the doors open, I realized the table in front of them was empty.

*We got it, my ass.*

"Axelle," my sister called and stood. I held my arms open for her as she glided over the stone and into my arms. "You look like shit."

I let out a chuckle and held her close. It had been far too long since I had seen her.

"Your beauty makes up for it," I said and waved to Cheryl who also stood to give me a hug, though Cyrille refused to move. I let out another laugh and pulled her daughter into my arms as well, planting a kiss on her forehead.

"It's so beautiful, Aunt Axelle," she said, and when she looked back up to me, tears were in her eyes.

My heart squeezed painfully.

"I am glad you like it, dear," I whispered. Cyrille pulled away from me and turned to pull her daughter into a hug as her sobs became louder.

"I didn't know something like this would set you off," Ash said, turning back to us. His face was twisted in discomfort.

I gave him a look.

"Where is the—"

"Sorry!" Nyx yelled from behind me, her voice startling me so much I couldn't help the small jolt that went through me.

Ash gave me a shit-eating grin and turned to Nyx. I turned as well, my heart stopping in my chest as I took her in.

Her long, dark hair had been pulled up into a high ponytail with only a few strands framing her face. She wore a knee-length pink dress that had floppy bows on her shoulders. She wore small strappy sandals, and I couldn't stop my eyes from running down her legs and—

*Get a hold of yourself.*

I was acting like some sort of horny teenage boy. I ran a *sex club,* for god's sake and bare legs were what turned me into this mess.

Cyrille gripped my arm and let out a noise, pulling me from my daydream of running my tongue—

"Nyx!" she exclaimed and left my side to look at the tray in her hands. "I didn't think you would pull out all the stops."

I had been so preoccupied with her dress that I hadn't even looked at the tray she was holding.

In her hands was a wood tray, and on top of it were drinks that matched the color of her dress. To the side of them were small stacks of mini sandwiches.

"I tried to do the best that I could with what I had," she said and sent my sister a sheepish smile. "Luckily, the liquor cabinet was packed, and I found enough leftover lemonade to make a boozy pink lemonade, though the sandwiches could use some work."

*Lemonade I made.*

I couldn't help but marvel at what she put together. It was such a small gesture, but it was enough to cause my chest to warm.

"It's perfect," I said before I could stop myself. When all eyes darted toward me, fiery anger rose in me.

I was angry at her for being so goddamn tempting and angry at myself for being such an infatuated idiot.

"Sit, please," Cyrille said and steered her to the tables.

I didn't miss the lingering heated gaze that Nyx gave me, and my sister sure as hell didn't either.

When we sat down, I was lucky that I wasn't sitting directly next to Nyx, but it became worse as I realized that I had no choice but to sit right across from her and right next to my suddenly quiet sister.

Clearing my throat, I took my seat and took my drink along with the rest of the group.

"Congratulations are in order," Nyx said, sending a soft smile to Cheryl, who sat at her side. Nyx took her drink and lifted it to Cheryl, who flushed under the attention.

"Congrats," Ash said as well, sliding his arm around Nyx, who gave no indication that she hated his touch.

*I don't want your son.*

What is the truth? Did she hate him? Was she the cheat I thought she was?

"Thank you both," she said and turned to me, raising her glass. "And thank you to Aunt Axelle. This ceremony is going to be more than I ever dreamed."

I gave her a soft smile, heat spreading in my chest regardless of the tension that was between Nyx and me. I was happy that they were here, truly.

"I'm more than happy to help," I said. "Besides, *someone* has to use it."

Cyrille let out a light laugh.

"Cyrille," I chided, already hearing the words out of her mouth before she spoke.

My sister had the tendency to mock my permanently single lifestyle.

"I still hope for that wedding," she said and took a sip of her drink. "I promised to be your best bridesmaid."

I rolled my eyes.

There had been a time when I dreamed of the wedding I was throwing for Cheryl... but that life wasn't for me. Not anymore, at least. There had been only one woman that I had ever allowed close enough to even *think* of marriage with, and she—

*Stop it.*

My eyes shot toward Ash, and as if he read my mind, he cleared his throat and let out a short chuckle.

"Maybe there will be another wedding sooner than you think," he teased, his eyes drifting to Nyx.

*This was not a fucking save, it was a jab.*

My stomach twisted so painfully I was sure I would double over in my chair. I gritted my teeth and gripped the thigh of my pants, forcing myself to take deep breaths.

White-hot fury ran through me.

*He couldn't be thinking of marrying her, could he?*

"How cute," Cyrille said. "How long have you been together?"

"Seven months," Ash said, his smile getting bigger.

Nyx gave Cyrille a forced smile.

"Still early for that type of planning, isn't it?" I asked.

Ash's smile dropped, and Nyx shifted under his arm.

*Fuck, why couldn't I keep my goddamn mouth shut?*

"Oh, I don't think so," Cyrille said. "After all, I got married to Luke after only six months. I knew it then that he was the one, and I couldn't wait to have all the beautiful—"

*"Okay,* Mom," Cheryl said, obviously hearing this story way too many times for her liking.

"Where did you meet?" she asked, turning to Nyx.

"He was an ex-client of my company," Nyx answered.

I lifted my brow and tried to get Ash's attention, but his eyes were drawn to Nyx, a small smile on his face. In this moment, he looked like he really liked this girl, and maybe it wasn't so hard to imagine that he loved her enough to marry her.

*God, I was fucking disgusting.*

It was almost enough for me to overlook their lies.

"Naughty," Cyrille chided, a glint in her eyes.

A shrill ringing from my pocket cut through the tense air and I let out a deep sigh.

"Excuse me," I said with a smile and quickly got up and speed walked into the house, digging my phone out to see it was Jenny.

"You just saved me from the worst—"

Jenny's hard tone cut through the line, causing me to freeze.

"We have a rat," she said, her tone harsh.

Ice-cold panic was injected straight into my veins.

"Explain," I commanded.

Jenny, my partner in crime. The person who had helped me open up the club of my dreams. She and her partner had experience opening many of these types of clubs, some of which were even darker and more secretive than Club Pétale. The knowledge that they had done this before had been the one thing that made me comfortable to work with them.

But if she said we had a rat, it meant...

"Pictures, Ax," she said in an exhale. "Not enough to identify anyone, but enough to ruin the club's image of privacy. All over.

Facebook, Instagram, Twitter, hell fucking Reddit has a shit ton. It's bad, Ax."

"*How. Did. This. Happen?*" I asked, forcing every word out through gritted teeth.

I stormed to the kitchen, looking for water. My throat was tightening and my palms began to sweat.

Everything I had worked for. The only thing I had dreamed about for years... and it was about to be taken from me. And this wasn't just about the club. The people who went there... they were dangerous and held half of the world in their hands. If this got out, they would never trust me again, or worse... it would be my head.

"Someone we invited," she said. "I am having our men take a look, see if they can at least determine which date it came from. Then maybe—"

"No maybe," I growled and grabbed a glass that was on the counter. "Find them *now*. Get Sloan on it. She'll fix your mess."

"I'm trying, Ax," Jenny said, her tone exasperated. "Please understand, this has never happened. In all the times—"

The glass slipped from my hand and shattered across the floor. Losing any bit of control I was holding on to, I threw my cell phone at the adjacent wall hard enough to cause it to break open, a mess of shards and metal flying everywhere.

*Fuck. Fuck. fuck.*

I had been distracted, *that's* why this happened. Because I was too busy—

A warm hand gripped my bicep, and it broke through the cloud of anger just long enough so I could turn and meet Nyx's eyes.

Then all hell broke loose.

I took that ponytail of hers in my fist and yanked it, a sharp whine exhaling from her mouth.

Her face was twisted in pain but there was something that lay just beyond it, something that made my mouth water.

"You did this," I fumed. "Don't you come in here and fucking—"

"What was that noise?" Cyrille asked, her voice sounding too close for comfort. I stared at Nyx, watching as her chest rose and fell with each deep gasp of air she took.

"Nothing," I called out, still keeping my hand threaded into her silky hair.

Her lips were parted and begging for me to kiss them. Her hand had come up to grip my shirt in a panic, and we were so close her chest brushed across mine.

"A glass slipped," I said, pushing Nyx away from me painfully. "I want you out of this house by tomorrow morning."

I left her to clean up the mess and stormed straight to the gym to work out this anger.

---

"Even I have limits, Ax," Sloan said from the other end of the phone. "I can try my best, but there is no way I can get you a person—"

"Sloan," I growled, unable to hold back my anger. I had spent hours going back and forth between her and Jenny, trying to figure this out before any of our patrons did, though by the vibration of my phone, I just knew the emails were pouring in.

*So much for fucking rest.*

"I know," Sloan said, her voice dropping low. "I *know,* Ax. Just trust me and the others, okay?"

I let out a sigh and ran my hands through my hair.

"You know I trust you," I muttered and hit my mouse, lighting my computer screen up.

In front of me, I had all of the photos that Sloan had managed to piece together from the internet and with each new one that came in, my stomach clenched and bile rose in my throat.

Luckily everyone listened to the rules and kept their masks

firmly on their face, but there was still a risk of one of the employees being outed. They were not required to wear masks. It was a way to put the patrons at ease.

It was like we were telling people that because you are trusting us with this part of yourself, we will trust you with our identity. An even trade that would make them more likely to come back.

Everything I had done, even in the smallest details, had been to promote the privacy and comfort of our patrons.

Because these were not just any people that we were dealing with.

Actors.

Politicians.

World-renowned professors.

For god's sake, I had a secret service member in my top-tiered client list.

Risking these people's identities risked my own as well.

"Don't stress, Ax," she said in a voice softer than I deserved. "Shield the calls I know you are getting. Ensure them everything is fine. Then get back to your family time. I will let you know when I have an update."

I almost snorted when she mentioned my *family.* I wanted nothing more than to run away and straight into the chaos that awaited me at Club Pétale.

"Fine," I muttered. "Thank you, Sloan."

"Don't thank me yet," she joked. "I have another picture coming your way that you aren't going to like."

Just then, a picture popped up on my screen that made my entire being still.

*"Shit,"* I murmured.

"Yep, look, I got to—"

Her voice was cut off by the loud beeping sound coming from my phone, indicating I had another call. Looking at the caller ID, I let out a sigh.

*This was going to fucking hurt.*

"We have it under—"

"Like *hell* you have it under control," a raspy voice came from the other end, cutting me off.

*Blake.* The person I was *least* looking forward to hearing from.

She was the member of the secret service that just so happened to be at the club the night these were taken. But she wasn't a person who just showed up to fuck around. No, Blake liked to push herself. She liked to be *watched.*

And the picture that just came in?

If you looked closely, you could see the very edge of her thigh, the bright-red ropes that were tied tight against her skin, and a small flash of a riding crop. It wasn't enough to incriminate her, but it was damn close enough to scare anyone that had been there.

"I performed that night, Ax," she hissed. "And now you are telling me that there are pictures of it floating on the internet?"

"No one will know it's you," I insisted. "You are registered under a private name, one of the few people I give that option to. There have been no discernible pictures of your body. You wore a mask—"

"Do I have to remind you where I fucking work, Ax?" she hissed. "I could get suspended, or worse. There is no telling what would happen if—"

"Calm down," I said in the softest tone I could manage. "I have it under control."

A new email came in from Sloan that lifted the weight off my shoulders and allowed me to breathe again, only if it was just for a moment.

"My people just confirmed that they had all the images taken down from the sites and narrowed down a list of potential suspects," I added after skimming the email. "I promise, Blake, I wouldn't try to harm your reputation. Don't forget that it is mine here too. I don't wear a mask in the club."

There was a pause from the other side.

"That's a lie," she whispered. "I saw you that night. You were leaving a room with someone. You had a mask on."

I froze and cleared my throat.

"That wasn't—I wasn't—"

"You don't have to explain it to me," she said quickly. "I was doing aftercare, and I caught you just as the door closed. I didn't mean to pry... I just thought you should know in case anyone else calls you." She let out a deep sigh. "I am forgiving, Ax. I understand what you are going through and empathize... but others are not."

"I know," I said and leaned back in my chair. The darkness of my room began to feel like it was crowding me. "Thank you, Blake."

She let out a huff.

"I did nothing for your thanks, Ax," she said. "I will await your update."

And with that, she hung up on me, and I was left to look over text after text as they came in. All threatening me if their identities ever got out.

I prayed to whatever gods out there that none of them found the motivation to follow through on their threats.

# NYX

There was no compromising with these two.

Ax wanted me gone and Asher insisted that I stay, neither of them showing any mercy.

"She hates me, Asher," I said with a loud sigh and flopped down onto the bed. "I think I should go."

It was a coward's way out. I knew that if I wanted to face this like a real adult, I would force Ax's door down and make her face me. I would explain to her exactly what Asher had done to me and maybe even warn her that he knew of the club.

Because if he had seen me, who's to say he hadn't seen the both of us?

But no, instead of taking the chance, I found myself back in Asher's room, sulking.

"Are you fucking kidding me?" he growled and rolled over on the bed.

He was shirtless, in only a pair of boxers. Once the sight would have stirred something in me, but it did nothing for me now. Maybe he felt that too, and that's why his eyes narrowed at me and he looked at me as if I had done him some great disservice.

A part of me wanted to spill that I fucked his mom, just like I had told Ax last night. Just to get back at him for being such an asshole, but that little nagging reminder of the pictures on his phone kept me on a tight leash.

"I tried," I said in a hushed voice. "I made the fucking sandwiches. I dressed nice. I literally did everything that you told me, and she *still* hates me. I am just going to ruin this if I am still here."

He rolled his eyes and cast a glare toward the door.

"You had one job," he said, his voice turning cold. "To get them off my fucking back."

His anger was palpable and swirled around us, causing the room's air to turn thick.

*What had Ax done to make him like this?*

"I don't think it's such a big deal," I said and turned toward him. "It doesn't seem like they really car—"

"I care," he said, interrupting me and turning to glare at me. "You didn't have to grow up with them, Nyx. The pure *disappointment* on her face is enough to send me spiraling. I needed *one* thing to show her that I could do, and she fucking hates you."

Silence spread between us. Images of my extended family looking down on us as I begged them for help flashed through my mind.

I knew all too well what it felt like to be looked down on. To be viewed as less than just because I couldn't reach their impossibly high standards. It had taken me years to break away from their mold and stop caring about what they thought before I could finally live my life the way *I* wanted... but that doesn't mean that their words and looks of disappointment ever left my mind.

At times, that just got more bearable.

And I didn't pretend that I knew Ax well enough to speak on how she had been as a mother... but there was something uncomfortable settling in my stomach when I thought of what Ax had done to him to make him feel this way.

"Ash, maybe just—"

"Go apologize to her," he demanded. "Right now."

I raised a brow at him. That was *not* the reaction I had expected from him.

"Apologize?" I asked and shot a glare at the digital clock on his nightstand. "It's almost midnight. She's probably—"

"Did you forget?" he asked, his hand coming to grip my chin.

I started to fucking hate the way he grabbed me and had the sudden urge to spit in his face.

"Obviously not," I hissed and jerked my head out of his grasp. Anger flowed through me freely, and for a moment, I seriously considered whether or not it was worth it to just quit my job.

It had taken me months to find this job, and even then, it had taken me *two years* to get to where I was now. If I couldn't find a job in time, I would lose my apartment, and that was something I couldn't think of.

My mother was always an option, but that was a last resort. She had a house in Oregon with enough room, but I refused to let that be an option. She had bought it in the time we had no contact, when she was recovering... but that didn't mean that I would be able to forgive her.

At least not yet.

I had let her back in my life for an update here and there, but I didn't tell her where I worked, or lived, for that matter. We didn't talk like we once did and at times, it felt like I didn't even have a mother. But even the pain from the loneliness was better than the pain of what she had put me through.

*Fuck it.*

"Fine," I growled and swung out of the bed. Without hesitation, I walked toward the door.

"Are you wearing that?" he asked me.

I paused, my hand already turning the doorknob. I was wearing something similar to last night, though this time I had taken his boxers as those shorts were obscenely stained with my own wetness.

I turned, feeling a bit of the anger from earlier swirl into something a bit more mischievous.

"Why?" I asked and ran my hand up the oversized T-shirt, pulling at it to show him that I also wasn't wearing a bra. "Worried your mom will find something she likes?"

His face went stone cold and panic seized my heart. Then slowly, a sinister smile spread across his face.

"I knew you were a dirty whore," he said and cocked his head to the side. "But I didn't know you would stoop so low as to try and fuck my mom. She has *standards,* you know."

Heat exploded in me and flushed my face. I bit my tongue, a metallic taste spreading across my tastebuds.

The urge for those sinful words to escape my lips increased tenfold, or better yet, the thought of marching down to her room and fucking her loud enough for him to hear would be just the thing to get back at him for those words.

*Standards.*

I wanted to fucking laugh.

"Fuck you," I growled and flung the door open, rushing down the hallway as his laughter echoed behind me.

Little did he know, there was no fucking way that I would be going to apologize to her. She had made it clear that she wanted nothing to do with me, and it hurt more than expected.

We had spent *one* night together, but it had been all that I had been thinking about. I imagined waking up in her arms after a wild night together. Imagined the way her warmth and comfort would be the thing I needed to finally relax into after so many years. I remembered the fire she started in me and how strong yet simultaneously weak she had made me feel when she had full control over me.

And the other night...

I bit my lip as my core began to ache.

I had gone to bed horny and unable to keep the way she looked at me out of my mind. Whatever had happened between us the other night had been far more addicting than even the first time had been.

The way her hand had gripped my throat, the way she fucked me mercifully against the door—

I sighed aloud as I entered the kitchen. It was dark with only the light of the moon shining through. I navigated my way to the bar cart and decided on a glass of white wine.

When I couldn't find a wineglass, I settled for a whiskey one. I wasn't picky. I just needed to reel myself in before I did something I regretted.

"We have it under control," Ax's voice came from somewhere farther away in the house. I looked around the kitchen for a place to hide as the sound of her bare feet against the floor moved closer, but there was nowhere unless I was willing to crawl into a cabinet.

I leaned against the kitchen counter and took a large sip of the wine, my eyes focused on the hallway I knew she was about to come out of.

*So much for fucking avoiding her.*

There was something between us, pulling us together over and over again. I knew she must have felt it too because we seemed to always find ourselves face to face no matter how unlikely the situation was.

Like being invited to her niece's wedding as her *son's* date.

"Yes," she said with an exasperated sigh. "I am sure. We have already narrowed down the list and gotten most of the sites to take them down."

She passed the threshold and froze when she saw me there.

I heard a voice on the other line but couldn't make out the words. She strode over to me and my breath caught when she didn't slow to a stop. I gripped the cool counter and braced myself, ready for her to come at me like she had earlier.

But she surprised me.

As soon as she came close enough for our chests to touch, she passed me while keeping her eyes locked on mine. Her gaze slowly trailed down to my lips and then as quick as the moment happened, it disappeared.

She leaned back, the wine bottle in hand, and took a swig straight from the bottle. She kept her eyes on mine and slowly took drink after drink as the woman on the other line kept talking.

My eyes locked on the way her throat moved as she pulled the wine bottle away. A drip of the alcohol escaped her plump pink lips and traveled down her bare neck and to her slightly exposed chest. She was wearing a loose tank top that showed off her prominent collarbones and dark tattoos that ran across her chest and down her bare, toned abs. She wore loose joggers that hung low on her hips and the white band of her underwear peeked out behind her shirt as she reached behind her to place the wine back on the counter.

She leaned against the island, her eyes trailing my body just as I had hers.

*This* was why I didn't want to see her.

As soon as we were anywhere near each other, there would be this electrifying tension between us. My body was already wound so tightly because of the last few months without visiting the club, and the other night was just the cherry on top.

"I would never put you or your clients in danger like that," she said, her tone low. "You forget I am a regular of the club as well. It's my reputation as much as yours, and if anyone was in danger of retaliation, it wouldn't be you."

My heart lurched when I realized she was talking about *that* club.

I leaned forward, trying to hear what the person on the other line was saying, but she held up her hand, keeping me frozen in my spot. My first instinct was to obey her. My body had reacted before my mind could even keep up. My second instinct, the one that stemmed from pure spite, was to lean closer to her. *Touch* her like I had longed to.

But *Asher* wanted me to apologize to her, or at least make sure that we were on good terms, and I knew that if I listened to the whispers in my mind, that I would be kicked out faster than I could even blink.

So I stayed still, like the good girl I was supposed to be. She even raised her eyebrow in response, but I saw the flash of satisfaction on her face. The same one she wore *that* night.

She may have had her emotions under control and learned how to keep a stone-cold mask, but there were times that it failed her ever so slightly.

When she was mad, her jaw would tic and her eyes would darken.

When she was happy, her eyes would light up.

When she was satisfied and in control, her demeanor changed. It was slight but you could see it in the way her lips pulled into a smirk and the way her head tilted back ever so slightly. It's as if she was looking down on you and reveling in the way you submitted to her. In that moment, she allowed herself to fall into the pride that was swirling inside her.

And that little change had me *addicted*.

If this was any other situation, I would have longed to mention it. Loved to see how she reacted when she knew that I could see *right through her*. But this wasn't any other situation. I was already in the shithole for the obvious hatred Ax had for me, and while it excited me to goad her, I would control myself.

*For now.*

"I will," she said. Then with a short goodbye, she hung up the phone and placed it on the island behind her.

I let us stew in silence for a moment before the need to know what she was talking about got so bad it made my skin itch.

"So the club—"

She held up her hand again, sending me a glare. I frowned and leaned forward to grab the bottle from behind her, but her warm hand on my wrist stopped me. I swallowed thickly, looking back up at her.

"You should be preparing to leave," she growled.

I yanked her hand off and brought the bottle to my lips, just as she had. I relished in the small bit of intimacy of our lips touching the same glass bottle before throwing my head back and taking a gulp.

I slammed the bottle down on the counter, probably far too hard, but luckily it stayed intact.

"I talked to Asher," I said and rolled my shoulders so I was standing straight in front of her. I refused to be weak. Refused to have her push me around. I needed to get Asher to delete those pictures, and I wouldn't let *her* fuck me over. "He won't let me go. So if you want me gone, you have to ask *him*."

I applauded her control, though I knew it was slipping. Her hands were balled at her sides, and I could hear her teeth grinding together. The veins in her neck popped and she took a deep breath.

"And what did you tell him, *love?*" she asked.

A burst of arousal shot through me and settled deep in my belly.

"I asked to leave," I admitted. "Said you didn't like me and that I didn't want to ruin a family event."

Her hand gripped the side of the counter.

"Then why are you still here?" she asked. "If you knew no one wanted you here, then why would you stay?"

Pain pricked my chest. *That* hit a bit too close to home. So much so I felt my eyes sting.

"Have you even talked to Asher?" I asked, taking a step forward. "Like *actually* talked to him?"

"Are you insinuating I don't know my son?" she growled, leaning down so her face was inches away from mine.

"I am saying that if you *really* cared about who he was dating, you would have known that he feels incredibly pressured to bring a date here," I said through clenched teeth. "He wants to *please* you. Make you *proud*. Yet you are too full of yourself to see what's really going on here."

There was a pause between us, and her eyes trailed down to my lips. My mouth dried and my tongue shot out to wet my lips.

"And what's really going on here?" she asked.

It was a double-edged question, and I knew she wasn't just asking about Asher and me. She was asking about *us.*

*What were we doing?*

Meeting in the middle of the night, sharing a bottle of wine, and looking like we were ready to jump each other at any moment was not what I should be doing with my boyfriend's mother. And now the house was full of people that could possibly catch us.

The thought made my hair stand on end and my breath catch... but I couldn't tell if it was panic or excitement that filled me.

"Ask your *son,*" I whispered, my eyes trailing to her lips and then back up to her eyes.

She straightened, pulling away from me, the spell between us broken. The cool air around us had turned into something hotter, and the buzz of electricity was still there crackling under my skin even as she put space between us, telling me all I needed to know.

"Tomorrow morning," she said and took a step back. "*Gone.*"

I rolled my eyes and took another sip of the wine.

"Tell that to your son," I hissed.

She crossed the space between us, her hand coming up to just lightly brush my throat. It was a threat. Reminding me that she could easily grab me and I would have no choice but to listen to her.

"You are a grown woman—"

"Ax? Nyx?" A light voice came from behind Ax. Her eyes widened, and then she turned. Cyrille was at the end of the hallway, an empty glass in her hand and wearing a nightgown.

*Fuck.*

"Come to join us?" Ax asked, her voice steady and not at all sounding like she had just been caught with her hand around her son's girlfriend's neck.

Cyrille leaned to the side, and I grabbed the wine, waving it in the air and smiling at her.

"Looks like there are a few of us who can't sleep," I said,

trying to keep my voice steady and my tone light. My heart was pounding in my chest, and my palms began to sweat, my grip on the bottle becoming slick.

"Wedding nerves," Ax added, then turned to send me a warning glare before pulling the bottle out of my hands and walking over to her sister.

"I never say no to a party," Cyrille said, though I couldn't see her face as Ax's front covered her entirely.

"You and Nyx will party alone though," she said and turned to place the bottle back on the counter. "I am far too old for this and had far too much to drink."

Cyrille was watching Ax intently then her eyes flashed to me. There was something in the way her blue eyes locked onto me that made me feel as though she was staring right through me.

"Better this way," she said and waved Ax off, grabbing the wine and coming toward me. "So we can *gossip.*"

She let out a small giggle, and I gave her a small smile, taking my long-forgotten glass and holding it up to her.

"Do tell," I teased and took a sip. I looked over Cyrille's shoulder to Ax, who was still staring at us. I waved her away. "Thanks for the wine, Ms. Blaise. Have a good night."

There was a tense silence that fell around us then she turned back toward the hallway.

"Good night, *Elayne*," she said and walked down the hallway.

Shock hit me like a punch to the gut, but I didn't have time to let my thoughts linger in the fact that *she* used the very name I had taken in the club.

"Elayne?" Cyrille asked and took a sip straight from the wine bottle. The heat that had coiled in my belly disappeared, her action causing the spell that had fallen over us to snap completely.

"A nickname," I said. "Sometimes Asher calls me it."

She looked at me like she knew I was lying but nodded anyway. A sense of relief filled me, and I filed Ax's move away for later when I had enough of a brain to think of how to get back at her.

"It's nice of Ax to do something like this," she said and looked around the house. "We were really close growing up, and family means a lot to us, so to have Cheryl's wedding—" She cleared her throat. "Sorry, it's just been emotional."

"I understand," I said and laid my hand on her shoulder, giving it a light squeeze.

"I just wish Asher's mom was still with us," she said, her voice cut off by a choked sob.

I couldn't stop the confusion from twisting my face. She sent me a pitiful look.

"He didn't tell you?" she said.

"I thought he was adopted," I said and leaned against the counter, my mind whirling. "I didn't know his biological mother was in the picture."

She let out a heavy sigh. Dread weighed deep in my stomach and I could taste the sourness of the bile that threatened to rise in my throat.

"Don't tell them I told you," she said in a stern tone.

I nodded and made an *X* on my chest, heart pounding loud in my ears.

"Cross my heart."

"I like you," she said with a smile, but it fell off just a moment later. "Ax and Hannah were together for a few years. When they had gotten together, Asher was already two, and when he was six, she..."

*Shit.*

I didn't know what to expect with this family, but it certainly wasn't *this.*

"If it's too hard, it's okay," I said with a forced smile. The lie tasted sour on my tongue.

She shook her head.

"She was shot," she said.

The air was still around us and blood whooshed through my ears.

*She was shot.*

Asher's mom was shot when he was six, and Ax's partner was—

"*Fuck,*" I breathed and threw back the rest of my wine. She refilled it for me without me having to ask. "Why? I mean—*shit.*"

Cyrille gave me an almost amused look.

"Anyone would be curious," she said and took my hand in hers. It was just as warm as Ax's. "No one really knows. All we know is one day, Ax opened the door and there she was. She had been there all night in the cold and bled out before dawn."

A chill ran through me, and I had to clamp my hand over my mouth to keep me from running to the sink. I liked to think that I could handle a lot. I've loved true crime documentaries, I even thought I would major in forensic science... but to have a heart-breaking death happen like this to people I knew and was involved with...

It made my heart hurt so bad I was sick to my stomach.

"And Asher's father?" I was unable to help myself.

Cyrille let out a noise.

"A deadbeat, though we couldn't get much information from her," she said. "All that we knew was that he was dangerous and maybe abusive as well. To her and Asher, Ax was their saving grace."

"Jesus Christ," I muttered.

"I know. Poor family. She has been closed off since then," she said, sadness weaving through her tone. "She threw herself into work and only came up for air for Asher, but even then—"

I removed my shaking hand from my mouth and placed it over the one that was intertwined with hers.

"It was lacking," I said, finishing for her. Asher's and Ax's relationship was becoming much clearer now.

She hummed.

"I just hope that this wedding can do something for her," she said. "She had been... *different* in the last few months. She calls more, and when she does, it's like she actually listens. And it's been forever since we came here. It's something."

I swallowed thickly and nodded.

"It sure is," I murmured, looking out into the dark house.

My mind whirled, but I was left with one powerful emotion that sucked the air out of my lungs and threatened to drag me down to the deepest parts of hell.

*Pity.*

I pitied both of them so strongly that it caused my chest to ache and the wine to turn sour in my mouth. All of a sudden, *I* felt like the asshole.

Here I was stepping into their relationship, which had already been strained due to Asher's mother being fucking *shot* to death. The blackmail pictures felt minor in comparison to what he was trying to get through.

"Damn it," I muttered and took another sip of my drink.

"Tread carefully, Nyx," she said. I looked toward her, but her eyes were locked on the wine bottle. "One heartbreak was enough to destroy this family for over twenty years. Let's try to avoid another one, or else I'm afraid I may never get to see my sister happy again."

*Fuck.*

With that, I downed the rest of the wine and hoped to god these next few days would go by in a flash.

# Nyx

"You are toeing the line, Nyx," my boss, John, said over the phone. He had called me right at six a.m. in response to the time-off request I had sent to him.

Luckily, I had been able to slip out of Asher's bed, my head pounding from the wine last night before he woke up.

"Hold on," I whispered.

I sped down the hall, trying to find an unlocked door. The air was chilly and the cold ground against my bare feet was unpleasant at best. It took me only a few minutes before I found an open door and slipped into the room.

I closed it with a click and leaned my head against the wood with a sigh.

"I know it's not the best time—"

"Not the best time?" he echoed, his voice rising. "They are coming to see *you* tomorrow, and if you are not here, you might as well kiss this project goodbye."

I bit down on my tongue, trying to reel in the anger that was threatening to explode inside me.

"I know, John," I said with a sigh. "It's just, something came up. I can work from my laptop, but there is no way I can—"

"Nyx," he growled, cutting me off. "If you are not here

Tuesday first thing in the morning to welcome our newest clients, I cannot promise you that you will have a desk when you get back."

"John," I said in an enraged gasp. "I have worked for you for over *two years,* you can't possibly—"

"I think I have made myself clear," he said. "Today and from Wednesday on, you can have off, but tomorrow is a no-go."

Then the line went silent.

"Are you fucking kidding me?" I asked aloud and stared at my phone.

I had been with that bastard for longer than most employees. I worked my ass off to get this client, and he couldn't even give me time off? And to threaten to fire me because of it? Who the fuck does he think he is?

"Well, I guess you better get back," Ax's voice said from behind me.

I jumped and swung around to see her standing mere feet away from me. She had on a soft-looking beige sweater and slacks. Her hair was slightly damp and there was a strong scent of cologne in the air that I hadn't smelled beforehand.

I looked around at the scene before me and realized that I was in some type of study. There was a desk behind her and behind it were three large windows that looked over the back of the property and the wedding venue.

She took a step forward, calling my attention back to her.

"That sounded rather serious," she said. There was an almost teasing tone to her voice. "Looks like you will have to leave early after all."

*No, she was condescending.*

She thought she'd won.

I sent her a big smile and opened the door.

"Why don't you come have the conversation with Asher and me?" I asked. "Maybe if you are with me, he can't force me to be here."

Her lips twitched, and she motioned for me to leave.

"Go ahead," she said. "Though I doubt he's awake."

With shaky strides, I walked down the hallway, trying to remember which door was his. All the doors looked the same and if it was not for Asher, I would have gotten lost long ago.

"You're gonna pass it," Ax called from behind me.

I turned to the door to my right, and heat flushed through me.

"Right," I muttered and turned to knock on the door.

There was a shuffling inside the room and a groan before the door was opened, and Asher's messy hair and pinched face came into view. He was still only wearing the boxers from last night and didn't even look ashamed to be seen in such clothing.

"What?" he groaned and leaned against the doorframe.

"My boss called me in," I said and shifted my eyes to the floor, unable to hold his heated gaze. My heart was pounding in my chest and I felt the wine from last night rise in my throat. Volatile emotions mixed inside me. I was angry, worried, sad, fucking panicked.

Ax was watching me beg her son to let me go. Asher saw me as a traitor for trying to ruin the only plans he could think of to win his mother's praise. And I couldn't stop thinking about how this poor family had been treated by the world.

The threat of losing my job was almost minuscule in comparison to all this... but I needed to put myself first. I couldn't continue to hang on to their every word and emotion and try to make it easier for *them.* I needed this job, and that was the end of the conversation. I wouldn't let myself feel bad, no matter how much the feelings were gnawing at my insides.

"Can't you take some time off or something?" he asked, his voice turning hard. I tried not to look over to Ax, and at this point, I wasn't sure if he had even seen her yet.

"I tried," I said quickly. "But Anneu is coming tomorrow—"

"I don't give a damn about your client," he growled. "I told you—"

He moved to step out into the hall and froze when he finally saw Ax standing there.

"It sounded pretty important," Ax said and put her hands in her pockets. Her eyes shot toward me then back to Asher. "I overheard her in the hallway. Her boss seems like a hard-ass and it's not really a big deal if she can't be here for it."

My heart swelled when I heard her trying to stand up for me, but it ached at the same time because I knew that she was only doing this because she wanted me out of her life.

And now I was here, the only thing standing between them. Without me, they wouldn't have been having this argument. They would probably be eating pancakes or whatever shit they do on a Monday morning.

*One heartbreak was enough to destroy this family for over twenty years. Let's try to avoid another one, or I'm afraid I may never see my sister happy again.*

My chest ached.

"I don't have much gas in my car to make the trip," he said, his eyes traveling back to mine. "Are you *sure* you can't convince them otherwise?"

"I'll take her," Ax said, breaking our stare down. Asher's face twisted in disgust but he quickly righted it before she saw. "I have to go into the office anyway."

It took everything I had to force myself to keep Asher's stare.

"Do you have to go all week?" he asked. "If it's just tomorrow, can you just go tomorrow? Come back for the ceremony?"

"I think it's best if I—"

"I can drop her off today and pick her up on Wednesday night so she can be here for the ceremony on Thursday," she said, cutting me off.

I waited with bated breath to see what Asher would say. He looked to his mom, then back to me. I knew there were things he was dying to say. You could see it bubbling under his skin, just begging to be free. He was angry, anyone could see that.

"Let me get ready so we can talk," Asher said, then shot a look toward Ax. "We will meet you in the kitchen. I'm sure Aunt Cyrille will be up soon."

Ax lingered, I could feel her eyes on me but she didn't say anything else as she walked past us. I felt a brush of heat as she passed me. We were so close our skin was almost touching, but it was over as quickly as it came.

As soon as Ax's footsteps receded, Asher grabbed my shirt and pulled me into the room.

"What the fuck do you think you are doing?" he hissed and pushed me against the wall. Pain pricked at the base of my skull.

"I am getting along with her," I hissed back and gripped his wrist. "Like *you* told me."

"You were supposed to *stay here,*" he growled. "Why can't you just use your laptop?"

I glared at him, placed my hands on his chest, and used all the strength I had in me to push him away. He tripped and was sent flying to the floor.

The shocked look on his face shouldn't have satisfied me as much as it did.

"I am keeping up my end of the deal," I said. "My boss will fire me if I do not show up there tomorrow, so those little *pictures* you keep wouldn't mean much if he was going to fire me anyway."

He scrambled to his feet.

"If you leave today with her, I *promise* you that you will have much more to worry about than those *little pictures,*" he threatened.

I rolled my shoulders back and instead of engaging with him, I chose to beeline to my suitcase.

He tried to reach for me, but I snapped my hand away from him.

"You are backed into a corner," I hissed. "*That's* why you insist on making empty threats. I will be back like I promised, and I will finish this wedding with you. If anything, going against your mother will only make it look weirder."

He paused and looked toward the door. No doubt trying to think of all the different ways he could blackmail me into staying.

*But I was only going to be gone for a few days, so what's the big fucking deal?*

He let out a sigh and dug for his phone. I closed my eyes and swallowed thickly, trying to rein in my emotions. Seeing Asher's phone was *not* something I was looking forward to.

When I took a deep breath and opened my eyes again, I saw the picture of my application staring back at me. There was a picture in the very left-hand corner. One I had taken off my Instagram. I had gone to the botanical gardens and wore a short, flared baby-blue dress. Once loved that picture but seeing it here in his dirty hands made me begin to hate it.

He turned it back to me and began reading off from it.

"Nyx Morgan, age twenty-six, submissive," he read, his voice far too loud.

My heart lodged in my chest.

"Stop," I commanded and took a step forward.

He took a step back but kept his face blank as he continued to read off every one of my dirty secrets.

"Open to choking, biting, impact play, overstimulation, degradation, *consensual nonconsent, sharing*—Jesus, Nyx," Asher said with a bitter laugh coming from his lips. His eyes narrowed and there was a cool look on his face. "I knew you were fucked up in the head, but this?"

The person in front of me was not Asher. Or at least not the Asher I knew, because this man... he had the heart of a monster. I could see it in the way he looked down on me. The way his jaw clenched and his lips turned down. He wanted this to hurt.

"You don't get to judge me for this," I said, though my voice had lost its power. "That was *private* information, and you have no right—"

"Did you forget that I am going to hand this to your boss?" he asked, his brow rose. "I will even have it hand delivered while you are meeting with him if you want to test me."

I didn't want to cry in front of him, but tears were threatening to spill over anyway.

"What do you want from me, Asher?" I asked. "I *have* to go, or your blackmail is moot. Your mom even offered to take me. Can't you just let it go?"

He threw his phone to the bed and stalked toward me. I walked backward, ready to run out of the room but he got to me faster than I could escape. His hands clutched at my shirt, and he forced me to the wall causing pain to explode from the base of my skull.

"You cornered me," he growled. "*That's* why I am letting you go. Don't think for a second that I don't know that you concocted this little plan of yours. If you tell my mom *anything* about this, I will leak this not only to your work but to that fucked-up family of yours as well. Do you understand me?"

The pinch of pain shot a burst of clarity over me and the need to cry was washed away with a tidal wave of anger that swept through me. I pushed him off of me with all my strength and sent a stinging slap to his face.

He stilled, his head still facing the opposite wall. His skin had already started to redden.

"I will go to work," I spat. "Then I will come back here to finish this job. That is it. I won't stand for your *shit* any longer. We have the terms of our deal and I will not let you throw me around outside of that. Do *you* understand *me?*"

I spoke the words with as much venom as I could muster and hoped that he didn't feel my hand shaking as I slapped him.

His lips quirked and he ran a hand through his hair. When his gaze met mine, I didn't waver and continued to glare at him, waiting for an answer.

"Your file didn't mention this," he mused and rubbed his hand over his cheek. "Though I guess anyone could guess what gets you off. I will stick to the deal as long as you stick to yours."

His last words surprised me, but I didn't let it show because the anger from his words was still swirling about.

I wanted to do so much more than slap him, but I made it a point to control myself.

Straightening, I turned toward the door and paused, opening it just the slightest bit before looking back at him with a smirk.

"Did you pull your *mommy's* file as well?" I asked and regretted the words as soon as they left my mouth.

He slammed into me faster than I could make out. His hand gripped my hair and a pained cry left my lips.

"Don't *test* me, Nyx," he growled in my ear. "I will ruin your life. You think all I have is stupid blackmail? Think again, *cunt.*"

He pushed me to the side and escaped to the bathroom before I could get another word in.

# Ax

"I didn't know you were coming back, sir," Yvon said on the other line, his voice coming out muffled.

He was most likely eating breakfast or still in bed. I had told him I would be gone for the week and to take it off, but I guess things changed. And by *things,* I meant a disastrous anomaly that went by the name *Nyx.*

A twinge of guilt hit me when I realized that calling him would mean that the vacation he had probably been waiting for may never come. I took pride in treating my employees well. I gave them almost unlimited time off. Gave them freedom in their work. I didn't like to keep many rules other than the necessary ones we needed to keep our work safe.

But here I was, ruining it for my star employee over a woman.

I made a note to treat him to something later.

"It won't take long," I said and shifted in my seat. "We are on our way now."

"We?" he asked.

I cleared my throat, my eyes locked onto the woman currently looking way too comfortable in the back of my car. I—*unfortunately*—didn't have my limo with me as it was too flashy for our little town and that meant that Nyx and I were squeezed into the back of my SUV.

Luckily, most of the staff had come back so I wouldn't be forced to *drive* us there, but at least then we would have had more space. I had leaned all the way to the car's door in order for our legs to not touch but Nyx seemed to have the exact opposite approach and was currently taking up as much space as she could next to me.

I had a feeling she was doing it on purpose.

She had worn that goddamn baby-blue dress again, and her legs were spread wide, her shoe *almost* hitting mine. She looked at me, a smile pulling at her lips.

She was *definitely* doing it on purpose.

*A little fucking vixen.*

"Me," I corrected. "Just me."

She rolled her eyes and looked back out the window.

Her demeanor had taken a sharp turn as soon as we climbed into the car. In front of my son, she was meek, reserved, almost... *scared.* She was but half of the woman she was when we were alone and nothing like the vixen that had walked into my room. She was shy then too, but there was a power to her. She was confident and sure of herself.

In front of Ash... she was but a shadow of herself.

It made me unreasonably angry. I had no reason to be, she wasn't my problem... but it still didn't stop the nagging feeling that I had that *something* was off here.

But I was worried that if I tried to dig too deep that I would get myself stuck and unable to crawl out. I would become even more obsessed than I already was.

"I can meet you at the club—"

"I just wanted to warn you," I said quickly. "I will probably call for your services later today and maybe later this week. Sorry for the abruptness."

There was a pause. I looked out my window, watching the large farms as we passed. The residents of this small town had been awake since dawn and I caught some of them as we passed, though none made a motion to wave.

They liked to save face in public and dote on us as they would any other resident, but inside they all saw us as the same.

*We were outsiders, and we didn't belong.*

"Not at all, sir," he said. "I look forward to seeing you."

"You too," I said and hung up quickly. Feeling the weight of Nyx's stare, I turned to look at her and raised my brow.

"Can I help you?" I asked.

She shook her head but continued looking at me. I let my eyes wander down her body to the light soft swell of her breasts in the sundress. I felt myself flush when I realized she wasn't wearing a bra.

*Fuck.*

She shifted, causing the dress that fell to her knees to hike up, showing her soft thighs. The same ones that looked so delicious with the red palm marks on them.

"You work a lot," she noted.

I couldn't help the snort I let out.

"How could I not?" I asked.

She cocked her head, then turned back to the window. I took her in then, it was easier when she wasn't looking. Her soft, unmarred skin and state of dress led me to believe that she probably had a comfy childhood, much like Ash. But Ash couldn't cook for shit, so she must have had parents that were more attentive than I was.

I wanted to know where she learned it. How she had found herself in New York. What drew her to my club. I wanted to know many dangerous things but all of those just made the pit bigger, so I kept my mouth shut.

"Do you ever get tired of it?" she asked, the suddenness of her blue eyes drilling holes into me caused me to suck in a deep breath.

*I do get tired.*

And evidently getting tired led to the circumstances right

now. If I didn't get tired and allow myself a night with a match, I never would have met her. If I didn't get tired, I would have never allowed Asher to go so long without speaking to me.

And if I never got tired, Hannah would have never been thrown on my doorstep with a bullet between the eyes and her skin marred with brands.

When I didn't answer she let out a sigh.

"What's with you and my son?" I asked, unable to help myself. Her lips twitched.

"What's with the club?" she shot back.

I clenched my jaw, irritation rising in me.

*Why the fuck couldn't she just give me a straight answer?*

"That's frankly none of your business," I said, my tone turning hard.

She smirked. *She fucking smirked at me.*

"What I do with your son is also *none of your business,*" she said and crossed her arms over her chest. A smug expression worked its way to her face.

I gripped the fabric of my pants. The space was too small and while there was a divider between us and the driver, he wasn't Yvon, so anything that I said or did in here could reflect badly on me.

"That's my *son,*" I growled. "I have a right to know what you are doing with him and if you plan to tell him who you *really* are."

"And I am a patron of the club," she said. "I want to know that my time there was private. From the looks of it, that may not be so true."

My entire body froze and blood rushed to my ears.

*What did she know?*

"You haven't gone for *months,*" I spat, feeling panic rise in me so quickly I became dizzy. "Your membership is all but expired. You don't have a stake here, nor would I trust someone like you, who is an obvious liar with a double life, with *anything* about the club."

The smile on her face was so large it pissed me off. I wanted to force her over to my seat and wipe that goddamn smi—

"How did you know I hadn't gone for months?" she asked.

*Fuck.*

I lunged forward, grabbed her chin, and forced her face close to mine.

"What the fuck are you playing here?" I growled.

Her smile dropped, and her eyes were wide as they searched my face.

"I'm just s-saying that I didn't think you'd notice if I was gone," she choked out. "Before, I thought you were another patron, but—"

"Don't finish that sentence," I warned.

I didn't want to cross this line. I *couldn't.* Her knowing anything other than what she already knew was asking for trouble. Not only was she fucking around with the both of us, but it had just proven that she was more cunning than I originally thought.

And in my business, that meant death.

"I didn't mean—"

"*Don't,*" I warned. "You will sit there—*silent*—for the rest of the ride and when we drop you off at your apartment, you will get your shit and you won't talk to my son or me until I pick you up on Wednesday night. Understood?"

Her face turned a bright red before she nodded. A sick, twisted sense of satisfaction ran through me at her sudden submission. Before I could stop it, another thought popped into my head.

"Use your words."

Her face turned hard and her eyes narrowed.

"I understand, *mommy,*" she said.

I pushed her away and sat back in my seat, forcing myself to look out the window or else I may very well do something I regret.

I was so angry when I reached the club that I brushed Sloan off completely when I entered the workroom. She let out an annoyed huff as I beelined to my office.

I slammed the door behind me harder than necessary and walked toward my desk. I didn't even sit down. Just opened my laptop and typed furiously until I had Nyx's file in front of me.

I quickly sent it to my phone and made note of her address and place of employment.

I looked down to the section where we asked them to divulge their current relationship status and my fists balled when I saw a green *single* attached to her profile.

"It was a fucking lie," I growled.

When I saw her previous BDSM experience, I froze.

*Some degradation.*

*Light impact play.*

*Overstimulation.*

*Bondage.*

I was instantly pulled in.

*When did she do all of that?*

My eyes scanned the rest of the document and an uncomfortable heat settled low in my belly when I read over what she was open to.

When I got to *sharing,* I slammed my computer shut and fell into my seat.

*I shouldn't be looking. I shouldn't have let myself go this far.*

But even as I thought that, my hand found my phone and I put in her address. She was far from the club and lived in an apartment that did *not* reflect what I had assumed about her upbringing.

It took me two seconds to decide to ring Jonson.

"Please *stop* calling me," he groaned. "Don't you have anything better to do than—"

"Nyx Morgan," I said, then rattled off her address. "Give me everything you know. Family, schooling, upbringing, *everything.*"

He let out a loud sigh, and I heard the clicking of a keyboard in the background.

"I'm going to need something in retur—"

"Payment will be in the lockbox in your spare third room," I said then paused. "And I'll introduce you to someone from the secret service."

It was a gamble if Blake would accept this or not, but I prayed that she did.

He let out a huff before he typed on his keyboard some more. My phone buzzed and when I looked, I had an email from him with a comprehensive compilation of everything that made Nyx, Nyx.

"Wait a minute... how did you—"

I hung up on him and opened my computer to devour the information in front of me. To my surprise, Nyx did not have the background I thought she had while growing up.

From what I could gather, she was raised by a single mother who grew up in Georgia. She was from a hyper-religious family, the type that would go to church every Sunday, volunteer for the potlucks, and even had a few stories on them in the newspaper, all revolving around their religion.

Her mother had disappeared from the records for a few years when she was nineteen and came back with a young Nyx in her hands. There were a few photos here and there, some school pictures, though none of it warmed my chest like I thought it would.

Instead, a sense of dread weighed over me as I looked over picture after picture seeing the young smiling child turn into a solemn adult.

It was her mother's arrest record a few years back that caught my attention.

"*Fuck,*" I moaned and ran my hand down my face.

Her mom got *nine* years for drug trafficking, the maximum sentence, and got out in seven because of good behavior. Disgust unfurled in my stomach, but it wasn't because of her mom. No... it was because of *me.*

Because of people like Ryder. I may have had limits and standards, but we all worked in the same business. I knew all too well how the families of those that got prosecuted for what *we* do ended up.

But Nyx... I looked at the files and counted the years.

Nyx should have been around twenty-four when her mother was let out and that must have been—*seventeen.*

Nyx had been seventeen when her mother was taken from her and she was forced to fend for herself. I spied a record of jobs and low-income apartments on Jonson's list, and I couldn't help but feel for Nyx.

She had grown up in a situation that had forced her to see the world's ugliest truths when she was still a *child* and had somehow made a life for herself.

And suddenly, just like I had predicted, the files had fueled my obsession and the only thing I could think of was Nyx. I wanted to show her the life that was possible.

I had been there, desperate to live my own life by any means. I took job after job until I couldn't work anymore, just so I could reach my dream. I wanted to show her what lies at the end of the tunnel.

*No wonder she had been so freaked about her job.*

Even if I regretted it later, things would have to change between us from here on out.

# Nyx

I should have been excited for sometime off but instead, staying alone in my apartment with nothing better to do was the worst possible punishment I could have been given.

Tuesday had come and gone.

My boss was not shocked to see me at work and the talks with Anneu had gone smoothly. Their PR and marketing heads were similar in age to mine and much less intimidating in person. I was shocked by how easy they were to work with and it took a huge weight off my shoulders.

But with the disappearance of that excess weight... came *dangerous* thoughts.

Thoughts about Ax of course.

Asher was but a buzzing, annoying fly somewhere in the back of my mind. I knew he was there but I didn't particularly care to find, or think, of him. I was content to ignore him until it came time to face him. And *hopefully* he really was just bluffing when it came to the consequences of leaving.

I played with the thought of showing up to the club. Or maybe even seeing if I could reserve Ax again... but my conscience told me that I should just find my vibrator and fucking let it go already.

Let *her* go.

I couldn't help the chemistry and tension between us, but I could sure as hell think twice before I tried to egg her on again.

Now that I knew about what had happened to Asher's mom, I knew that what I was doing with the both of them was incredibly fucked up. I had so many questions running around in my mind.

*What did she look like?*

*How did they meet?*

*Who shot her?*

The last one was grading at my insides every time I looked at Ax. I knew she had to know something. How could she not? Ax had even more questions that plagued my mind. I knew now that she had to have a higher position in the club than she let on, but that club was new so what the hell had she done to build up their infinite amount of money?

She seemed like a much harder worker than Asher, but there was no way she could accumulate that much wealth on her own, right?

Even if she gave off the air of a no-bullshit worker, I really doubt that she had to get her hands dirty. When her hands roamed my skin, there were no calluses or rough patches, nor did I think someone with so many servants would have ever had to be in a position like that.

I couldn't imagine what she must think of my apartment. Her face had remained cold and unfeeling when she dropped me off in a slightly run-down building that had paint peeling off the side. It wasn't in the greatest neighborhood and a room here was the size of a closet in her home.

But if she saw the inside, I'm sure—

"I need to get a fucking hobby," I moaned and sat up from the couch.

It was only eight in the morning and I still had the whole day ahead of me. I had already made myself a cup of coffee, read some poetry, watered all my plants... but then I had nothing else left to do.

Usually my weekends were filled with relaxation and short walks to the shops nearest my place, but never did I have to think about what to do on a weekday.

Getting an idea, I jolted out of my seat and ran to my closet. I shuffled through my clothes until I found a loose T-shirt and baggy jeans. I threw them to the bed and searched for the next item.

Unlike early this week, I had time to actually pick something out for the wedding and after meeting Cheryl and her mom, I wanted to make sure I actually tried to look good. They were both really sweet and the least I could do was make sure that I looked decent.

I caught a glance at the color scheme from the kitchen this morning as the workers were putting up the roses and other decor. Something blush would probably look best and maybe some strappy heels...

I froze when I didn't find the dress I was looking for.

*I could have sworn that I had something to wear that would have looked good.*

Cursing, I dove for my phone on my bed and checked my credit card balance. I didn't know if I would have money to splurge this month on clothes. This apartment, transportation to work, food, coffee, and some new books were usually all that I could afford with the measly salary from the design agency. Anything else would put a strain on my budget and...

I let out a heavy sigh when the balance finally loaded.

*Maybe something from the clearance rack at Macy's would do.*

I pulled on my fresh clothes, grabbed my tote bag, and headed for the door. When I heard Ms. Pruitt's voice in the hallway, I froze. I waited to see if she would be entering her apartment anytime soon, but after a few more moments, her voice continued on.

I wasn't really in the mood to talk and didn't want to explain why I was home on a Wednesday but I guess I had no choice.

I pulled the door open and froze when I saw Ms. Pruitt's door open and the old lady herself leaning against the doorframe. Her eyes were alight and there was a rare smile that spread across her face. And next to her, in all her glory, was Ax.

She wore a full suit today, complete with a tie and vest, and the way the soft gray fabric stretched over her muscles caused my mouth to dry. Her tattoos peeked out of her cuffs and stood out on her knuckles, her tie was loosened, giving her a polished yet rugged look all at the same time.

Her eyes shifted from Ms. Pruitt to mine and it took me until that moment to realize that she, too, had been smiling. The act sucked the air out of the tiny hallway.

"Nyx," Ms. Pruitt said in a teasing tone. "Where have you been hiding this one?"

If the heat in my face hadn't been obvious, it sure had to be now. Each word hit me harder than the last and caused butterflies to explode in my stomach.

*Fuck, why couldn't I chill for just a moment?*

"Hiding is an... interesting way to put it," Ax drawled, her voice light but it caused my skin to prickle all the same.

"What are you doing here?" I asked and turned to pull my door shut and locked it.

"Oh, don't be rude, Nyx," Ms. Pruitt chided. "She was waiting on you and you know it."

I turned over my shoulder to send Ax a look who just smiled at the elderly lady and motioned for me to head down the hall with her.

"I'll talk to you later," I said in a hushed whisper and waved to Ms. Pruitt. She shot me a shit-eating grin before giving me a thumbs-up and slamming her door a bit hard in her excitement.

I let out a sigh and looked back to Ax but she was already halfway down the hall and to the elevator.

"I have things to do," I told her as I ran to catch her at the elevator.

"Then I will drive you," she said and stepped into the elevator, leaving me open mouthed and shocked. She motioned for me to join her in the elevator, her handsome face twisting in confusion.

I snapped out of my shocked state and stepped in with her.

She pressed the parking garage button, and we rode in silence until I couldn't keep my questions in anymore.

"Why did you come early?" I asked then added quickly, "And how did you know which apartment was mine?"

The elevator dinged and she stepped out.

"I finished work early," she said simply.

I paused in my steps. She stopped and turned around when she realized I wasn't following her. The underground spot was humid and the sound of squeaking tires against the linoleum floor filled the silence between us.

"I didn't bring my clothes," I said and turned back to the elevator. "I can go—"

"You can wear Cheryl's," she said and turned back to the parking lot. A sleek black limo pulled up in front of her and a man with a scarred face and single blue eye stepped out of the car to open the door for her. He looked at me with something in his eye, but I couldn't tell if it was hatred or something else.

"I was actually going to go get a dress right now," I said and clutched my tote as she turned to glare at me. "It's only a few blocks, we can walk."

"No," she said and turned back.

Sharp bursts of anger rose through me.

"I am not going in the fucking limo," I growled. "You may like the attention but I *don't.* And besides, this is *still* my day off. You can't just come in here and change my entire schedule around just because *you* got off work early."

The sound of my rising voice bounced off the concrete walls. The driver looked toward Ax. She stayed silent for a few moments before standing up straight and fixing the buttons on her jacket.

She nodded toward the man who frowned but closed the door, nonetheless. She turned back to me with her lips in a thin line.

"Lead the way."

"How'd you know?" Ax asked from behind me, causing me to jump and for my card to slip out of the reader.

The barista in front of me gave me a pitiful smile and moved our cups to the start of the bar.

I finally entered my card into the reader, feeling the burning gaze of Ax on the back of my neck.

"It'll be ready in a moment, Nyx," the barista said. I smiled and nodded to her.

I had become a regular in the café. It was a small family-owned shop that had exploded in the last year. They were known for their unique flavors, including honey-lavender, strawberry shortcake, marshmallow, and red velvet lattes.

It was nice to see growth, but it had made it hard to frequent because of the crowds. Though it seemed Wednesday at eight forty-five may have been a sweet spot. Many people had left as soon as we had entered, making me believe we just missed rush hour.

I quickly walked to the end of the bar and waved to the barista who was making our drinks.

Ben was a favorite of mine. His bubbly personality and bright smile always seemed to make my day better. Though his smile disappeared as soon as he saw my overly disgruntled shadow.

"How did you know?" she asked again, causing me to jump.

"I worked as a barista for a long time," I answered, turning to her. "You walk into any coffee shop looking like *that* and the barista will immediately start pulling the shots for an Americano."

She bristled and stared ahead at the barista working.

With a small triumphant smile, I faced forward as well.

"I didn't know you were a barista, Nyx," Ben said in a light tone before putting my iced cinnamon bun latte on the counter. It had been my favorite guilty pleasure, and I was overjoyed to be getting another one on a nonweekend day, even if my credit card was crying because of it.

I grabbed it and put my straw in, taking a healthy sip of the sugary goodness.

"Yep," I said with a smile. The memories of working through college flashed across my mind. It had been a lot of early mornings and sleepless nights but I did what I had to so that I could live. "In college, so it was a while ago."

Ben rolled his eyes and put my second iced cinnamon bun latte on the counter.

"You are what, in your midtwenties, girl?" he asked.

I rolled my eyes and grabbed the second one.

"Something like that," I muttered.

He shook his head and let out a chuckle.

"And she was right, by the way," Ben said, looking behind me. "I was already pulling the shots."

He placed her hot Americano on the counter and she stepped forward to take it.

"Thank you," she said and nodded to him.

He gave me a look, but I just shook my head, hoping he wouldn't mention anything.

"See you on Sunday," I said and held up my latte to him and the girl at the counter in an attempt to wave to them.

They both waved back.

"Do you normally drink two coffees?" she asked as we stepped out of the shop.

"I already had one today," I said with a smile and walked down the sidewalk and toward my favorite bakery. I wouldn't be able to buy bread but it would be nice to at least stop by since I was close. "But this isn't for me."

She was silent after that, presumably sipping on her coffee and enjoying the nice walk, though I doubt she was a person that would enjoy walking around the city for *fun.*

It took only a few moments to get to the bakery but when we did, I felt a bit of nervousness fill me. Annette owned this place with her husband, and I couldn't help but feel nervous that she would ask about Ax.

Anyone else would ask me when I saw them next... but I was afraid she would pry too much and I honestly didn't want to lie to her.

I stopped at the door, trying to maneuver myself so I could open it but Ax stepped close behind me and put her hand on the door above me before pushing it open. My heart lodged in my throat and heat rose to my face.

Her earthy cologne enveloped me, and her warmth singed my skin. I cleared my throat and stepped into the bakery seeing Annette right away at the counter, helping a customer.

Her eyes widened when she saw us, but she quickly smiled and continued helping the customer in front of her.

"Get something for breakfast tomorrow," Ax commanded me. I gave her a look.

"Don't you have chefs for that or something?" I asked.

Her jaw tensed.

"I doubt Cheryl will want a full meal and most of the day she will be in makeup and dress, so she will need some type of snack that is easy to eat," she said.

I shrugged but didn't go to the breads right away. Instead, I went to the counter and stood in line until it was my turn.

"Nyx!" Annette yelled and reached over the counter to give me a hug. "Aren't you supposed to be at work or something?"

I gave her a sheepish smile and pulled away so I could give her the coffee. She accepted it with a thankful smile though her eyes lingered on the woman behind me.

"I have the day off," I said with a smile. "Have to get some shopping done."

She leaned to the side.

"And you, Axelle? Doesn't that little niece of yours have a wedding soon?"

My blood ran cold. *Annette knew Ax?*

I had thought that this place had been my safe haven. A place all to my own where the outside world couldn't reach me... and now I had to share that with Ax?

I turned to look at Ax who was staring at Annette with a soft smile.

"I'm here to pick up Ms. Morgan," she said, causing another burst of shock to run through me.

*When did she learn my last name? Did Asher even know my last name?*

Annette let out a light laugh. I turned to her with a forced smile.

"So formal," she jabbed.

"I think it's a part of her character," I whispered loudly to Annette.

She let out a small giggle and then a gray-haired man peeked his head out of the back. I swear I could hear Ax's teeth grinding against each other. Scott sent me a contagious smile.

"Ax? And Nyx?" he asked. "I never thought I'd see you two together."

My insides heated when I realized what type of *together* he meant.

"Bread," Ax commanded from behind me.

"Ah yes," I breathed and started to show Annette which breads I wanted, leaving Scott and Ax to themselves.

Ax went to the counter and began quietly chatting with him, and I got so into my talking with Annette that I forgot that she was even here until the shop had descended into silence.

"Where did you get this?" she said, her tone deadly.

Annette and I both froze and met each other's eyes before looking toward Ax and Scott. Scott gave her a look. The register was open in front of him, and Ax held crushed bills in her hands.

She put her coffee down with care and opened her hand to spread out the bills on the counter.

"*Who* gave you *these* bills?" she asked, her voice holding no heat, but the aura around her had plunged the shop into a tenseness that caused my heart to skip a beat.

Scott leaned forward, dropping his voice to a whisper, but I heard him loud and clear.

"You did."

"Take them," Annette said quickly and thrust the bag of bread and pastries into my hand. "Take them and take Ax and get out of here."

I opened my mouth to speak but she interrupted me.

"*Please,*" she whispered. The panic in her voice stirred me, and I grabbed the bag before marching over to Ax.

I grabbed her hand and pulled it, forcing her to look at me. Her face was twisted into a snarl and her eyes had a sort of heat to them that had my entire being wanting to flee from this bakery and never return.

"Let's go," I said in a soft voice. "I have to buy a dress for the wedding and if we don't hurry, we will never make it back before dinner."

It was a lie, we both knew it, but she nodded anyway.

"See you on Sunday, y'all," I said with a wave and left our half-drunken coffees behind us.

# Ax

I couldn't even enter the store with Nyx.

Not that it would have been a good idea anyway, but as soon as I saw that poorly made fake money in the old man's hand, I knew that I was moments away from exploding. If I had followed her into that store, I was sure that I would have lost control on either her or some poor innocent soul that was working there.

Hell, I wanted to destroy Scott as soon as I saw those bills. I was ready to. Him and the whole shop.

If Nyx hadn't been there to pull me out of my rage-induced haze, I didn't know what I would have done.

"Sir?" Yvon asked from the front seat. The divider was down, and it was just him and I in the limo.

I had taken my jacket and tie off while I was waiting for her and currently sat with my head back against the seat, staring at the black ceiling of the car.

My mind was buzzing.

"Do not lower the divider, no matter what you hear," I said. "Take us straight to the house and turn straight back once we leave."

"Yes, sir," he said and rolled up the divider.

I pulled out my phone and dialed Jonson's number. As always, he picked up on the second ring.

"Agent Jon—"

"I fucking *told* you I didn't want any of that trash in my stores," I growled. "So why am I finding that shit?"

"Damn it, Ax, you can't keep calling me like this," he grumbled. "What are you talking about?"

"The *money,* Jonson," I reminded, trying hard to rein in the violent emotions swirling inside me. "It's in my businesses now, and I told you I did—"

"The money?" Jonson echoed. "I have no idea what you are on about. I sent you the guy so you could use him how you see fit. How the fuck am I supposed to know anything about your... *businesses?*"

"You promise me right now that you had nothing to do with it," I ordered.

The door opened and a hesitant-looking Nyx stepped in with a bag of clothes and my card still in her hands. A part of me was pleased she treated herself with my money... but did she have to buy so much shit?

She tried to hand it to me, but I waved her away and shifted in my seat, spreading my legs farther. Her eyes followed the motion.

"I don't even know what you are talking about—"

"You know exactly what I am talking about," I hissed. Nyx's eyes widened, and her tongue darted out to wet her lips.

"I don't, Ax, really," he said with an exasperated sigh. "I don't know how it got into your stores. All I did was refer him to you. I have done nothing else."

"If I find out you are lying, you will wake up to your toenails being pulled off one by one," I growled.

"Jesus, Ax—"

"And send me his boss's name," I commanded.

"I don't give up my—"

"Jonson," I interrupted in a clipped tone.

Nyx jumped in her seat.

"*Fine,*" he hissed. "I'll get back to you in a few—"

"Hours," I interrupted. "Four at most."

"Ax—"

"Is the guest's bedroom window fixed yet?" I asked, letting my eyes trail down Nyx's form. She was dressed casually today, but that didn't take away from her beauty. And lucky for me, it would seem those clothes would be easy to take off.

"Six," he shot back.

"Five," I growled. "Take it or leave it."

"Taking it, don't fucking bother me until then."

He hung up on me, and I threw my phone onto the seat adjacent to me. With my eyes still locked onto Nyx's, I knocked three times on the car's roof and Yvon started to drive.

Nyx stayed silent as we pulled out of the city. Every second I was with her in this goddamn car made it that much harder to concentrate. Made it that much harder to breathe. And Jesus fucking Christ, did I want to pull her to me and see if she tasted the same as all those months ago.

"What happened?" she asked after twenty minutes had passed.

Her eyes were fixed on the bag of clothes in her lap, and mine were fixed on her. I had memorized every part of her. The way her breathing started to become erratic. The way she pushed her thighs together as if I couldn't tell what she was trying to do. The way her cheeks flushed when a particularly delicious thought crossed her mind.

I was losing myself in her.

There was nothing outside of this car that I could even focus on besides her. Asher, the fake money, the leaked photos... all of it disappeared into the background and in its place was *her.*

I couldn't do anything to reel myself in at this point. The anger, lust, and pure need had begun to consume me and I was sure that if I didn't have her lips on mine in mere minutes, I would combust.

"Put the clothes on the ground," I ordered and slowly unbuttoned my cuffs. She slowly put them to the side of her and placed her now empty hands in her lap.

"I don't think—"

"Safe word," I said. "Tell it to me."

"Pineapple," she breathed, her eyes going wide.

The small remembrance of our time together caused electricity to dance on my skin. This time wouldn't be like the last. We were no longer strangers now. I knew what that little file said about her, and I couldn't stop myself any longer. I was going to fuck her until I had my fill, and then, I would stop.

Like an addict, I allowed myself one last hit, promising that afterward, I would never allow myself the sinful delight ever again.

But we all knew how much of a lie it would be.

"I have found myself unable to wait," I said. She leaned forward and my eyes snapped toward hers. "Sit still and stay there."

She slowly leaned back.

"Yes, *sir,*" she purred.

*God.* I almost groaned aloud at the sound of *sir* on her lips once more. I rolled my sleeves up, once, twice, a third time before speaking again, fully aware of how her eyes had locked onto me.

"This ends after this," I said. "We do not speak of what happened here or in the club that night to anyone outside this car. Do you understand?"

She hesitated for a moment before nodding. I didn't have to remind her of her mistake, she straightened and let out a light, "Yes, sir."

"Clothes off," I commanded.

She hesitated, and I saw a spark of defiance, but it was gone as soon as it came and she rushed to take her clothes off. She started with her shirt and unclipped her bra. When her pert breasts and rosy nipples were bared to me, I couldn't help but suck in a sharp breath.

Heat coiled in my stomach and my mouth went dry. I licked my lips, wishing I could taste them.

"Pants," I commanded.

She took off her pants and underwear in one fell swoop.

"Open."

She spread her legs for me, showing me her already wet and swollen pussy. Her breathing was heavy now, her breasts rising and falling with each inhale. Her lower lip was between her teeth as she tried to keep a hold of herself.

"Do you want me to touch you?" I asked her.

"Please, sir," she said in a breathless moan. She spread her legs even farther, but I stayed in my seat.

"Show me."

Without a single ounce of hesitation, her hands trailed up her sides and around her breasts. She used one hand to pluck her nipple and the other teased its way down her stomach until it reached her swollen clit. She looked at me and a sick, sharp burst of pleasure rose through me.

"You may continue," I said and watched as she rubbed back and forth on her swollen clit. Her movements were hard and hurried. She was chasing a single orgasm out of many and I wondered briefly how many I could give her in the car ride we had together.

She let out a strangled moan and threw her head back.

"Don't stop until you make yourself come *at least* twice," I said and began rolling up my sleeves.

If she heard me, she gave no indication of it. She continued to rub her clit, her body writhing under her touch. Her pussy was so wet it began dripping on the leather seats and I had the strong urge to make her lap it up with her tongue, but I resisted.

Anger rose in me when she came. She let out a loud whine and her body jerked as her orgasm ripped through her. But it wasn't the act of her coming that angered me.

It was because she didn't even look at me as she fucked herself.

"Stop," I growled.

She forced her eyes open to look at me but she did not stop

rubbing her clit. She let out an even louder moan and dipped two fingers inside of her.

"*Fuck,*" she gasped and began to fuck herself. Her entire hand glistened with her own cum and the sounds of her moans and gasps filled the car.

Then when the triumphant smirk spread across her face, I lunged forward and pulled her off the seat, forcing her to the ground. I slammed my lips to hers in a bruising kiss and pried her mouth open with my tongue.

She moaned into me and tangled her cum-covered hands in my hair. Her legs wrapped around my waist and she began grinding against me in search of friction.

I nipped at her lips and trailed kisses down her neck and took a hold of one nipple in my mouth, sucking it lightly. When I bit down, she arched into me.

"More," she commanded. "Please, *sir.*"

The car was more cramped than I would have liked but I managed to kiss down to her sopping cunt where I latched onto her clit and sucked it, hard.

Her thighs wrapped around my head and her fingers tugged at my hair.

I gripped her thighs, digging my nails into her skin, and feasted on her. I didn't care for air, nor did I care that her grip on my hair had become painful. All I could think about was how starved I had been. How deprived I have been to have kept this from myself.

Everything about her, from the way her thighs fit around me to the way my name sounded on her lips to the way she tasted, was as if it came from the devil himself. She was the sweetest yet most forbidden treat he could have given me, and I fell for it *every fucking time.*

"Fuck, Ax," she gasped.

I licked the length of her pussy before latching back onto her clit. I should have punished her for calling my name but I couldn't because it sent waves of heat through me so powerful I was losing my mind.

She came with a whine and I leaned up to replace my tongue with my fingers.

"I wish I had my toys here," I said and plunged two fingers inside her. Her back bowed. "You would look so beautiful tied up, my ropes so tight, your skin would be red after. I'd leave you like that until you've come so many times all the fight leaves from your body."

Her pussy tightened around my fingers and I ground the heel of my palm into her clit.

"Someone is a liar," I purred. "First being a brat, now this? What's next? Are you going to come on my hand when I call you my *little whore?*"

She had to cover her mouth to muffle the sob that escaped from her mouth. I pounded into her and curled my fingers inside her. She was squeezing me so tightly I knew that she would be coming soon.

I leaned forward and brushed a kiss to the inside of her thigh before biting down on it.

It was the thing that sent her into an orgasm so violent I had to place my free hand on her lower stomach so I could continue to fuck her.

"Say it," I growled. She shook her head wildly.

"F-fuck you," she choked out. Her eyes widening as soon as she realized what she had done.

I smirked and pulled my fingers out to force them into her mouth.

"*Dirty* mouth for my *dirty* little whore," I cooed and leaned down to lick her nipple. "What are you? Tell me."

She bit down on my fingers and I pulled them out to grab her throat, squeezing the sides of her neck just hard enough to make her breath catch. The way her eyes lit up was dangerous because they only added to my desire for her.

"I'm not *your* anything," she said, though her words became weak when I pulled her nipple into my mouth and sucked.

"Say it or I won't let you come," I growled and looked up at her. I trailed the hand that was on her stomach to her clit and rubbed slow circles in the abused flesh. "Say it, Nyx. Tell me you're my little whore."

She whined when I pulled my hand away.

"Ax—"

"*Sir,*" I corrected.

Her eyes flashed open and a wild smirk spread across her lips.

"I'm *daddy's* little whore," she said.

*Fuck.*

The words shouldn't have affected me as much as they did, but it caused my own core to clench and wetness pooled in my underwear. With a growl, I lunged at her, capturing her lips in mine before spreading her legs and rubbing the heel of my palm on her clit.

Her arms wrapped around my neck, and she pulled me to her, making our bodies flush. Her kisses were wild, crazed. She gripped at my hair, my shirt, then she tugged so hard on my vest that I heard the buttons rip from the seams and fly somewhere around us.

I wrapped my hand around her waist and pulled us up so that I was on my knees and her legs were spread across my legs. I pulled back, taking in her flushed face, swollen lips, and wild hair. She was beautiful in the messiest of ways.

"Show me then," I whispered and curled my fingers inside her. "Ride *daddy's* hand like the *whore* you are."

She kept her eyes on me, and her hand wrapped around my shoulders as she planted her hands and began to rotate her hips on top of me.

"That's right," I cooed and planted kisses on her neck. She let her head fall back with a moan. "Make yourself feel good."

She whimpered when I brought my thumb to her clit.

"I need mor—"

We were cut off in a sudden turn. She fell forward, pushing me back and causing my back to hit the seat. This position was much more comfortable though, because she easily straddled my stomach and continued her movements.

Her breasts were at the perfect place for me to lean forward and take a nipple into my mouth.

"Fuck, Ax," she moaned. "Please. Please, more, I need—"

I cut her off by gripping her waist to stop her movements and taking over.

She stiffened and leaned forward to put her hand on the seat behind me. Her wetness was dripping all over my hand and onto my vest. Small droplets of sweat fell on me, and I leaned back to watch her face as she squeezed around my fingers.

I had seen her come so many other times before this, but in that moment, it felt different. Her eyes were closed, her mouth open, and her head slightly tilted back. Her face was relaxed and euphoric all at the same time.

She may not have realized it but during this moment, she had fully given control to me. The once shy, inexperienced woman had learned when to take what she wanted and when to sit back and trust her partner.

And in that moment, that was what I felt like.

*A partner.*

The person that brought her over the edge again and again, the same person she trusted enough to give up full control to, and I—

*Didn't fucking deserve that.*

There was a dull throbbing in my head as reality crashed down on me. I had let myself fall too deep. Let myself become too intertwined with her. When did I stop looking at her like a one-night stand? When had I fallen so deep that there was no turning back?

Not only did I not deserve it, but it scared the living hell out of me. The last time someone had trusted me like this—

"*Sir,*" I corrected, needing some type of distance between us. "It's sir to you now."

# Nyx

I don't know what I expected from her.

But it was definitely not for her to fuck the life out of me on the floor of her limo then pull away from me like she just had. There was something this time about how she corrected me.

A coldness had seeped into her voice and the warmth and fiery passion that had filled the air around us got sucked right out of the car.

*Pineapple.*

The word was just on the tip of my tongue. I didn't want this to stop... but I didn't want it like this. I wanted her because she made me feel warm. Made me feel safe. Taken care of.

But this was cold. We were back to strangers now.

She was under me, her warm-honey eyes looking at me as if I had made some grave mistake. Her lips were drawn into a tight line but still swollen from our violent clashing. Her hair stood up at all ends after I had literally tried to yank it out. Her clothing was wrinkled, and the vest that had once looked so primed and regal was now torn apart and missing buttons.

"I'm sorry," I whispered, looking down at her. Though at that moment I wasn't sure exactly why I felt the need to apologize to her.

She pulled her fingers out of me and gripped my hips.

"You're for—"

"Thirty minutes out," came the voice of the driver from the speaker above us. I jolted and looked up to the ceiling.

"One more," she growled and pushed me back so I was on her thigh. When she guided my hips to move against her leg, my hands flew to her chest.

"Pineapple," I breathed. She stopped immediately and let go of my hips like they had burned her. "I'm sorry, I just can't—"

"It's okay," she said in a low tone. "Tell me what you need."

*What I need?*

What I need is to forget about the outside world. To forget about all the kinds of fucked-up shit I was doing and focus on the person in front of me, but even she...

Even she had just shown that whatever had been between us had just been in my imagination. It was small, but I saw it. Just like when she looked at her family with warmth in her eyes, so small it was almost unnoticeable, but I saw that.

Just like I saw the disgust in her eyes.

"I need to put my clothes on," I said slowly.

She nodded and sat up, reaching behind me to grab my discarded clothing.

I placed my hands on her shoulders, panic welling up inside me. "And space, please."

She paused and leaned back to look up at me. There was something—maybe uncertainty—that crossed her face, but I couldn't be sure because it was gone too fast.

"Okay," she said and leaned back against the seat.

I slowly got off of her, painfully aware of how much of a mess we made. Wetness covered my thighs, pussy, and her vest and pants were starting to stain. When I was finally able to maneuver myself off her in the unstable car, I saw that I had also made a mess of her pants.

*You realize four is unacceptable, don't you?*

Her words from *that* night played over and over again in my head. Shame rolled through me, making it impossible to look at her as I dressed. I could feel her eyes roaming over my body as I struggled to put on the clothes.

"Let me—"

"Please don't," I snapped, glaring at the offending hand that tried to steady me so I could pull on my pants.

Her eyebrows pushed together and her jaw was clenched. She was trying really hard to listen to my boundaries and act like a good caring domme, but it was obvious how much she was struggling.

It just made me feel worse. I shouldn't be taking my own shame and anger at the situation out on her.

When I finally got my clothes back on, Ax was already sitting back in her seat, looking over her clothes with a frown.

"What happened today?" I asked, crossing my arms over my chest.

Her eyes shot to me for a moment, then out the dark tinted windows.

"Something at the shop wasn't right," she said. "I'm sorry for taking it out on you. That wasn't right of me. I didn't mean to be so rough."

*Fuck.*

My heart twisted at the vulnerability of her words.

"That's not why I—" I took a deep breath. "I liked it. *A lot.* I just... don't want you to regret any of this."

Because that's what it looked like. She understood exactly what we were doing and the consequences that it had on her relationship with her son. She knew that the moment we just had wasn't just a *last time* and we would never think about it again.

What we had done just hurled us toward both the end and beginning of whatever it was we were building. And the horizon had no other promise than hurt.

She pushed her fist against her lips, eyes looking at the moving scenery outside.

"I regret everything about meeting you," she murmured, her voice barely louder than a whisper.

Pain exploded in my chest, but I worked hard to not show it on my face.

"Talk to him," I pushed. "I *promise* you, it will be enlightening."

She let out a huff of a laugh but there was no humor in her expression as she turned to me.

"*Enlightening,*" she reacted, the word coming out like a curse from her lips. "And what is it that I should ask him, hmm? Why his girlfriend—the only one he has ever brought home, by the way—was at *my* club and in *my* bed only to show up months later on his arm?"

*Her club.*

It wasn't a surprise really, though I suppose nothing was with her. Just her existing had been the biggest surprise in my life. Scratch that, her being Asher's *mother* had been the biggest.

I chewed on my bottom lip and dug my fingernails into my palms. I wanted nothing more than to tell her, but I was already toeing a line with Asher that I couldn't risk.

"Ask him..." I smiled when a particularly sick idea came to mind. "Ask him why he got that shiny new car of his."

Ax shook her head.

"He said it broke down on him and he got the dealership to replace it," she said, eyeing me.

It was my turn to laugh now.

"I didn't know you allowed Asher to use *your* money without any restrictions or oversight," I teased. "I mean, if you don't think there is anything weird about a new Porsche breaking down in the middle of a packed street, then I suppose that's just your prerogative."

Her jaw flexed and the tension was thick in the air between us.

"If you know so much, why don't you just tell me?" she asked.

I shrugged.

"Same could go for you and why you almost bit Scott's arm

off," I said. "Plus, the last thing I want to do is... get between you."

She rolled her eyes, the most expression and attitude I had seen from her to date.

"That's exactly what you want to do," she snapped. "That's all you've been poised to do. Since the moment you walked into my—"

Her words were stopped short by the car coming to a halt.

Without waiting, I grabbed my bag of clothes and climbed out of the car.

"Nyx—"

I cut her off as I slammed my door and walked toward the house, ready to destroy everything and anything in my path.

*If she wanted me to be the bad guy, the sick evil temptation that was ruining everything for her... then so be it.*

"So how did you two meet?" I asked Cheryl and Rob as they put the final touches on the thank-you gifts.

Since I had come back early, we had decided to do some last-minute tasks that had been pushed off. For Cheryl and Rob, this meant signing thank you cards and for me it meant wrapping up the small gift baskets Ax had purchased for the guests.

Ax was content to leave them the way that they were, but Cheryl had insisted that they needed something a little *more* and I wasn't about to fight her. Not on the night before her wedding at least.

She had been a nervous ball of energy since I arrived, and her family hadn't made it any better. Her mother, father, and siblings had been permanently banned from helping out or even speaking to her.

Not that I blamed her. Cyrille's knowing look and perfectly timed jabs scare the hell out of me.

*She had to be some kind of witch or something.*

As if she heard her name in my thoughts, she came waltzing out of the French doors armed with lemonade.

"We grew up together," Rob interrupted before Cheryl could yell at her mom. Her face was already red and her lips formed a small pout. "Didn't date until after high school though. After that, there was no one else."

I gave them a warm smile and thanked Cyrille for the lemonade.

"I love weddings," I said and placed another wrapped package on the floor next to me.

"Me too, dear," Cyrille said and placed a hand on my shoulder. It was obvious she had no intention of leaving anytime soon. "Everyone is so happy and joyful. Family comes from all over to celebrate the happy couple."

I sent her a smile.

"It's all just very lovely," I said and started on the next present. "I haven't been to many so every time I go I try to soak in every minute of it."

"You sound like my sister," Cyrille said with a small laugh. "But I think she likes the idea of weddings more than the actual wedding. Did you see her earlier? It looked like she swallowed a bug."

I winced and tried to focus on my present as memories of the limo assaulted me.

*That was all me.*

"I can't wait for it to be over," Cheryl said. "Don't get me wrong, I am super excited but it's just all so..."

"Exhausting?" I finished for her with a grin.

She nodded and sent Rob a shy smile. He grabbed her hand and placed a small kiss on her knuckles.

Seeing them together like this caused my chest to ache. I wasn't in a rush to get married or find my "true love"... but years of dating assholes—Asher included—wore me down. And don't get me started on whatever was happening with me and Ax.

All of it just proved that I was nowhere near achieving what they had.

"Have you been to Paris, Nyx?" Cyrille asked. I jumped when I realized I had zoned out looking at the happy couple.

I shook my head.

"Never even been out of the country," I said with a sheepish smile. "Though I would love to go."

"Mine and Ax's parents are from there," she said with a sigh. "We try to visit every few summers. Maybe next time you can tag along."

I didn't look over the fact that she hadn't mentioned Asher.

"I don't speak French," I said and moved on to the next present. "But I wouldn't turn down the offer for a vacation."

She let out a light laugh and patted me on the head.

"Most of us don't," she said. "My parents were too obsessed with making sure we knew English to ever try and teach us *real* French other than curse words when they yelled at us. Ax is the best but she doesn't use it often."

My insides heated at hearing Ax's name.

Hearing all this information about her... felt kind of *wrong.* She would never have agreed to share this much with me. Even so... I wanted to know more. *Needed* to know more.

"Does she go with you back to France often?" I asked, trying to keep my voice light.

"Not at all," Cyrille said with a huff. "She's *constantly* working. It's like she never had a day off in her life. Even with all this money, she still works like she has none."

I grimaced at her tone. I grew up with a single mother who had less than... reputable habits and caused us to have to scrounge a lot for money. I understood the struggle of trying to build some type of wealth only for it to be taken away from you by some unforeseen circumstances.

If I was in Ax's position, I probably would have done the same. I was still mad at her, *hurt* from earlier... but I understood this part of her.

"It's the mindset," I explained. "I don't mean to assume about how it was like growing up, but I didn't have much growing up and struggled. Even now I try my best to keep a roof over my head and even though I make much more than when I started out... I still revert back to my old habits. I think it's a way to assure you will always be safe and protected."

There was a silence after my words and I looked up to Cyrille as heat spread across my face.

"Ah sorry I didn't—"

"No, you're right," she said with a small smile. Her expression had turned wistful as she looked out to the wedding venue. "I guess I just hoped that she would treat herself better. I worry about her, you know."

I forced a smile to my face and grabbed her hand.

"She's lucky to have someone as caring as you to think of her," I said. "She probably just wants to make sure you and Asher have the best life you could. I know if I was her, I would be the same. She is the oldest sibling after all, right?"

She shook her head, a smile spreading across her face.

"She is actually the youngest," she said in a whisper. "I don't really act like the older sister, do I?"

Heat spread across my face and I stammered for an apology.

"I am not *that* sensitive," she said with a laugh. "She has just always been the one to take care of the family. Even when she was young. I remember when I was in middle school she would sneak me her allowance to make sure that I had enough to eat. Worried about my weight loss. Little did she know I was trying to diet."

I couldn't help but smile at her. The image of little Ax giving her sister lunch money would be burned into my mind forever.

"I can see that," I whispered. "There is a lot of love in your family. Your parents must be proud."

Cyrille gave me a small smile before patting my head.

"Asher is lucky to have such an understanding girlfriend like you," she said.

And just like that, I was pitifully slammed back into my body.

Whatever warm emotions that had filled me during that time vanished and there was a sour taste on my tongue.

"I'm sorry," I whispered and stood. "I'll be right back."

As I was making my hasty escape, I didn't miss the sight of a lingering Ax leaning against the side of the French doors. She watched me with narrowed eyes as I escaped.

# Ax

It was a ploy, I just knew it...

So why did the credit card statement show exactly what she had alluded to?

It was impossible to miss, but I had been so... *distracted* with myself—my business—that I hadn't even realized how much money Asher had been blowing on useless things.

Cars, expensive clothes, and heaps of jewelry. Though I had yet to see Nyx wear any type of jewelry and there were pages and pages of receipts for various high-end shops.

I chalked it up to her own personal preference. After all, she hadn't had *that* hard of a time accepting my money, so why not Asher's?

A knock sounded on the door of my study and I turned just in time to see Asher's head poke through the small space, the light from the hallway lighting the room. He smiled and stepped over the threshold.

"Such a hermit," he joked. "No light, staring at a computer, and glasses to top it all off."

I forced a smile and took off the blue light glasses I used for work and swiveled around in my chair to look at him.

"I thought you said you had problems with your car," I said.

He shrugged and rocked back on his heels.

"I did," he said. "Porsche went ahead and replaced it."

I gave him a long hard look but stayed silent.

His eyes shifted to the computer behind me and he let out a sigh.

"Look, I don't know what she told you—"

"She? Nyx?" I asked and cocked my brow. "What does she have to do with it? I just want to know why you bought an entire fucking car without letting me know. You would have gotten away with it if my people hadn't been careful and flagged it for me."

I don't know what made me want to lie to protect the person that was single-handedly ruining my life.

He rolled his eyes and looked back toward the door.

"Someone poured sugar in my gas tank," he said after a moment and looked back toward me.

"Sugar?" I asked. "Who would do that? They know it would ruin—"

Ash let out a groan.

"I know she had to have said something," he growled. "*Nyx* did it, okay?"

"No," I said and shook my head. "Nyx? Why would she do that?"

It didn't make sense in my mind. Nyx may have been many things, but I knew she wouldn't have done something like that, right?

"I cheated on her, Mom," he said. "She found me on my desk fucking a girl and decided to get back at me by ruining my car."

The air was sucked right out of my lungs, and I found myself floundering for words.

*I don't want your son.*

*It's complicated.*

*... he feels incredibly pressured to bring a date here.*

Suddenly the tension between them, the anger from Asher I saw in the hallway, they were lying about how they met… all of it started to make sense.

He was trying to save face… but why?

"Asher," I moaned and ran my hand through my hair. "Tell me you didn't."

When he was silent, I peered back up at him. His entire body was tense.

"Why is she here—"

*"Because you won't leave me the fuck alone about it!"* Ash yelled, his voice bouncing off the walls.

I sat there stunned as he glared at me, his chest heaving with each intake of breath.

"I didn't mean to—"

"She's here because I fucking asked her to, okay?" he growled. "I *tried* to bring someone you liked. I *tried* to show you that I was fine and could live up to your insane fucking exp—"

"Asher, I don't expect—"

*"Don't you fucking lie to me,"* he hissed. "I felt too fucking ashamed about cheating on the only girl that looked at me as more than a wallet and forced her to come here, okay? We broke up almost four months ago."

Four months. *Four* months.

I ran my hand over my face, feeling the exhaustion weighing on me.

"I'm sorry, Asher," I said with a sigh and looked up at him.

His chest was heaving and his face was flushed. I stood to go to him but he took a step back, the action causing my chest to twist in pain.

I didn't want this to happen to us nor did I realize just how shitty I had been to him. If he had felt such pressure to live up to my expectations, I had to have gone wrong somewhere, even if I didn't do it on purpose.

The last thing I *ever* wanted was for Asher to feel the pressure

I had while growing up. I wanted him to get the best out of life and live the life we all wished we could have.

*I fucked up.*

"I didn't realize that—"

"You don't realize a lot," he snapped back. "Ever since Mom died, it's like your blinders have been on. You don't realize anything because you don't *see* anything other than your work."

The dig about his mother caused his words to spear my chest.

"I have to work so we can afford this lifestyle," I said, though I knew it was a poor excuse. If his mother was still alive, she would never have allowed this to happen.

He let out a noise of frustration and threw up his hands.

"That's your excuse for being an awful parent?" he growled.

I sighed and ran my hand through my hair while looking at the bank statements on my computer.

"I *tried,* Asher, I *am* trying," I said and looked back to him. "I'm sorry if you felt pressured to bring her here be—"

"I felt pressured?" he asked and shook his head. "I knew I shouldn't have brought that *bitch* here. Couldn't keep her damn mouth shut. She was the one that told you, didn't she? I'm not stupid."

Anger and panic rose in me so sharp it made my head spin.

"Don't call her that," I growled. "You were the one that *cheated* on her and tried to cover it up. If you would have just been honest—"

"Since when are you besties with her?" he asked with a raised brow.

"I-I'm not," I stuttered, losing my cool.

I didn't want to have this talk, especially not about Nyx. My mind was already whirling with the thought of Nyx not *actually* being with Asher. This whole time I had been *killing* myself thinking that I was fucking his girlfriend.

Though fucking his *ex* wasn't much better.

He eyed me and then cast his gaze to the ground, letting out a loud sigh.

"I'm sorry, Mom," he said, his voice barely above a whisper. "I just thought that maybe bringing her here would make you happy."

I let out a sigh of my own.

"Just seeing you has made me unbelievably happy, Asher. I've missed you." I said earnestly. His smile made my chest ache because I knew that if he had any idea what Nyx was to me, I would quite literally *never* see that smile again.

He walked over to me, unprotected and threw his arms around me. The last time he had given me a hug was when he was graduating high school and he had grown a whole foot taller since then, causing the top of his head to come up to my forehead. He leaned his head in the crook of my neck and I wrapped my arms around him, inhaling his scent deeply.

"I've missed you too," he said, exhaling and sinking into me.

The day of the wedding had to have been one of the worst days of my life to date.

I had stayed up all night, tossing and turning, remembering what Ash had said about Nyx. I don't know what was worse.

Me fucking his girlfriend...

Or me fucking the ex he cheated on yet still obviously had feelings for.

The way his face twisted when he mentioned the way he fucked her over and then when he called her a bitch...

I have never felt my blood boil so intensely.

I loved Asher with all my heart but goddamn, in that moment, I was ready to burst.

It took all my strength to pull myself out of bed and dress in something remotely presentable though I didn't care about my hair or obvious bags under my eyes. I tried my best to stay away from Nyx and Asher for most of the day, but when it came time to prepare for the guests, I had to force myself out into the world.

"Ax," a hesitant voice called from down the hall behind me. I didn't have to turn to know it was Nyx.

I straightened my suit and took a deep breath before facing the person that had single-handedly turned my world upside down. I didn't even register my sister standing next to her at first because I was so taken aback by the beauty that stood in front of me.

Nyx's black hair fell down her back in waves with two small twists pulling most of her hair out of her face. Her makeup remained light but there was a shine to her face that made her look like she was positively glowing.

Her dress was a deep-blush color that matched the wedding colors and meshed well with her skin. It was a silk-like material that had a sweetheart neckline and sleeves that hung slightly off her shoulders, showcasing her collarbones and neck in a way that made my mouth water. Memories of my lips trailing her throat and chest flashed through my mind and when she took a hesitant step forward, her smooth leg peeking out of the slit of her dress, my heart began hammering in my chest.

"Claudia is waiting," my sister said from beside her.

I tried desperately to pull my attention from Nyx, but my body wasn't responding to my mind.

"Sorry," I managed to choke out. "Is she in the dress already?"

When Nyx's gaze cast downward, the spell was broken and I was able to shift my eyes to my sister who gave me a knowing look.

"Yes," she said and held her hand out to me. "And she desperately needs the company of her aunt to continue on."

"She's nervous," Nyx added and turned, giving me a look at the top of her bare back as she did so.

I nodded and swallowed thickly.

"Go on, sweetie," my sister said to Nyx. "Tell her we will come in a minute."

Nyx nodded and walked down the hall and around the corner without another glare toward me, her heels lightly echoing throughout the empty hallway.

I walked toward my sister and ran my sweaty palms down the front of my suit jacket.

My sister clicked her tongue and reached forward to fix my tie, which I just now realized was the same blush that Nyx wore.

"Should I be worried?" she whispered.

I cleared my throat and looked straight ahead toward where Nyx fled from.

"Worried about what?" I asked, though we both knew I was well aware of what she was asking.

She let out a huff.

"Worried that I'll find you and her in a broom closet while your *son* is missing his date," she hissed.

My eyes trailed back to her, her words hitting me so hard it knocked the air out of my chest.

"I have more control than that," I muttered and pushed past her.

She didn't fight me on what I said but the unspoken words swirled around us.

*Are you sure? Because the way that you looked at her said the exact opposite.*

To my sister's merit, it wasn't a broom closet.

I found myself forced close to Nyx in a worse way than I ever thought possible.

We were assigned to sit right next to each other and Asher was on the other side of her.

The ceremony was beautiful, tears were shed and I watched with a full heart as my niece married the person of her dreams. His family was sweet and welcoming and surrounded my sister and me for far longer than I would have liked, but I endured because it made them happy.

And then the reception started and I was forced to a table on the edge of the property, our backs toward the apple trees that surrounded the place. The sweet scent of their wilting blossoms cut through the mixture of sweat and sweets. Normally it would have put me at ease, but now it only worsened my anxiousness.

I had picked this spot previously, thinking that this would be a great place for Asher and me to talk after the ceremony. I had chosen only a few other people to sit next to us, but those seats remained empty as people drank and mingled on the dance floor.

Leaving just the three of us, and I swear to *god* if Nyx's leg brushed across mine one more time, I was going to go insane.

"I'm going to get drinks," Ash said and stood abruptly. "Want anything?"

"My regular," I said with a forced smile.

His eyes lingered on Nyx and his hand reached out as if to touch her, but he pulled back at the last moment.

"Champagne, Nyx?" he asked.

She sent him a smile that made heat flow freely throughout me.

*Jealousy is a fucked reaction, Ax.*

"Yes, please," she said and paused for a moment. "Or if there is anything stronger, I would appreciate it."

A smirk flitted across his face.

"I got you, babe," he said and left the table.

I let out a loud sigh as he disappeared into the crowd leaving just Nyx and I behind.

"Why didn't you tell me?" I hissed and turned to Nyx. Anger shot through me when she gave me a look.

"Tell you what?" she asked with her brow raised.

Her leg bumped into mine under the table again and I let out a growl before grabbing her, though rougher than I probably should have. Skin touched skin and I realized that her dress had fallen, leaving her leg bare under the perfectly placed tablecloth.

She sucked in a sharp breath of air, her face flushing.

"That Ash had *cheated* on you," I said in a low tone.

Her eyes shot out to the crowd and she sat back in her chair, giving off an air of ease and confidence but underneath the table her legs were so tense they began to shake.

"It wasn't my place," she said and licked her nude-colored lips.

"So, you decided to ruin his car?" I asked. "Do you know how much it cost me?"

"Yes," she said, turning toward me. Her face had hardened and there was a slight smirk on her lips. "I know exactly what it cost you, and if you were so worried about money, you would have caught that purchase *months* ago and we wouldn't be in this situation now."

My jaw clenched and I grasped her bare leg tighter. My fingers ached to climb higher and to check if she had worn underwear tonight.

I hoped she didn't.

I don't know if it was my tiredness or the relief of finally knowing that Nyx and Asher were not together, but I felt a brush of confidence light in my chest and the words were out before I could stop them.

"You look good in my money," I murmured in a low voice and made a show of trailing my eyes down her body. For the first time all night, I allowed myself to selfishly take in her body. The dress fitted perfectly to her and the color of it brought out the smoothness of her skin.

The party fell away around us and all I could focus on was the sharp rise of her chest. The neckline was low, almost scandalously so, and it would have been so easy to grip the hem and bare her plump breasts to the world.

Just as easy as it would be to slip my fingers between her legs.

If I were a better person, I would have been able to control myself. I would have been turned off by being here in front of all these people, including her ex, but if anything, it fueled me. I wanted to watch her squirm, trying her hardest not to let anyone know that I was fucking her under the table and in front of them all.

I wanted the cry from her orgasm to be lost in the heavy bass of the music and for the flush of her cheeks to be attributed to her drinking.

But we would know better. And that scandalous piece of information would be enough to fuel me for the rest of the night.

"I don't get it," I murmured, watching as my words caused her to jump.

Her eyes shot to mine and her tongue darted out to lick her lips.

"Don't get what?" she asked. Her voice had a noticeable shake and it caused my head to swim.

"A lot of things," I answered. "Why you even got with Asher to begin with. Why you played this little game with him. Why you showed up at *my* club, requested *me*."

She paused, her eyes flashing to mine.

"I wanted someone experienced, is all," she said. Her eyes flashed back to the party and narrowed in on something, my guess was Asher.

"And most of all, I *still* don't get why I can't stay away from you," I said in a low tone.

Her breath caught, and there was a slight blush spreading across her cheeks.

It was a lie though. I did get it.

Nyx was beautiful, kind, she was a survivor. She kept her volatile and ugly emotions deep inside her only to be pushed out when forced... and it *intrigued* me. She was the first person who had ever been able to make me so completely and totally reckless.

And it was not me. Not the me that I had been carefully crafting all these years.

So this... this was me being selfish. This was me giving in to my desires even though I knew how dangerous they were.

"He's coming," she whispered and my gaze shot over to see Asher moving through the crowd with two glasses in his hand. I shifted in my seat and placed my elbow on the table to lean my head on my palm, making it look like Nyx and I were in a pleasant, casual conversation.

Against my wishes, I pulled my hand away just as Ash came to our table.

"I have to go get mine but here are yours," he said.

"Thank you," I said and reached the hand that was gripping his ex's thigh to the glass of whiskey.

"Looks like you two are getting along," he said playfully and handed her a large glass of what looked to be a Long Island.

"She was just telling me about her biggest client," I said, the lies coming out smoothly.

It hadn't taken much digging to find out about this client. Apparently they were kind of a big deal, which made sense why her boss was so uptight about her meeting them, but that didn't give him an excuse to be an asshole.

I had done a little digging on him too. Turns out he tried to get away with a bit of tax fraud this last year, so if worse came to worse, there were things that could be done to make his life a living hell. All it would take is a few calls to the right people and he would be in cuffs faster than he could start that fancy new Porsche of his.

"Ah yes," Asher said. "How did that go, by the way?"

She shifted under the attention and took a sip of her drink.

"They were nice," she said. "Very young, though most of the company is. They left happy, and my boss finally got off my back when he saw that they preferred me over him. Think it scared him a bit."

A smile pulled at my lips.

"Why not just work for them instead?" I asked and brought my cup to my lips. "Sounds like your boss is a dick."

Nyx's eyes widened before letting out a small laugh.

"Language," she chided. "But I'm not sure. I have been there for a few years and it took me a while to get to the point I'm at now."

I nodded.

"You'll be more valuable to another company," I said. "Moving every few years will increase your salary instead of just staying in one place."

She mulled over the thought for a moment before Asher interrupted.

"I'll go get my drink, feel free to continue," he said and disappeared back into the crowd.

I didn't hesitate to slip my hand back under the table and grip her thigh.

She sent me a glare.

"What do you think you are doing?" she asked.

"What does it look like?" I asked and hooked her leg over mine, letting my fingers trail mindless patterns on her skin and getting slowly to the spot that made my mouth water with each movement.

Her eyes darted around the party and her hand gripped the drink so hard her knuckles turned white.

"He's going to come back," she muttered.

I smiled when my hands brushed across her damp underwear.

"Then you better keep a lookout," I said and applied light pressure to her core. She swallowed, her eyes widening.

"There are people around," she said but her legs spreading for me under the table gave me all the answers I needed.

"Safe word," I reminded. "Tell me it."

"Pineapple," she said, but it was barely audible over the music.

Satisfaction unfurled inside me when she shifted again. I couldn't keep the smile off my face.

"Tell me," I whispered and shifted so I was facing the party. No one was looking our way, and even if they had, they would see us looking like we were deep in conversation. I grabbed my drink with my free hand just for an extra touch. "Do you like it? Having so many people around us but not one of them knowing that I'm going to fuck you under this table?"

Without warning, I gripped her underwear and pulled them down just enough for me to run my fingers down her wet folds. Her gasp was concealed by the bass of the music.

*Perfect.*

# Nyx

Her words caused my skin to light and my stomach to clench.

I shakily brought my drink to my lips, trying desperately to cover my flaming face. I had long ago lost sight of Asher and foolishly hoped he wouldn't come back.

Ax's hand left me to tug my underwear down even more.

"Take them off," she commanded.

I helped her take them off, only to watch her grab them and put them in her pocket. Her hand was back to my thigh in seconds, forcing my leg back over her legs, this time wider, so when she brought her hand back to my dripping pussy, she would easily be able to fit two fingers inside me.

"Tell me," she said and used her thumb to rub my clit as she pumped in and out of me slowly. "Are you getting off on knowing that I'm going to make all these people watch you come?"

I couldn't hold in my moan.

I wanted to hate it. I wanted the vulnerability of the entire thing to make my stomach turn and to use the shame that washed over me to make me find this whole situation disturbing...

*But I fucking loved it.*

I loved the secrecy of it. I loved the wildness and risk of it all.

It would take only a single person to come back and ruin this entire thing and for us to be outed to the entire wedding.

"Yes, *daddy*," I whispered and reached my hand down to my clit, replacing her thumb.

She froze for a moment before shifting and picking up her pace, ramming her fingers into me in a way that must have been obvious for anyone to see from afar, but her face was so stone cold they probably would have just overlooked it.

"Oh god," I moaned and picked up the pace on my clit.

White-hot lava replaced my blood and every movement of her fingers combined with mine was making a delicious heat coil in my belly.

"Faster," she mumbled and my eyes moved across the crowd to see Asher's familiar form walking through the crowd.

I imagined Asher coming here and seeing Ax's fingers inside me, watching me come while still inside me. My pussy clamped down so hard on Ax's fingers I had to hunch forward, unable to keep my collected demure.

I peeked up to see Asher getting taken aside by a few of the guests, his eyes trailing to mine.

My body seized, white spots flashing across my vision as I came violently around Ax's fingers. Her eyes were glued to my face, but I forced my head to the table. To anyone else, it may have looked like I was just resting, but Ax and I knew better.

And now so did Asher.

I let out a choked sob as my pussy fluttered around her fingers, my own fingers furiously rubbing my clit, trying to ride out this orgasm as long as possible.

"Dirty, *dirty* girl," she whispered and pulled her fingers out of me before wiping them on my thigh. The act was humiliating and hot all at the same time.

After I caught my breath, I straightened my posture and looked back at the crowd.

Asher was gone and not a soul was looking at us. My clit was swollen and aching and my pussy was begging for more, but I knew at this moment that was not possible.

"I need more," I said and shakily took a sip of my Long Island.

She let out a laugh that made my insides heat.

"Well, it looks like we are both going to be disappointed tonight."

I didn't speak, letting her words sink in. And just like in the car, whatever was happening between us became painfully clear.

*This is not anything more or anything less than what just happened, and still, even now, it is filled with regret.*

That lying son of a *bitch.*

"I don't know where you got that information from, but I swear I would never—"

"Put the risk of our brand and our client's brand at risk?" my boss finished for me.

It was a normal Monday. The sun was out and there was only a slight warmth to the air, promising that today should have been a good day, but again I was lied to horribly and as soon as I stepped foot on the property of my workplace, I was called into my boss's office.

And then he started to lecture me about brand safety and the risk I was posing to our clients, without even divulging what I had *done,* though I knew for sure it had to be something with Asher, because what else could it be?

That slimy bastard had really gone against his word.

*Did you forget that I am going to hand this to your boss?*

I had done everything he had asked for. Played the good little pet. I smiled and laughed with his family and pretended to be the most doting girlfriend in the world, all so that he could turn around and get me fucking fired.

"I wouldn't," I promised, my voice rising an octave. "Please just tell me what is going on."

I was panicking, and it was showing. My anger was rising, but so was my worry. I was sweating buckets by then and it felt hard to breathe.

I stared at my boss, willing him to believe the innocent act... but it was lost on him. His beady eyes narrowed in on me and wandered down my body. I couldn't tell if he was criticizing me or checking me out.

He sighed and turned his screen around to show me a picture, but it wasn't the one that Asher had threatened me with.

This one was much worse.

It was still me, but instead of being taken outside of the club, it was from the inside and while I had my mask on, you could tell that it was me. I was in front of the girl who had checked me in and next to me, partially hidden, was the semi-naked girl that had brought me up to my room.

I swallowed thickly, not letting the raging emotions inside me take over my entire being.

"What is this?" I asked. "And isn't this a form of sexual harassment, you showing me a half-naked woman on your *work* computer?"

His entire face turned a bright red and he quickly turned his monitor back to him. It was his turn to panic. I kept my gaze sharp as I glared at him.

"That's you," he said. "In the dress and mask. And you should know that our company has a strict—"

"You cannot prove it is me," I said and stood on surprisingly sturdy legs. "I am walking to HR to file a complaint. You may think this is okay, but it isn't. No matter how small the company or what our relationship is, this is unethical and will be considered harassment."

"Like I said," he stammered after clearing his throat. "We have a very strict policy regarding—"

"What about your policy on harassment?" I interrupted. "Do

you know what *one* sexual harassment lawsuit can do to a company? I could literally bring down this entire fucking company with so much as *one* post."

He straightened in his chair and let out an offended huff. His face was so red he looked like a walking tomato. His breathing was heavy and he looked like he was about to burst.

It was that picture. The small man in his too-big chair, looking down on me for something that should have no shame attached to it at all. That picture was the one that made me realize that no matter what, he was not the boss I wanted to work for. He was a selfish, greedy little bastard that didn't know how to take no for an answer.

He stammered for a response but didn't find one in the time it took me to turn on my heels and walk out of his office. I held my head high as I walked through the office, many heads turning to look at me.

I ignored them, not letting the shame of what they probably just overheard get to me.

*I wasn't at fault here,* I tried to remind myself. Trying to stoke the anger so it overpowered the need to curl up in a ball and cry my eyes out.

When I got to our HR manager, her door was already wide open for me. She sat at her desk with a large stack of paperwork on the surface. Her curly hair had been pulled into a bun and her tired face looked even more sunken with the hard overhead light.

"Linda, he can't—"

"Nyx," she interrupted with a warm smile. "Close the door, dear, would you?"

I did what she asked and sat down in the chair across from her.

"It's sexual harassment—"

"Nyx," she said in a soft tone.

"You can't even prove that was me—"

"*Nyx,*" she said more firmly this time.

I bit my tongue and pulled my hands into my lap. My control

was slipping and my hands began to shake with anger. But it was more than that. Of course, I was pissed.

I was pissed at my boss.

Pissed at Asher.

Pissed at Linda.

But I was also utterly ashamed.

For the first and last time, I jumped into the deep end and tried to find something that made me truly happy. I had taken precautions and made sure that I wasn't tied back to the company but still... they found out.

Everyone in there must have heard and even through the thick panes of glass that separated me and the rest of the team, I could feel their burning gaze on my back and the judgment in their stares. It was humiliating.

Now everyone would know what happened there. They all knew that I had some *sick* and *twisted* fantasies. So much so that I had to go to a fucking BDSM club to get my fix. Shame and embarrassment burned my skin and I found even just keeping Linda's pitiful gaze was too much.

"There are multiple pictures," she said in a low tone. She shuffled through the folder of papers and pushed one toward me. When I got the courage to look at the paper, my eyes began to water.

It was a printout of my application to Club Pétale. Complete with my headshot and it listed *all* of the things that I was looking for while I was there.

"How did you get these?" I asked, my voice barely above a whisper. When I met her gaze, I couldn't stop the tears from overflowing. "*Who* gave these to you?"

"This was left in a package sometime over the weekend," she admitted and pushed the files toward me.

I peeled back the folder with a shaky hand and bile rose in my throat at the first picture. I slammed the folder closed, then grabbed it in its entirety and held it to my chest, the weight of it threatening to bring me down to the floor with it.

"This is appalling," I muttered. "This is blackmail. You can't just—"

"*Nyx*," she said again. Her tone sharp. "You signed a contract. You knew from the beginning that this company was strict on its employees and their image is their biggest concern because without this, the client—"

"I *know,*" I stressed. "But can't you see this isn't as simple as you guys are making it out to be? Someone is doing this because they *want* this to ha—"

"You went there *willingly*," she said, her fingernails clacking on the desk. "You signed up to become a part of this. And now that these pictures have come to light, we have to act."

I wiped the stray tears from my face, even more embarrassed knowing that I would have to leave this office looking like I had just broken down.

"Linda, please," I begged. "I need this job. Without it, I cannot afford to keep my place."

She let out a sigh.

"I know, Nyx," she said. "Trust me, I know. But these are the rules and as much as I want to nab that bastard for humiliating you like this... my hands are tied."

I leaned back in my seat, letting the situation sink in. Everything I had tried so hard to avoid the past few days had blown up right in my face. I knew Asher's words were too good to be true. He was an asshole and I should have learned how good of a liar he was when he started cheating on me.

That man could lie with a straight face if a gun was put to his head.

"Do I still get my sign-on bonus for Anneu?" I asked after a moment had passed.

She gave me a smile.

"I was able to negotiate it for you," she said. "That asshole wanted to take it for himself."

Now that brought a smile to my face.

"HR shouldn't call employees assholes, Linda," I chided playfully, pushing down the lump in my throat.

Two years. Two years I had been working here to provide a life for myself and it vanished in mere hours.

"Then employees should not force you to look at a picture with a half-naked woman in it," she said. "I warned him not to show anything, but he didn't listen, so you bet your ass he will be the next one in that seat."

A sense of comfort spread in my chest.

"Thank you, Linda," I said and grabbed my bag, folder, and my application to Club Pétale before standing. "Don't be a stranger."

She gave me a smirk.

"Oh, I won't," she said. "Expect a call from me soon to tell you all the juicy details of my conversation with him."

I shook my head and turned to walk out, not once looking back at my team or the boss that had shut me out.

# Ax

Sloan leaned over me, her chain hanging off her body. She was so close her skin brushed across mine and for once, I didn't find her teasing funny.

"It's bad, Ax," she said, her voice husky and sounding like it was overused.

If I didn't love her so much, I would have had her beaten for her annoying tendencies and lack of personal space already. Sloan has only been with me for the last few years, but she has become one of my favorites and one of the most valuable workers here at Club Pétale.

Like many of my work relationships, we found each other under some not-so-perfect circumstances. But this time, it had been my life on the line. A bit of miscommunication between me and a gang a few counties over.

Sloan was with them at the time and had spoken up for me, saving me from a bullet to the head. It wasn't long before I approached her to come work for me. At the time, I didn't know how skilled she was with cybersecurity until we were more than a year into our friendship.

She stood and ran a hand through her dyed-silver hair. The sides were shaved down and there were tattoos just beneath the short hair and traveled all the way down her neck and arms. She was taller and slimmer than I'd like to keep around, but she had proven more than capable.

She was about the age of my son, if not a bit older, but her maturity and intelligence had shown that she was older than her years. Her brown eyes held a light even in this dire situation and her skin was painted with freckles. There was a single piercing on the bridge of her nose and another on her lip.

"How bad?" I asked and leaned back in my seat.

She moved to sit on the edge of my desk but I gave her a look. She rolled her eyes and shifted on her feet.

"They used an employee ID," she said. "*Your* ID. Are you sure you only accessed it once last week?"

I nodded.

She ran her hand over her face.

"It says you've accessed these files multiple times over the last *few months, Ax,*" she said.

Anger fanned through me. Not only was the problem with the leak *getting worse,* but they had hacked into my system *and* Ryder had been a pain in the fucking ass.

How could I focus on my club here when another one just got hit by Ryder? I had no idea who his contact was in the New York police force, but when I got my hands on them, I was going to fucking kill them.

They had taken the whole club out and started to arrest the pseudo-owners. Luckily though, my people worked on loyalty. But that didn't mean that I could just sit here and take it.

"Why did no one flag it?" I growled.

She sent me a smile that made my blood boil.

"Why would they?" she asked. "You're the boss. It's your place. It's only right that you—"

"*No,*" I growled. "Only you and your team are supposed to have access to these files. It doesn't matter if I'm the fucking *President,* if someone is in here without authorization, *you* flag it."

There was a silence that fell over us.

"I'll fire them," she said. "Will that do?"

"Will that do?" I hissed. "These have been leaked as well as pictures from *inside* the club. N*o*, it will not do, Sloan."

Her eyes widened and she gnawed on her lip.

"I knew that... but the fact that they used *your* log-on is the most troubling," she said and grabbed the chain on her neck, tugging on it sharply. "I'll have them do some more digging. Can you send me the newest photos? I'll see what else we can pull from them."

"You should have already—"

"I am not a miracle worker, Ax," she snapped and walked around my table. "Let me do my job. Send me whatever new photos you have and I'll take a look at the log-on information."

I didn't say anything else and let her walk out of my office. When she shut the door with a soft click, I launched out of my chair and threw everything that was on my desk to the ground in one swoop.

I didn't stop there though, I tore everything out of my drawers, threw the papers all around, all while Sloan's words raged through my head.

*Who would do such a thing, and how fucking dare they try to make a mockery of me like this?*

As soon as I got a hand on whoever did this, I was going to make them pay. I had tried to do this the nice way, to put my past behind me. I tried to build a normal living for myself but it was becoming clearer and clearer by the day that the past was going to catch up to me sooner rather than later, and I was going to have to do things I wouldn't be proud of.

"Damn it," I growled and grabbed the picture frame that was lying on the ground and threw it at the wall.

Glass and wood shards flew everywhere and it was the only thing that was able to pull me out of my angered haze.

With a sigh, I walked over to the destroyed frame and picked it up, careful of the sharps of glass. I flipped it around to see a picture of a smiling Asher the day he graduated from college. He hadn't aged much since then, but there was a carefreeness about him in this picture that made me want to scream.

*What had happened since then?*

It had been two weeks since the wedding and he had gone back to ignoring me. I tried to actively reach out to him. I called him on my way home from work, messaged him. Fuck, I even tried to find him on social media, but there was no trace of him.

For all intents and purposes, he was a ghost.

I had a feeling he had to have found out about Nyx and me, but I would have expected more anger. Someone like him would have ripped my door down and took his anger out on me until he was satisfied. And I would have let him too. After some separation from her, I honestly could not understand what had come over me.

I was better than this.

I wasn't a weak woman that would break just for a taste of the forbidden. I had a life, a family that I had worked hard to care for and because of *her,* I had been distracted.

So much so that I let someone jeopardize everything I had been working for.

*I pray that Sloan can find that rat.*

The day after my breakdown, I received a call from Asher. I picked up on the second ring.

"Asher," I sighed. "I've been worried about—"

"I need a favor," he said, his voice coming out gruff and like he had just been sleeping.

I straightened in my seat. For the first time, Asher had come to me with a problem and even though I knew it shouldn't have excited me, it did.

Because he chose to call *me* after everything.

"Anything."

# Nyx

It was bordering on three weeks being jobless when I received a call from Asher.

Up until then, he had been ignoring my calls. I had texted, emailed, and called at all hours. I even drove to his work and stood outside for hours on *multiple* days, only for him not to show up. I thought that maybe he had been watching me and carefully avoiding me when I was there to ambush him, but when I pulled aside his coworkers, they all told me he really hadn't shown up.

It was almost worrying. Maybe he had gotten kidnapped, or worse. My mind, of course, went into overdrive as I sat in the parking lot, looking at the clouds and hoping to get a glimpse of him...

But then I remembered that he was the entire reason that I was stuck without a job and having to scrape by.

I had a small cushion of money, but it wouldn't last me long. Even just before I received the call, I was looking at my mom's contact information and debating whether or not to call her and ask for help. I was worried that since Asher had broken his promise to *not* tell my boss, that he may have broken the promise to not tell my overly religious family as well... but if that was the case, my emails and social media would have been blown up a long time ago.

I quickly picked up the shrill ringing phone before I missed his call. All the anger boiled up inside me and I couldn't wait to rip into him. I was almost giddy because of it.

"You fucking asshole, I'm going to kill you—"

"I have a job for you if you do me a favor," he said, cutting me off. His voice was just as harsh as it was when he was threatening me in his mother's home. He had lost the nice guy act completely. His tone was curt and cold as ice. I could hear a bit of noise muffled in the background but I couldn't make out anything notable.

"Fuck you, Asher," I said. I was seething, and hearing his cold tone only made me that much angrier. "You're the reason I lost my job in the first place. I trusted you, and you sent those pictures—"

"Do you want it or not?" he asked, annoyance clear in his tone.

"Why do you think that I would ever take anything you gave me?" I scoffed. "You have already proven to me how much of an asshole you are. I don't trust you for one moment."

He let out a heavy sigh and there was a pause between us as he weighed my words. He had taken so long to sit in the silence that I would have thought he had hung up if not for the muffled sounds in the background.

"Where are you?" I asked, breaking the silence. "I tried your work, and no one knew—"

"It's legit," he said, his tone softening. "Just a favor and I promise you that I will get you a new job. One that you will love."

"Will you tell me why?" I asked. "I followed through with everything—"

"We can talk about it when you come," he said. "Now, do you want it or not?"

I thought about it for a moment. Honestly, I didn't want it. I wanted to stay as far away from him as possible and try to recoup my losses. Working with him on yet *another* favor would probably hurt me more than it would help me.

But I needed it and like I said, I never was able to stop letting toxic people back in my life.

"What do you need me to do?" I asked hesitantly.

There was a low chuckle on the other end.

"Dress in that slutty outfit you wore to the club and meet me in your parking lot in fifteen," he said. "I'll tell you on the way."

Instant regret washed through me and all hopeful feelings I once had about this interaction disappeared.

*Fuck.*

He hung up the phone, forcing me to hurry off my couch and hope that I could find that damned dress.

"Asher," I warned as his hand slipped around my waist.

He steered me into the building where he threw the valet his keys and sent me a smirk like I should have been impressed with him.

"Calm down, Nyx," he said, his tone condescending. "These are the types of people you like."

*I knew I shouldn't have fucking trusted him.*

"You haven't told me what we are doing here yet," I hissed and grabbed onto his shirt as he pulled us through the lobby. "Or why you outed me to my work."

The place we walked into looked like an ordinary upscale hotel, complete with freshly waxed floors and multiple glittering chandeliers. Valet and staff greeted us as we walked in, all wearing clean suits. The air smelled of light lavender and there was a faint clanging of glasses and shattering coming from the bar in the lobby.

I tried to peer into the bar to see what type of people I was dealing with but he quickly pulled me across the room and to the elevators that waited for us. I tried desperately to keep up while also trying not to trip over my heels.

My feet were already beginning to ache and the fewer answers he gave me, the more nervous I got.

The elevator smelled like it had been freshly cleaned and there was a mirror on the interior, giving me a look at how we looked together. Asher had worn a T-shirt and jeans, which made me feel completely overdressed in my dress and heels.

"We are meeting some people I work with," he said, his tone light. "And you are here to play a part."

I gave him a look.

"And why did you go back on your promise?" I asked.

He shook his head and let out a bitter laugh.

"Because plans change, Nyx," he said, his eyes glancing toward me before going back to the mirror-covered door. When I followed his gaze, I saw he was looking at me through the reflection.

"What changed?" I asked, swallowing thickly.

He shifted.

"Letting my *mom* play with your pussy at a *family* wedding," he growled. "You thought you were slick, but I know an orgasm face when I see one. Remember, I used to play with it as well."

The world froze around me.

"Asher, I—"

"Don't," he said. "If anything, I should be thanking you because now you are here and I need all the help I can get."

I didn't know what to say. I knew we would get caught but... not like this. Not in an elevator with Asher. There was an awkwardness that filled the air between us and even though he had been the bigger asshole, I wanted to apologize for what I had done.

"What part do you need me to play?" I asked, my tongue feeling heavy and my heart beating fast in my chest.

"My *whore*," he said and when the elevator dinged and the doors opened, he pulled me into the room.

*Yep. A big fucking mistake.*

I was hit with the scent of cigarette smoke first, strong enough to tickle the back of my throat. I had to force down my cough and blinked a few times to take in the scene in front of me.

We had entered one of the penthouse suites. The entire space was open, only to be divided by short walls that didn't do anything to cover the sounds of sex floating through the air. The room was dim besides a few lights and there was heavy music that was so loud I could feel the bass in my chest.

As soon as we stepped in, the people who were sitting on the various couches that littered the space turned to look at us. I had never been one to judge anyone based on how they dressed or looked but I swore in that moment I had stepped into a literal gang den.

Men wore outfits similar to Asher and there were scantily clad women surrounding them. Some were playing cards while others were smoking, and the sour smell lingered underneath all the cigarette fumes... it was something a lot harder than nicotine.

I tried to school my expression, but this was like walking into my literal worst nightmare. Not only were we the center of attention in a place I *really* didn't want to be, but dark memories threatened to overtake me.

I had tried to push away the trauma of my childhood and the life-altering drugs my mom had been on... but the smell and the effects it had on the people were all too familiar. The dilated pupils, the various people passed out on the ground looking at nothing or nodding off.

The images of trying to wake my mom, screaming at her to get up after finding her on the floor after a day of school, filled my mind.

*No. I couldn't be here.*

My throat felt tight and the room felt as though it was closing in on me. The anger that I had been honing and looking forward to letting out on Asher changed into something sharper, scarier. Sweat poured from my skin and I took a shaky step back.

"Asher," I whispered, my voice holding a slight shake to it.

I didn't want to see this. I couldn't. I like to think that there was a lot that I could handle. I had been on my own since I was seventeen, for god's sake. I had seen some things, but this—*drugs* —it had always caused the same visceral reaction in me.

"Play your part, baby," he whispered and pulled me farther into the room.

I flinched as a random rough hand trailed my leg. I couldn't tell who it was from, but I also refused to make eye contact in fear that it would signal me as an outsider. He pushed past the people on the couches until we were pulled past the kitchen and to the side of the room that was partitioned by a small wall that did nothing to hide the noises from beyond.

Lead filled my gut and I was starting to get a bad feeling about being here.

"I won't fuck you here, Asher," I growled under my breath as we approached the other side of the suite.

He let out a laugh and shook his head. The action caused me to flush with anger and embarrassment.

"I don't like sloppy seconds, baby," he jabbed.

When we stepped around the wall, I had to bite my tongue to keep from making any noise. There was a large bed in the middle of the area, the whole right side of the room was made of glass, and the writhing, naked bodies were shown to the world.

On the bed, there were three men and a single girl. The girl was sprawled in the middle of the bed while her head lay off of it. One of the men was between her legs pounding into her with muffled grunts. Another was fucking her face, causing her to gag on his cock. The other had his hand on her throat while she was furiously jacking him off.

"Fuck, this bitch is going to come already," the guy between her legs huffed out.

A dull throbbing ache started between my legs and I couldn't help but admire the woman as she came. Her loud sobs filled the room only to be muffled by the man fucking her face. When the one between her legs looked up at us with a smirk, panic shot through me.

I averted my gaze, my face heating, only to meet eyes with another man. He was much older, with salt-and-pepper hair. He was sitting in a love seat off to the side, dressed in a suit and tie. He gave off an air of confidence and power, if not for the girl that was on her knees in front of him, deep throating his cock.

He leaned back, his eyes shifting from the people on the bed to us. There was something in the way his eyes bore into us that made me feel disgusting. His eyes trailed down my body and his hand came to pet the girl's head before pushing her down.

Her gags could be heard over the music.

"Asher," the man said and pulled the woman back only to shoot ribbons of cum on her face. All while looking at us.

*Disgusting.*

"Ryder," Asher greeted, his arm wrapping around my waist and pulling me closer. "Looks like I missed a party."

Ryder let out a snort and pushed the girl away before pushing his soft cock back into his slacks. The girl caught herself before falling to the ground and didn't even hesitate to join the others on the bed when Ryder stood. When he walked over to us, I couldn't help but shrink back into Asher. Ryder noticed and smirked.

"Is this the lovely Nyx?" he asked and held out his hand.

Asher's fingernails dug into my side. *A warning.*

"Yes," I said with a fake smile on my face, though I am sure my flushed cheeks gave away just how uncomfortable I felt being here. "It's nice to meet you."

When I put my hand into his, he jerked me out of Asher's arms and into his. He made a show of bringing my hand to his mouth and leaving a wet kiss on the back of my hand.

"Likewise," he murmured. "Asher, why don't we go outside? I'm sure your date would prefer something a bit more... *private.*"

I swallowed thickly. I didn't want to be here, that was for sure, but the idea of going somewhere *private* with these two caused my stomach to twist.

"She can handle it," Asher said from behind me, his hand trailing my back. "Whatever you prefer, Ryder."

He shot Asher a look before pulling me to the back of the penthouse. Beyond the glass, I could see a brightly lit pool and various lounge chairs. Before we went outside, I spotted stairs to a loft off to the side, though I was pushed out of the room before I could spy what was up there.

The outside air hit me like a slap to the face and the small dress that I wore did nothing to protect me against the cold. Ryder sat down in one of the comfy chairs that littered the area and motioned for me to sit down in the one across from him with Asher.

Asher sat first, then his hands found my wrist and tugged me down so that I would be forced to sit on his lap. He shifted us and sat farther back in the chair so I was sitting between his legs. His arms wrapped around me and his chin rested on my shoulders.

As much as I hated this asshole, I wouldn't give up the warmth he just provided me.

"Relax," he whispered in my ear, his hands trailing down my sides and running up and down my thighs, chasing away the chill on my skin with his own body heat. "You just need to *act* like my whore, not bend over for me. Unlike you, I don't like a fight."

Shame and anger flooded me at his audacity. I knew I deserved it for what I did with Ax, but that didn't make it any less painful.

"Fuck you," I whispered.

Ryder watched us with a heated gaze and Asher said nothing of my cursing.

"It's done," Asher said, raising his voice slightly to travel across the space between us and Ryder. "After this, it should be easy to get what we want and we can move into phase three."

Ryder's face split with a grin so slimy it caused bile to rise in my throat.

I have no idea who this man is or what Asher has gotten into, but nothing good came from this. I may have come to dislike Asher and hate him for what he has done to me... but he had to have known that what he was doing here may very well ruin his life, right?

"Good," he said and trailed his hands over his lips. "I am assuming we can have this done by the end of summer?"

Asher let out a small chuckle.

"Maybe sooner," he said. His hand trailed a little too high up my thigh, pushing up my dress just slightly and pulling Ryder's gaze down. "I'm thinking our little diamond in the rough can be *very* convincing."

His hand slipped under the hem of my dress, brushing far too close to my panties for my liking.

Feeling bold, I wrapped my hand around his wrist and stopped his motions. I expected him to get angry, like he had back at his house, but instead he just sat there, not moving his hand.

Ryder let out a laugh.

"I'm sure," he said. "Though I have to say, I'm not fully convinced this will be the nail in the coffin you think it is. Remember who we are facing here. I am trusting you because of your insight but if I'm being honest, if anyone else came to me with this half-baked idea, I would have put a bullet in their skull."

Blood rushed through my ears and the sounds of the world were drowned out. My chest felt tight and my throat was closing in on itself. The spike of fear through me was so potent I could taste its sourness on the tip of my tongue.

*Shit.*

This man was even more dangerous than I imagined.

Asher's nail bit into my thighs and maybe normally, I would have yelped at the pain, but right now, it was the only thing anchoring me to this moment. I wanted to get up and flee. I didn't want to be here. Not with Asher and certainly not with *Ryder.*

"I'm positive this will work," Asher growled.

Even at the threat, Asher seemed to feel no fear. He was *angry.* Even though he was facing a man who could quite literally kill us where we stood. A part of me was impressed while the majority of me screamed at him internally to knock it the fuck off.

"Asher..." I said in a harsh whisper. The words were hard to force out due to the panic still having a choke hold on me.

"Shhh," he whispered, his lips brushing the side of my throat. "This is not a conversation you want to be in."

Ryder stood up and straightened his suit before walking over to us. His hand brushed across the side of my face. This time I couldn't help but flinch. He gave me a tight smile.

"If it doesn't..." he said, his hand trailing down my neck. "I will expect to be compensated fairly. After all, just this week, over fifty of my men have been cuffed and I am starting to run low on stock. That's a big loss."

His eyes locked on mine, and then without another word, he turned back the way we came.

"Feel free to stay as long as you'd like," he said before disappearing back into the house.

I turned in Asher's arms immediately, eyes wide and panic and anger swirling inside of me.

"You have gotten yourself in deep shit, Asher, and I want no fucking—"

One of his hands clamped down on my mouth while the other tangled in the hair at the nape of my neck.

"You did so good," he said in a light tone though there was a hardness in his expression that caused my blood to freeze. "Don't ruin it with that attitude of yours. My patience has begun to wear thin."

I swallowed thickly. His eyes were narrowed and there was a grim expression on his face. At this point, I didn't know what to believe when it came to Asher. He had played far too well and was constantly jumping back and forth between this harsh, cruel demeanor and the person I had originally fallen for. I didn't have those feelings for him anymore, instead, they were replaced with fear.

*God, I was so screwed.*

When I didn't say anything, he slowly pulled his hand away.

"Now," he said with a smile crossing his face. "I think I promised you a job, did I not?"

I fucked up bad in my past life.

Because how else could I explain the shitty turn my life just took?

Not only did Asher get me involved in something that was totally illegal and life-threatening, but right after, he dropped me off at the club that had ruined it all.

And I didn't even get a mask now.

*Just go in and ask for my mom, she's waiting for you.*

Those were the last words he said to me before he literally pushed me out of his car and left me in the cold. He had refused to divulge any information about what had just happened and acted as if we didn't just narrowly escape with our lives. I pushed and prodded on the way over here, but his lips were sewn shut. He didn't elaborate on how he knew she had touched me at the wedding, nor did he explain why he was pushing me back to her.

And now I had a bigger problem to take care of.

I looked up at the house in front of me. Nothing had changed since the first night I had visited but there was something inside me that felt as though the property in front of me was utterly unrecognizable.

The light music that was filtering out of the house caressed my skin, enticing me to step forward and into the place that threatened to uproot my life for the second time.

I didn't fully understand what Asher was trying to accomplish and why my pretense was needed at that meeting earlier, and I had a feeling this wouldn't be the last time he would rope me into this.

He knew about the wedding... but did he know about what happened at the club?

I had spent days combing over the files that they dropped off at my work, but there had been no mention of who I had been paired with for that night and there were no pictures of us together. There were pictures of me walking through the club, my eyes lingering on the people there... but it was oddly clean.

At least of me.

The only thing really incriminating is that I went there, not what I had done there.

With a deep breath, I walked up the steps of the house. Two of the bodyguards stood on either side of the entrance, already poised to step forward and stop me from entering.

"She's working tonight, boys," a husky voice called out from behind me.

A warm arm wrapped around my shoulder and I looked up to see a woman with silver hair, freckles splattered all over her face, and an impressive amount of face piercings and tattoos.

Well... only two piercings, but that was saying something for me. I was terrified of needles.

Her dark tattoos peeked out of the shaven sides of the side of her head and trailed down her neck and disappeared behind her clothing.

I jumped when a familiar face stepped up next to her. It was the scarred man that drove us to Ax's house. My face flushed when I realized he knew *exactly* what we had done in the back seat.

"Sloan," the man to our right greeted us and waved us in. "Don't scare this one away."

Sloan, which I assumed was the girl that currently held me hostage, laughed and pushed me forward.

"No promises," she said and gave me a wink. "You look cute, darling. Ax will eat it up."

Anger unfurled in my belly. I didn't come here to be a joke to them.

"I didn't say you could touch me," I said and stepped out of her hold.

A beaming smile split her face, and she nudged the driver next to her.

"We got a feisty one, Yvon," she teased. "Maybe she'll give Ax a run for her money, you think?"

The sides of Yvon's lips twitched before he stepped past me and pushed the door open.

"She already has, if my memory serves me correct," he said, a deep chuckle coming from his chest.

My face heated.

Sloan laughed again and pushed me through the door.

"Is a man even supposed to be in here?" I asked quickly as Yvon followed us into the club.

We were immediately hit with loud music and low voices mingled with moans. My skin heated and I wished for nothing more than to have that mask back, but neither Sloan nor Yvon had one, so I assumed they must work closely with Ax and be exempt from the mask-wearing policy.

"It's for work. And unlike you and Ax, I am able to separate work from pleasure," he said and walked off toward our right and toward the staircase. The lady at the front looked us over with wide eyes and an open mouth.

Sloan let out a low whistle.

"You must have made him mad," she said with a small chuckle.

"I didn't do anything," I growled and followed after him with Sloan close on my heels. "I saw him all of one time—"

"Two," Yvon corrected and stopped suddenly on the stairs, turning to face me. "Two times and I don't take kindly to *cheaters.*"

I swallowed thickly. His blue eyes burned into me and I felt more exposed in front of him than I had ever before.

*What the hell was his deal?*

"I am *not* a cheater," I growled and took a step forward. "And if I didn't know any better, I would say you are jealous—"

"Oh, I fucking *love* brats," Sloan said, interrupting me by clamping her hand down on my mouth. "But Yvon isn't one to play, love. Come on, before we have to clean something out of the carpets."

Yvon and I glared at each other before he turned back toward the stairs with a huff.

I pushed Sloan off me and turned to glare at her.

"Don't fucking touch me," I snapped.

She licked her lips, trying—and failing—to conceal her smirk.

"I see why Ax dropped everything to dom you for the night," she said and pushed past me. "Let me know if you're open to trying another out. God knows it's been boring around here."

I couldn't even look at her as she passed me.

In part because I was so pissed at her comments... and also because her words caused a delicious heat to coil in my belly.

I rolled my shoulders and turned back toward the staircase to see both Sloan and Yvon waiting for me at the top.

Fuck Asher. Fuck Ax. Fuck Yvon. Fuck Sloan.

I was tired of being pulled around by everyone and expected to just *follow* their lead and do whatever they said.

If they were going to play this game, *then so was I.*

# Ax

"Let's share, Ax," Sloan said as she leaned against the wall, watching as an angry Yvon showed Nyx around the top floor of Club Pétale. There were three floors and an attic. The attic being used for my living space, while this floor would be where Yvon, Sloan, Jenny and I would work. Jenny didn't come around all that much, but I made sure to keep space for her and allow the others on Sloan's team to take the extra space if needed.

I had come out of my office to watch Nyx, unable to help myself. As soon as I heard that she had arrived, the same almost excited feeling filled me. I couldn't sit still and all I wanted to do was lock her up and keep her all to myself.

She walked the spacious workroom, making sure to look into each and every office as Yvon guided her. When I bought this space, I tore down all the walls and made us separate offices with doors, and the only windows were facing outward to the surrounding land. There were a few windows in the main room, a table, some chairs, and a small kitchenette. It was small, but it did its job.

The space was dark, but with the help of some soft overhead

lights, it fit with the vibe of the rest of the club. Nyx seemed to like it.

She may have put on a cool mask and only lifted it to throw a snarky comment at Yvon, but I could see right through it. Just like I had that night. She loved it here.

The thought made my chest warm.

"She marked on her form that she doesn't like to share," I murmured, letting my eyes trail down her bare legs.

"*No,*" Sloan said in a low, mischievous tone. "She put down that she didn't want to be shared *that night*. Don't lie to me."

White-hot rage made my blood boil.

"You looked at her file," I accused, venom lacing my tone.

"It is my job," she said. "Jealous?"

*Yes.*

But I wouldn't admit it to her.

Sloan and I had shared a sub on occasion. She was as much a pleasure dom as I was but liked to add a bit more pain and roughness to her sessions than I did, mainly through piercings, branding, and knife play. Though Nyx had shown me how easily I lost control around her, so maybe Sloan and I weren't so different at all.

A part of me didn't want to share Nyx, but it wasn't because of Sloan...

There was a two-part reason.

Sloan was charismatic and liked to joke often. She had a reputation in the club, but other than that, she was attentive and cared for her partners when they were together. She and Nyx would look good together. I hated to admit it, but it was obvious that I was much older than Nyx.

She didn't seem to mind, but I couldn't help but feel a bit wary that we weren't compatible because of it. I had worked my way through life to get to where I was now. I raised a kid, almost got married.

Nyx was still just figuring out her life.

And the other part, the reason that I didn't want to share...

was because I wasn't sure what Nyx and I were. Were we lovers? Not really, I had made that clear after not contacting her even though I should have. I hadn't set our boundaries and we never had a *real* talk about what we wanted from each other.

Besides random sexual encounters, that is.

We weren't friends, that was for sure... so who's to say that she wouldn't continue to go to Sloan after we were done? Maybe she would realize that I was too old for her, too uptight. Maybe she would look back on all the horrible ways I had treated her under my roof and realize I wasn't worth it—

*Get yourself together, Ax.*

No matter what, she was with Asher and even though he had hand delivered her to my doorstep, I knew that if I crossed this boundary *again* and he found out...

I couldn't risk it.

Asher came before everything and I had been far too distracted to see that, *until now.*

*"No,"* I said quickly after realizing I had been staring at Nyx for too long. "I'm not jealous."

Yvon was running over some rules with her, both looking like they were ready to break out into an argument. I had become enamored by the way her eyebrows creased and her hands clenched into fists.

She was a ticking time bomb waiting to explode and I found myself leaning forward, just waiting to see what would happen.

"Then you won't be mad if I fuck her over your desk and make you watch?" she asked.

"If that's what she wants," I said. "I've been wanting to do it myself for a while."

Her smile dropped but was quickly replaced with a bigger one as Nyx came closer.

No, Sloan wasn't the person I should be worried about. That had been my own insecurities talking. She was a player and didn't have plans to settle down. There was a person that she told me about once when she was so drunk she couldn't stand up on her own, but that person was long gone and Sloan used sex to fill the void she left.

But Nyx... she walked over to us and couldn't even meet Sloan's gaze. Her face flushed, and she sent a glare at Yvon before looking toward me.

*She should be acting that way because of me and me alone.*

"I'm guessing we work when the club does, is that right?" she asked me.

I nodded because I couldn't get the words out. I cleared my throat, earning a look from Sloan.

"I have a computer for you in my office," I said and motioned to the door behind me. "Come in and I'll give you all the details."

She gave me a soft nod, a weak gesture that didn't fit her personality at all.

I opened the door to my office and waved her in.

Sloan pushed off the wall and moved to enter, but I put my hand on her shoulder and stopped her.

"Not tonight," I said. "We have to set the boundaries. Sign the waivers. Give her some time."

Sloan let out a huff but stepped back anyway.

She knew as well as I did that if Nyx did not sign those papers that there would be no chance for whatever scenario she was thinking about.

"You got it, boss," she said and nudged Yvon. "Lighten up, dude. You look like you got a stick up your ass."

"That would be more pleasurable than whatever the fuck that was," he growled and turned before I could stop him.

Sloan gave me a look but I ignored it by turning abruptly and shutting the door in her face.

I marched toward my desk and motioned for Nyx to take a seat across from me. The room that I had once decorated with pride suddenly felt too bare in front of her.

I had matched my carpet, leather couch, and floors with the rest of the club's theme. The only change was my desk which was a rich mahogany and topped with various pens, papers, and pictures. I had a few erotic portraits hung on the wall and a shelf of knickknacks and books... but with her here, suddenly, it felt all too much.

Her eyes looked over everything, not missing a single thing. I didn't want her looking at me like this. It made it harder to separate things the way I was supposed to.

I sat down on my own chair and riffled through my desk, pulling out the three forms we required from every new employee and pushing them toward her. It had been a while since I needed these and I felt a sense of heaviness that fell over me as she looked over them.

I reached over to get a pen for her and placed it softly on the desk.

There was no going back after this. From then on, she would be at my side every day until she moved on or was fired, though, from her record, I doubted that she would ever do something that would warrant a firing.

"An NDA, an updated form listing out your boundaries and... kinks, as well as—" her small gasps and reddening cheeks told me she saw the one that I wanted her to see the most.

"What kind of work allows the employees to fuck each other?" she asked.

I licked my lips and sat up straight as heat exploded inside me.

"Language," I chided.

She sent me a look and her eyes skimmed the paper at a lightning-fast rate.

"Aren't you worried about the fallout?" she asked.

"Why would I be?" I asked. She was the first to question this document to this extent. A part of me was intrigued, the other annoyed that she was coming here to scrutinize our business.

"Not only are you running somewhat of a controversial place," she noted and leaned back in her chair. "But it's downright scandalous that employees are allowed to fuck each other. I am sure this would not be great if it was released to the press."

*Was that... a threat?*

I leaned back in my chair, grabbing the sides so hard the squeak of the letter broke through our silence. Nyx's eyes shot toward my hands.

"This is how we work," I said. "We are a literal sex club, Nyx. I don't expect my employees to keep it in their pants, but I do expect them to abide by our rules and want to ensure that nothing will fall on the company. If you sign that—"

"I can't sue *you* for sexual harassment," she said, indignation filling her tone.

Irritation and desire swirled inside me. I almost regretted sending Sloan away.

"We don't tolerate sexual harassment," I said. "And I will deal with it as I see fit"—less than legal ways, but she didn't need to know that—"but we need this, so yes, you cannot sue *the company.*"

She looked back down at the form with a frown.

"This doesn't—"

"Do you want the job or not?" I growled, losing my cool.

I cursed internally when her eyes shot back to mine, but instead of getting angrier like I thought she would... she smiled.

"Oh, I want it," she said, a sort of amusement in her tone. "Don't confuse my questioning with a lack of desire. I just want to know my rights before coming in here."

I sat forward, folding my arms over my desk and taking a deep breath. Her floral scent tickled my nose and my fingers itched to tangle themselves in her hair. The purple ends had faded, leaving an almost silvery finish to them. Today, her hair had been worn with light waves in it and would lightly brush across her exposed skin as she shifted in her chair.

The act of her coming up to slip it over her shoulder was more arousing than it should have been.

"Are you satisfied?" I asked.

Satisfaction purred in my chest as her face flushed.

*That's more like it, kitten.*

"No," she said, jarring me. "But I will be. Now before I sign this, go into detail about what you expect from me here. Leave nothing out. If I feel as though you are shorting me, I will walk out of this place and never look back. Money be damned."

*Jesus, this was going to be a long night.*

"If this is a false alarm, I will murder you myself," I growled into the phone.

The headache from last night had already returned full blast and without even looking at the clock, I knew that it was well before a reasonable time for me to be awake.

I grabbed my blanket and covered my face, trying to chase what little comfort I could.

I spent *hours* with Nyx last night explaining what we needed from her, including a redesign of our website and newsletter and working with Sloan to design an app.

She was not happy about the Sloan part, to say the least, and that alone took up a good forty minutes of fighting, but once we were done, the little kitten seemed to finally have calmed down enough to accept the position. Regardless of what was happening between us, I needed her more than I'd admit.

Jenny and Sloan were great for a lot, but I needed someone with a better handle on all things brand related and I didn't have the time nor understand all the nuances that go into setting up everything.

I was honest with her last night when I said that in the future, I have no idea what that job looks like and that I would be leaning on her to help guide us in the right direction. That was another conversation that took way too much time and contributed to the headache that was now coming back full force.

"Do I sound like I want to be up right now?" the very same devil growled in my ear. "I set up alerts and I was notified only moments ago. They are looking at the files now."

I tore myself out of my blankets and walked from my bedroom to my makeshift living room, where my discarded laptop lay waiting for me.

I didn't always stay in my place in the attic and preferred one of my various properties that were much more *spacious* than here, but I was too exhausted last night to even think of where I would be spending the night.

I opened my laptop and quickly opened the security footage of the floor below me. My heart stopped when I saw Nyx sitting in the empty office I reserved for Jenny with her computer open and two coffees next to her.

I looked at the time on my computer and was surprised to see that it was already ten o'clock in the morning. I told her she didn't need to be here this early, but I was learning very quickly that Nyx worked on her own time.

"No one but Nyx is here—"

"Of course, they wouldn't do it from inside. God, why do I even try?" Sloan growled, and I heard the faint sound of a zipper. "Go into the portal and look at your history, it's the best we can do until I get there. I don't have the best equipment for this here. Watch what they look at and write it down for me. I'll be there in fifteen."

"Sloan, you are thirty min—"

The line was before I could get another word in.

I grabbed my laptop and quickly tried to get dressed while watching the portal's history.

Whoever it was, they were taking their sweet time combing through our files. My eyes widened when the page refreshed.

*They are looking through our platinum members.*

Platinum members were of the highest rank. They were the people who held the most power in the outside world and had full access to everything and anything at the club. If their identities were leaked...

Without having time to button up my shirt, I ran downstairs and to my office, passing the open room Nyx was sitting in. I didn't even have time to look at her as I pushed into my office.

I didn't bother hooking up my computer to the screens and focused solely on finding a piece of paper and scribbling down every single profile they clicked into, what files they were looking at, and what time.

"Ax?" Nyx's voice wafted through the room.

"Not now," I snapped, trying to keep my eyes on the ever-changing screen.

*They are really fucking serious.*

The person combed through almost all of the platinum members. My heart was beating wildly in my chest when I realized that sooner or later, they would reach Blake's profile. There were many people that they had already looked at that could ruin my entire life, but Blake... I couldn't do that to her.

*I am forgiving, Ax... but others are not.*

As I was writing the fifth name down, I heard a familiar high-pitched siren that caused my heart to drop into my stomach. It only took a second for me to realize that there were multiple and they were getting closer the longer I stalled.

"Are you fucking kidding me?" I moaned and rolled my shoulders. The tension that had built in my body was becoming unbearable and if I wasn't careful, I might lash out at the wrong people.

Namely ones with badges and handcuffs.

I started to button up my shirt and turned toward Nyx, not caring that I was practically flashing her at the moment.

I had bigger things to deal with.

She was standing closer to my desk than I had realized. Today her hair was up in a bun on top of her head and she was wearing a matching navy linen set that caused her to look far too innocent. I couldn't tell if she was wearing makeup, but that didn't make her any less beautiful.

If there weren't multiple police cars coming to my club, I might have found it in me to compliment her.

"Watch the portal history and write down the names," I ordered and reached under my desk to grab the excess cash I had on hand for moments like these. This wasn't the first time Sloan had brought trouble to my literal doorstep. "I'll be back in a moment."

She didn't meet my eyes as I walked past her, her eyes were fixed on the computer as she ran toward it. Her urgency and eagerness to comply *almost* made the situation that much better. As I walked down the stairs, hearing the sirens get closer and closer, I was beginning to regret ever bringing Sloan into this goddamn company.

The door burst open just as I was about to reach for it. Sloan, with her motorcycle helmet still on, a wrinkled hoodie, and ripped jeans, rushed through, almost running straight into me.

"Thanks!" she yelled and slapped my back as she passed me, narrowly pivoting so only our shoulders brushed.

I mumbled curses under my breath and stepped out to see two cop cars pulling up and Sloan's motorcycle thrown on the ground. The lawn had been torn up where she rode through it and the police cars stopped only feet away from it.

*That will be pricey to fix on such short notice.*

I was thankful that the trees covered most of our property, though I knew the neighbors had already heard the sirens and were probably using them as one of their millions of reasons why we should be kicked out of the area.

The first cop dove out of his car, gun raised, while his coworker from the other cruiser rolled down his window to shout, "Hold up!"

The weight of the money felt heavy in my pocket as the familiar-faced cop got out of his car, his smile wider than it should have been for someone who just got led on a chase through the outskirts of New York.

"Kenneth," the other cop called, but he ignored him and practically skipped up the stairs to me.

He held his hand out and I pushed the money into his palm,

his other arm circling around my shoulders. To his partner, it would look like nothing more than a friendly hug, but the way his grubby fingers took the money out of my hand told me otherwise.

Just like many of the law enforcement out there, they got slimy when they got a whiff of money. I had learned when I was young and still working for others that you only needed to sniff out one dirty cop and the rest would just follow.

It helped win situations like this, but it didn't mean I enjoyed this part of my job.

"Misunderstanding," he said, pulling back with a smile. He winked at me before turning back to his partner.

"Name?" I asked.

He froze before letting out a sigh. His face was turned away from me so I couldn't see his expression, but by the narrowed eyes of his partner, I knew he wasn't happy about what I was asking of him.

He knew the drill by now. This was the third or fourth person he had brought here. You would think that they would have written off Sloan's motorcycle by now, but maybe the point was to line his pockets even more with my money.

"Dennis," he called and made a sweeping motion with his arm. "Meet Ax. Ax meet Dennis Walsh."

I nodded and waved to the man. He looked at me with a wary expression. One that a dirty cop wouldn't. It raised alarm bells in my head and made my palms sweat. He looked to be minutes away from calling for backup on both his partner and me.

"You drive safe now," I said and stood on the porch until they disappeared around the corner.

To be safe, I brought out my phone and sent the name off to Jonson with a quick note.

*Find me something good.*

And then turned back to put out yet another fire.

# Nyx

"So, you're some type of computer hacker?" I asked, sitting on the edge of Sloan's desk with two coffees next to me.

I had caught a glimpse of her office when Yvon was giving me a tour but I didn't have a chance to really look at everything in there.

Her desk sat in the middle of the room and had not one but *three* monitors on it with a huge processor on the left side that lit up with lights as she typed away on her computer. The windows behind her were blocked out by blackout curtains, leaving us in the dim lighting of her room. The overhead lights had been dimmed and the only strong light was the one coming off of her monitors.

There was a leather couch off to the side with a trunk of god knows what near the right side of it. A small rug decorated the middle of the room and besides the shelf off to the right of the entrance, I couldn't make out any of the decorations she kept in her office. It was just too dark.

It was a little bit into Sloan's personality that I didn't expect.

Sloan's face twisted at my words and a burst of amusement ran through me.

I think annoying her was my newfound hobby. Annoying Ax

had its perks but annoying Sloan... God, something about the way her jaw clenched and her attitude had been more than enough entertainment to last a lifetime.

And after seeing Ax this morning, disheveled and baring her tits to the world, annoying Sloan was a way to let off steam. Even remembering it now caused a low heat to settle in my belly.

"Don't be dense," she growled as she typed away on her laptop. "I went to fucking MIT. Hacker my *ass.*"

I raised my brow at her, my smile widening.

"Did you *actually* graduate from there? Or did you just go there for a semester or two and then drop out?" I teased.

She paused to look over her laptop and glare at me.

"I have better things to do than entertain you," she growled. "Don't test me."

I let out a sigh and turned back toward the open door.

I jumped when I saw Ax standing there looking at us. She had loose jeans on and a button-down that was slightly askew. Her hair was a mess and she wasn't even wearing shoes.

It looked like she literally rolled out of bed and made all types of nasty thoughts run through my head.

"That was two *grand,* you idiot," she growled and stalked toward us. Instead of going around to the side that Sloan was on, she stood right next to me, the heat of her thigh brushing across mine.

"That's chump change to you," Sloan grumbled.

Unable to help myself, I reached over and pulled at her shirt.

"It's uneven," I murmured and began to undo the buttons of her shirt.

Her smoldering gaze bore into me as I undid each button, careful to not touch her skin. I had already seen her bare chest under her shirt earlier but didn't want to push my luck.

I told myself that I was going to play this game too. That I wouldn't be treated like nothing more than a pawn with everyone involved, but that plan slowly began to dissolve as she watched me. I may have been able to keep a calm and confident facade on the outside, but inside I was freaking out.

Even Sloan's clicking on her computer paused when I reached the last button. I then lined up the sides and began buttoning them from the bottom up.

The room was so silent I felt as though the sound of my heart could be heard throughout.

When I reached the top button, I had no choice but to look her in the eyes. My breath caught in my throat when our gazes met and my face flushed.

"Buttoned or unbuttoned?" I asked.

"Buttoned," she answered, her voice still husky from sleep.

A smile spread across my face and I kept it unbuttoned and then went one further and unbuttoned another.

"It looks better this way," I murmured.

Sloan let out a light chuckle and the typing continued.

"I guess we can use my desk if you so choose," she said from behind me.

"No need," Ax replied, her eyes trailing my face.

With a shaky hand, I reached to my side and handed her the hot Americano I had gotten her this morning on my way over.

"It's still warm, I think," I whispered.

There was a tension between us, one that I hadn't felt since that night in the car.

"Thank you," she murmured and took the coffee from me. "Why were you here so early?"

"Usually, I'm up at six," I said. "It felt wasteful to just stay at home."

After staying here until three a.m., I had hoped to get some sleep in, but I only got as far as seven a.m. before my body forced me to get up. She nodded and took a sip of her drink. My eyes locked in on the way the muscles in her neck moved as she drank.

I had to look away and toward Sloan when I felt the heat flush up my neck. Sloan was already looking at me, her eyes narrowed.

"I have an IP address," she said. "But that's all. I need some more time to narrow down the rest."

"And how long until you find out who it is?" Ax asked.

"A few days," she said. "I already sent out some instructions to the team and will have some members of the team pull city and provider info and will try to narrow it down from there."

"Is someone hacking into your stuff?" I asked Sloan.

The sides of her mouth twitched.

"I'll tell you if you show me your tits," she said. "Maybe I'll even let you sit on my lap while I finish this. Show you what that MIT degree did for me."

Heat ran through me and my gaze shot to Ax. She was already watching me.

"She's the one in charge of this, not me," she said with a shrug. "Up to you."

"You can't just tell me?" I pouted.

Sloan's hand grabbed the back of my shirt and pulled me down. My hands flailed to catch me.

"Show them to me, baby," she whispered, her breath hot on my ear. "Maybe if you say please, Ax will suck on them for you."

"Sloan," Ax growled.

"Come on," she said and nipped my ear.

"I'm leaving," Ax said and turned on her heels, leaving the same way she came.

"Buzzkill," Sloan murmured and pushed me back to my sitting position. I watched her back as she retreated, a bitter feeling rising in me.

I wondered what had changed between us. The once passion-filled kisses and situations seemed to disappear moments after they showed up. Whatever had pulled her out of it in the car that one time seemed to linger between us.

And now that she was my boss, it seemed worse than before.

Maybe Asher had told her that he saw what we had done at the wedding.

I wondered if I should tell her what Asher was up to, or if that would be crossing the line. If I was a parent, I would want to know that my son visited drug-fueled parties with less than savory characters.

Asher had stopped talking to me since then, disappearing just like I wished he had so long ago... though given the most recent events, I refused to let my guard down just yet. But that's not the only thing that was on my mind.

Since seeing Ax again, all I could think about was Asher's mom and how much it must have devastated her to lose the love of her life. I understood now what her sister had warned me about. Ax didn't deserve the heartbreak, neither of them did.

The thought caused my chest to ache and guilt to grab hold of me.

"Don't let it get to you," Sloan said from behind me, stirring me from my thoughts.

I turned back to look at her. She was leaning back in her chair now, no doubt watching me stare longingly at Ax's back.

My face felt hot suddenly.

"I don't know what you mean," I said and jumped off her desk, smoothing my clothes down.

She let out a huff.

"Come on, Nyx," she drawled. "I know a crush when I see one."

I paused, grabbed my coffee and turned to take her in. Her hair was a mess around her head as well and she had bags under her eyes. She looked just as tired as Ax.

I didn't know what caused me to do it, but I leaned against her desk and let out a heavy sigh.

"I dated her son," I said. "And so it doesn't matter if I have a crush or not. I shouldn't have even taken this job to begin with."

She sat back and stared at me, leaving us in silence until...

She burst out laughing.

"You're telling me you're not fucking because you also had a piece of *Asher*?" she asked, her words barely understandable through her guffaws of laughter.

I lunged forward and cupped my hand over her mouth, careful to not spill the coffee in my hand all over the pricey-looking monitors.

"Shut up," I hissed. "She'll hear you."

She pushed my hand away and wiped away a fake tear.

"I can assure you that just dating Asher isn't going to make whatever that was go away," she said and leaned back with a sigh, as if the laughing had exhausted her.

"And what was *that*?" I asked, leaning back and looking toward the open door. Ax still hadn't reappeared.

"You tell me," she said. "Last I checked, I wasn't unbuttoning my boss's shirt."

My face felt like it was on fire. I cleared my throat and turned to leave.

"Don't worry," she said. "If she didn't want you, she wouldn't have let you do it in the first place."

I waved her off and continued to fast walk toward the exit, ready to get the hell out of her office.

"Stay out of it!" I grumbled.

She let out another laugh.

"Next time, get me a coffee too while you're at it!"

Two weeks have passed since I started working for Ax and we have created a sort of routine for ourselves.

Every day I would stop off at my favorite coffee shop and bakery. Get *four* coffees. And then catch a taxi to the office. It was manageable given that Ax paid me twice as much as my last job. I was able to catch up on rent, buy myself some clothes, and treat myself to a nice dye job.

I was beginning to enjoy life again and found solace in my routine.

Until today.

"You need to get laid, girl," Ben said as he handed me the tray of drinks. "Hair looks good, by the way, digging the pink."

I flipped the hair over my shoulder and sent him a wink. The purple was gone and now replaced with a pastel pink that was a bit much to keep up, but I was in love with it, so the extra trips to the salon were worth it.

"Ben," I chided playfully and slipped a five in the tip jar. "Your customers would be appalled to hear you speak like this."

He gave me a wink and leaned forward. The café was empty at this time. Morning rush had ended and the afternoon time with all the exhausted office workers and school kids was still hours away, leaving just me and the barista there to joke around.

I quite liked this part of our routine. I hadn't had friends for a long time and so being here with them to talk about life and other things was comforting.

It came along with the perks of working at a place that was only open at night.

"Seriously though," he whispered. "I mean, you look good, but you seem… tense."

I gave him a forced smile.

Even though I loved my new job, dealing with Sloan and Ax was beginning to wear on me.

Sloan was overbearing at times, a natural flirt. On more than one occasion, I had heard moans coming from her office and not too long later, I would see a red-faced worker come out of her room. Sloan would then come out and give me a triumphant look.

She had asked me, multiple times, if I would like to "try her out," but I was adamant about not fucking any of my coworkers. Especially not with Ax mere feet away from me… though that didn't mean it got any easier.

Every night I was surrounded by beautiful women and I would be lying if I hadn't had to bring out my own vibrator on an especially active night at the club.

I tried my best to stay away from the patrons when I could,

but that was hard when they were literally everywhere. Not to mention that Ax hasn't even looked at me since the day in Sloan's office.

Everything was professional—*cold.* It almost made me think that everything that happened with us had been a very real-feeling wet dream and nothing more.

"I am... tense," I said with a sigh.

The bell to the café rang but Ben ignored it, a wicked look passing his face.

"What about that sexy masc woman you were with?" he asked, lowering his voice suggestively. "She looks like she could *relax* you."

I grabbed the drinks with a huff, trying to ignore my reddening face.

"I'm leaving," I growled and turned, keeping his gaze. "Next time, I'm keeping your tip—"

Strong hands gripped my shoulder, jostling my drinks and splashing at least one of the cold coffees all over my blouse.

A loud gasp ripped from me and I turned to the person that stopped me from ruining *all* of my drinks.

"I'm so *sorry—*"

My apology got caught in my throat as I locked eyes with the beautiful honey eyes that haunted my dreams.

"If I knew you were so easily distracted, I would have come to accompany you more often," she murmured and looked toward Ben behind me.

"Do you have a rag?" she asked, then her eyes trailed down to my now ruined shirt. "And maybe a new... whatever the iced drink was that she ordered? Half of it spilled."

"R-right away," Ben said.

Ax took the drinks from me and motioned for me to take the spilled one.

With shaky hands, I took it and placed it back on the counter. My shirt had already begun to stick to me, and I was all too aware of how embarrassing this whole situation was.

Ben threw me a damp rag and gave me a shit-eating grin when his eyes met mine.

"I'll have that latte out for you in a sec," he sang and disappeared behind the bar.

I turned toward Ax with a sheepish grin and tried to wipe the stain out of my shirt. I had yet to go shopping with my newest paycheck, so this had been a staple in my wardrobe and as I tried to rub the stain out, I realized I would probably have to retire it now.

"We can get you something else to wear when we get to the house," she said and reached past me to grab the drink from Ben. My breath hitched as she invaded my space and her spicy cologne hit my senses. "Let's go."

She had turned toward the door before my mind caught up and I was there—once again—staring at her as she retreated. I hadn't expected to see her here. I thought that I still had at least forty minutes before I had to see her. It was a little silly, but I needed all of those forty minutes to collect myself and prepare to see her and now that had to be shortened into a mere four seconds.

"Go, bitch," Ben hissed from behind me.

I forced my stiff legs to follow her out, suddenly all too aware of just how ruined my outfit was.

Yvon was waiting for us outside, though this time, they'd chosen a black SUV instead of a limo, much to my relief.

"I have to give the coffee to Annette," I forced out as I climbed into the back of the SUV, far too close to Ax for comfort.

By Yvon's frown as he shut my door, I knew that we all remembered what had taken place the last time we were in a confined space like this.

"I know," Ax said with a sigh, shifting the drinks in her hands. She frowned at her lap and looked toward me. "Buckle my seat belt."

My body moved without thinking and I reached over to grab her seat belt. Only when our faces were centimeters apart did I realize my mistake. Swallowing thickly, I fastened her seat belt before mine, then took the drinks from her hand. I was careful to not touch her skin.

I worried about what she had heard, but she had her normally stoic face on, giving no indication that she had heard Ben tease me about *her*.

The car jerked forward and we were on our way down the familiar path to the bakery. It was only a few blocks away so we arrived rather quickly. I unbuckled my seat belt and bolted to leave, but Ax's hand splaying across my chest and pushing me back into the seat stopped me.

"Stay," she said and grabbed hold of one of the iced drinks. "Are they the same?"

I couldn't manage more than a nod.

She nodded back and left the car. I watched as she entered the bakery, but my attention was called back to the front of the car, where Yvon's icy gaze met mine through the rearview mirror. He let out a huff.

Irritation rose through me. Not only had I been *tense* as hell recently, but I had to deal with a stained shirt and now *him*. Yvon had not changed his opinion of me over the last two weeks and his attitude weighed on me more and more.

"What's with you?" I growled and took the chance to finally take a sip of the delicious latte Ben had prepared for me this morning. Even the sweet bitterness that ignited my tastebuds was not enough to get rid of the bad taste he left in my mouth.

"Were you really going to show up in *that?*" he asked.

I looked down at my ruined blouse and skirt. Before this, it had been a perfectly fine outfit. What gives?

"Now you are policing my outfits—"

He interrupted me with a loud groan.

"There is an event tonight, Nyx," he said and turned just so I could catch his bad eye. "You didn't forget, did you?"

I froze. An event—

*Shit. Shit shit shit.*

I *did* forget. I had been so busy running back and forth with all the new website updates and creating the brand portfolio that I didn't even look at the date.

Tonight would be a very special event that would bring the more important members to the club. It was an initiative I had heard on my first day and it would be used to help strengthen the ties with our members but... *fuck.*

Ax's door opened and she climbed in. I had to look back out toward the window in order to keep her from realizing how stupid I had been.

*Maybe I could just sneak out before it started? Not like they would need me, right?*

"Nyx forgot about the event," Yvon said before pulling away from the curb.

I shot a glare at him. I caught his smirk in the rearview mirror.

*Bastard.*

"I didn't," I mumbled and shot a glance to Ax.

There was a small light in her eyes and the corners of her mouth twitched. She grabbed her coffee from my tray and took a sip.

"I prepared for that possibility as well," she said and shot me a glance. "I have a dress for you."

"I don't have a mask," I said. My skin heated unbearably under her gaze.

"You don't need one," she said. "Just treat it like any other night. The more they can see of you, the more they will trust us and that trust is key to running a business like we do."

*Like we do.*

My stomach erupted in butterflies.

It was such a simple and ordinary, meaningless phrase, but at that moment it meant a lot to me. Because for the first time... I was treated like a partner instead of just an employee.

"I look forward to meeting them tonight," I murmured, looking back to Yvon in the mirror.

He had a frown.

# NYX

The dress was obscene.

It was a skintight, shimmery blush fabric that made my skin itch. On top of that, it was strapless, so I couldn't even wear my bra with it. If Ax hadn't been ignoring me the way she had, I would have assumed this was on purpose.

With a huff, I brushed my fingers through my hair. At this point, I was stalling. I had been in my office for over twenty minutes. Music had already started to filter through from the floor below, grating on my nerves. I had gotten used to the hustle and excitement of the club below my feet, but this was the first time since my night with Ax that I felt anxiety creep up on me.

I looked over my form in the mirror, frowning. The dark night was washed out by the dim light shining behind me, making my reflection all too clear. The girl in front of me was different than the one that wore the mask all that time ago.

Even though my nerves displayed on my face, there was something different about the way I held myself. I was no longer trying to hide in the shadows. Minimize my presence so I would be overlooked. The girl reflected back at me had confidence and fire in her that could have only been ignited through hardship and pain.

I hadn't pretended to have a perfect life growing up. I had

been through it all. Homelessness, an addict of a mother, a family that had shunned us. Life had beaten me again and again but never once had it forged someone like the woman looking back at me.

The door opened behind me, and I caught sight of Sloan. She was wearing a suit, looking much more like Ax than I had ever seen her before.

"Aw man," she joked. "I'd hope to have caught you naked."

I rolled my eyes, a smile spreading across my lips. Turning to her, I twirled.

"How do I look?"

She let out a light laugh.

"Perfect, though I don't think Ax's taste would be anything less than extraordinary," she drawled.

My face heated and I walked toward her, leaving my phone on the table.

"Flattering me won't make me fuck you," I said and pulled at her tie. Confidence burst through me, tingling at my insides, begging me to fuck with the woman in front of me. "It seems like you had enough of that earlier."

A wicked grin passed over her face.

Mere hours earlier, loud moans were coming out of her office. It was the norm for her, but I wouldn't admit just how much it made my stomach clench.

"Oh, baby," she purred and slipped her arm around my shoulders. "Is that jealousy I hear?"

I let out a laugh as she pulled me out of the room. The fear of the party below had subsided in that moment and I was enjoying being in the company of a friend.

Because whether I would like to admit that or not, that's what she was to me. Now what I did with my friends was another question entirely, but I appreciated her company and humor.

"Not even a drop—"

My words caught in my throat when I saw Ax standing near

the back of the room on her phone. I had seen Ax wear a suit on multiple occasions, but tonight she looked *sinful.*

She wore a white button-down with a tight black vest and slacks. Her sleeves had been rolled up to show her tattoos and the muscles in her arms jumped as she folded them across her chest. Her hair had been slicked back and her face tilted upward, showing off her long neck.

"I know," Sloan said with a wistful sigh, pausing so we could both take her in.

A dull ache started in my core and I knew that in seconds my thong would be uncomfortably damp. It was far too easy to imagine me and her in her office, as she fucked me on her desk. The thought of her still wearing that suit while I was completely naked and trembling in front of her would be a fantasy I may just be willing to kill for.

There would be no way I could concentrate on the party with her looking *like that.* All guilt and hesitation vanished in midair and I thought of all the possible ways I could lure her back into her office and beg her to fuck me.

"God, I am *so* fucked," I moaned and leaned into Sloan, praying she would give me the strength I would need to last through this event.

Sloan's hand tightened on my shoulder.

"My offer is still available," she said, dropping her voice into a whisper while Ax talked on her phone, unaware that we were still watching her. "If you want, I could take you right here and now, force her to watch as you come."

My body heated unbearably and my nipples stiffened, creating two obvious points in my dress. My panties were soaked now.

*Yes, please,* was on my lips and I almost uttered those words until Ax's gaze shifted over to us.

"That would be inappropriate," I murmured.

Sloan snorted and walked us toward Ax.

"The way you're panting over your boss is *inappropriate,*" she whispered, her hot breath wafting across my ear. "I bet the way you are currently creaming in your panties is also *inappropriate.*"

I made a noise of disgust and pushed her away.

"Language," I chided.

She laughed and pulled me back to her.

"Say that again after you see me perform tonight," she said. "I think you'll rethink your position on not fucking me."

I pulled my eyes away from Ax to look at her with raised brows.

"Perform?" I asked. "You? What will you do?"

She let out a chuckle.

"You'll see," she said with a teasing tone.

"I didn't think you liked to be watched," I said. A shiver went through me when I thought of what she would be doing in front of everyone.

"It's not the crowd that does it for me," she admitted, her hand squeezing my shoulder. "It's the control. Where it happens is not really important."

I nodded and was about to ask another question as curiosity burned at me but there was a clearing of a throat.

I jumped and looked toward Ax, feeling the heat wash over me once more.

Tonight was going to be torturous between the two of them.

"It's time," she said and looked at us both, her eyes falling on Sloan's arm over my shoulder. "I'll take her from here, you go get ready."

Sloan tugged on the end of my hair before leaving my side. She sent us a wave before leaving Ax and me alone in the office. The air was sucked out of the room and I had to avert my gaze to the ground.

"Are you nervous?" she asked and her fingertips trailed my arm until her fingers intertwined themselves with mine.

My heart skipped a beat.

*Now I was.*

"A little," I admitted, looking up at her. "I didn't know Sloan was performing."

There was a light smile on her face.

"Sloan's will be a little... intense," she said. "If it gets too much, you can retreat back here and no one will think anything of it. Just let me know before you go."

I nodded, though there was no way I would be missing this.

"I know we talked about the platinum members," I said. "Though I am not sure if there are any, in particular, I should be aware of."

She squeezed my hand, making me jump when I realized that I had forgotten about the gesture. She dropped it as if also just noticing.

"Blake and Payton are the ones that I will be looking out for," she said. "I will introduce them to you if we come across them, but other than that, I recommend you stay by my side. There will be many powerful people in the crowd tonight and the last thing I want is for you to get involved with the wrong person."

Something akin to excitement and a bit of fear traveled through me at the mention of the dangerous people mingling below these floors. This was a private, safe place, so the idea of danger here was more exciting to me than when I was forced into it with Asher.

"I am not planning to play tonight," I said, though it felt like a lie.

Ax realized that too and her lips quirked.

"That's for the best," she said and then looked toward the door to the stairs. "Let's get started, shall we?"

When she held out her arm to me, I took it without hesitation.

Let the party begin.

I... underestimated the kink.

And myself, evidently.

There was a crowd of more than thirty people pushed into the back of the house. All of the people there were mingling and dressed in varying degrees of clothing. Some had none at all, others were dressed in full suits like Ax.

When we entered, they all descended onto Ax like hawks but there were only a few that she introduced me to. Every time someone would come up to her she would meet them with a polite smile, call them by their assigned name, and talk about the various new additions to the club. Then we would leave and move on to the next group.

I stayed on Ax's arm, smiling at all of them. No one even took a second look at me.

Maybe at one time I would have liked that, felt safe... but after the fifth person, I was getting annoyed. I wanted to make them look at me. I had come all this way and settled into myself and my wants... just to be ignored?

Before I could speak up, I was thrust into a room where we would get to watch our first show.

The back of the house had been cleared for a stage in the middle of the room and there were a few seats up front while the rest of us stood in the back. When it started, I was glad that we didn't because it turned out I was not ready to see someone tied up and whipped until they came.

"That's Blake," Ax whispered in my ear. Her sudden attention to me caused me to jump and look back at her. She motioned for me to look back at the stage. "She has been our main for this show since we opened, though the person tying her has changed a few times."

I swallowed thickly and nodded.

Blake was currently on the floor of the stage, completely naked, with her hands tied behind her back and in a kneeling position. One of her legs was tied while the other remained free. The person who was tying her up would stop every now and then to lean down and talk with Blake before moving on, either to start with the whipping or, this time, it was a vibrator.

There were a few cheers from the crowd.

I had been excited to witness this, even a bit nervous... but now that it was happening before me, I didn't realize the effect it would have.

Blake threw her head back as her partner brought the vibrator to her clit. Her moans were drowned out as the crowd around us got more and more excited. A few people around us moved closer and others decided to start parties of their own causing me to shrink back into Ax who was positioned behind me.

"Sloan is coming on," Ax whispered in my ears, her hot breath wafting across my face.

I nodded stiffly, trying to ignore the heat in my belly. She was so close that her body heat seeped into my skin and when her hand would brush across the back of my thighs, I found myself wanting to lean fully back into her.

"Let me know if it's too much," she said, this time her hand coming to cup my shoulder.

Her touch burned.

"I'm okay," I whispered.

Sloan appeared on the stage before I had time to prepare myself. She had worn gloves and took her time looking over the masked Blake. Seeing Sloan without her mask up there in front of everyone caused me to stir.

Even among everything around us, I was somewhat worried for her but she didn't seem to mind. There was a light smirk on her face and she motioned for the staff to bring her something.

The something they brought her wasn't anything I was prepared for.

It was a surgical tray with various tools on it. She leaned down and placed a kiss to Blake's lips before pinching her nipple hard enough a yelp could be heard over the crowd and music.

It made the crowd go crazy.

When Sloan pulled away and started preparing the needles, I brought my hand to my mouth.

*Was she really going to use those? Here?*

Ax's grip on me tightened but I couldn't pay attention to her as I was pulled in by Sloan and Blake. It was quick. Sloan bent down and began speaking to Blake, but I couldn't hear them over the crowd and my own blood rushing through my ears.

She grabbed Blake's breast before pinching her nipple and then she pushed the needle against the sensitive nub. Blake and Sloan breathed in together and then she pushed through to the other side.

Blake was rewarded with a kiss from Sloan and her partner upped the vibrator until Blake leaned forward into Sloan. This time, I could hear her sobs of pleasure echo through the room and cut through the noise.

My pussy clenched so hard I was sure I was coming on the spot. I don't know if it was the sight of her tied up and coming or that the needle was still in her nipple when she did it.

"Nyx," Ax said and turned me so that I was facing her. "Are you okay? Do you need a break?"

My entire body felt hot and I couldn't even process everything I had just seen. I didn't want a break. I wanted to see more. I wanted to see what she looked like when she came again as Sloan pierced her or as her partner whipped her.

The look on her face and the cries were seared into me and the ache between my legs was unbearable.

I couldn't speak, so I just nodded. When I moved to go upstairs, she started to follow me but I waved her off and left her alone in the crowd.

I pushed through the guests in a hurry, trying to get to the safety of the office space upstairs.

There were only a few that tried to say something to me, but other than that, I got to the office safely and ran toward Sloan's office.

I wasn't thinking when I entered. All I knew was that her

office would have what I needed. I pushed through her dark office and rounded her desk, pulling open every single drawer. When I came up empty, I located the chest and pried it open, only to find it mostly empty save for a spare rope and paddle.

"Fuck," I growled and slammed the top closed.

I left her office only to freeze when I spotted Ax's office still open. I knew it was a bad idea before I even started toward it, but I couldn't help myself. The heat inside me was threatening to burst and if I did not get some pressure relief soon, I was sure that I would fall to my knees in front of Sloan or Ax or maybe even both.

And I was better than that.

I tried not to feel the intimidation as I riffled through the drawers and it was easy when I opened one that contained every toy imaginable. I grabbed the first vibrator I could find and made quick work of leaning against the table, pulling my thong off and bringing it straight to my clit.

I didn't care about any foreplay, nor did I want to take this slow. I *needed* to come now and a lot before I would be able to face them again. As the vibrator came to life under my hands, I couldn't stop the low moan that spilled from my mouth.

I couldn't stop the images of tonight flowing through my mind. The way Ax looked in her suit. The way Blake came after the needle pierced her skin. I bucked my hips against the vibrator, and a low whine came out of my mouth as my orgasm began to build. It was too slow for my liking.

The door pushed open, pulling me from my trance. Ax stood there, her eyes locked on me and her hands carefully rolling back the sleeves on her button-down.

"Shit," I muttered and dropped the vibrator. "Sorry, Ax. I got a little—"

"You're testing my patience, Nyx," she said in a low voice and walked toward me.

I swallowed thickly and averted my gaze to the floor only to find my discarded thong there along with the still vibrating toy.

Ax's shoes came into view and then slowly, she sank down to her knees. My breath caught and I met her heated gaze. She reached down and turned the toy off, all while keeping her eyes on me.

"You should be down there with the—"

"I can be wherever I want, Nyx," she said in a low tone. "And right now, I want to be here."

She stood to her full height then, towering over me only to slip past me and sit in her desk chair. The leather squeaked, breaking the room's silence.

"Ax, I—"

"Come here, Nyx," she said and patted her lap.

I swallowed thickly as my clit throbbed.

"And if I don't want to?" I asked and immediately hated that I did so.

"Up to you," she said and shifted in her chair. "Though I would very much like to help you with your... situation."

My situation, meaning my loss of orgasm and soaked cunt.

Steeling myself, I walked over and sat down on her lap, leaning back into her chest. The heat of her skin caused electricity to shoot through me.

"You've been... different since the last time," I said.

I shuddered as her hands trailed my bare thighs. Her touch was not at all hesitant as she pushed up my dress, her finger dipping to where my own wetness had covered my thigh.

"Because I knew that we shouldn't have done this," she said, her voice right by my ear. She nipped at my lobe, pulling a whine from me. "I should have stopped this the moment I found out you had been with Asher."

Asher's name caused me to freeze, but she started to massage my thighs. I let out a shaky breath before spreading them for her.

"Then why didn't you?" I asked. "Why are you here now?"

Her chest had been rising and falling in erratic movements, our breaths filling the quiet space around us. It was dark, and I knew she probably couldn't see me, but I had never felt more bared to her than in this moment.

She was stock-still, waiting for me to make a move. With a deep, shuddering breath, I spread my legs even wider and used my hand to grip her wrist.

"Because I can't seem to stay away from you," she said, still not moving. "You're my son's ex-girlfriend and now my employee. I should stay as far away from you as possible."

I understood her. As much as I wanted her, it didn't stop me from feeling bad about tearing them apart.

"We can stop," I suggested, though my aching pussy protested the idea. "I never wanted to come between you."

"Somehow," she mused. "I believe you. Though I have a feeling if you were just playing us, you would have told him already."

I couldn't turn to face her as the moment between us passed.

"He knows," I whispered.

There was another pause before her nails dug into me.

"What?" she asked, her tone turning hard.

*Shit.*

"He knows," I said and tried to turn to face her, but when I tried, her hand came up to my face and forced me to look forward. "At least about the wedding. I don't know about the other times."

She took a deep breath before she let go of my face. This time she did turn me so that we were facing each other. Her face had changed to a cool mask as she spoke to me.

"Why are you here if he knows?" she asked. "Why did he ask me for a job for you if that was true?"

I swallowed thickly, panic taking over my body. I didn't know if I wanted to tell her this.

"He got me fired," I said. "He blackmailed me and sent pictures of me coming here to my boss."

I had never felt coldness like I had in that moment. The entire air chilled and her face gave away no indication of what she was thinking.

"Pictures?" she asked. "He had pictures of you *here*?"

I nodded.

She let out a sigh.

"Fuck," she whispered. "*Fuck.*"

I moved to get up, but her hands were on my hips, forcing me back down.

"Listen, it's okay, just let me—"

She cut me off by forcing her lips to mine. It was a short kiss before she pulled away and looked at me.

"Please," she whispered. "Can we just forget about this conversation until tomorrow? If I have to go one more day without touching you, I'm going to go insane."

*Fuck.*

All the lost heat came back and hit me like a truck.

I nodded, a small whimper escaping my lips.

"Turn back around," she whispered.

I followed her command and turned, only to lean back against her chest.

"Yes, that's right."

Her hands came to rub my thighs again.

"Tell me what you were thinking about," she commanded, though it sounded more like a plea. "Distract me."

"You," I said quickly. "I was thinking about you. And Blake and Sloan's performance."

"I thought you didn't like it," she said, her hands trailing along the wetness on my thigh.

I shook my head.

"I liked it *too* much," I said.

She let out a strangled noise.

"Lift your dress, kitten," she commanded, her voice only a whisper, but the authority in her voice was clear.

With shaky hands, I pulled the dress up and over my ass, baring my wet cunt to the world. Her hand traveled to my center before cupping my pussy. A wave of heat went through me and I leaned farther back into her, my head lolling back to rest on her shoulder.

"Please, Ax," I begged.

The sharp sound of her hand slapping my cunt echoed through the room. A low whine slipped from my lips and I had to fight the urge to slam my knees shut.

"Try again," she growled and ran her fingers across my clit, chasing away the slight sting from her slap.

"Please, *daddy*," I moaned and dug my hands into the armrests at her side.

I was rewarded with her beginning to circle my clit.

"If I would have slipped my hand under your dress in front of all those people, would you have let me fuck you?" she asked, and finally, after teasing me, she pushed two fingers into me only to remove them just as quickly.

I struggled against her, spreading my legs so wide my thighs began to ache.

"Oh god, yes—"

I was cut off by her hand coming to pull down my dress, exposing my breasts. She tweaked my nipple with her free hand, pulling a moan out of me.

"What about it did you like?" she asked. "The people? The bondage? The whips? The piercing? Sloan?"

I couldn't stop the whine when her fingers left my clit. She leaned us forward, opening her drawer, the same one that I had riffled through before. My breath caught when she pushed us forward.

She reached for a pink one with a suction head and a G-spot vibrator before closing the drawer and having us lean back again in her chair. She shifted me so I was leaning against her right side and partially turned so our gazes were locked.

I licked my lips, the need to taste her burning at me.

"Put it in," she said and lifted the toy to me. "Do you need lube?"

I shook my head and closed my shaky fingers around the toy.

Her hands left me to zip down my dress, and before I knew it, it was bunched around my waist and every single dirty fantasy I had with her fucking me fully clothed in her office was about to come true.

When she settled again, her hands reached down to spread my pussy lips open and she watched as I inserted the toy inside me. The stretch was delicious. When I waited too long to turn it on, she took the initiative but made sure to put it on its highest setting.

Sharp but muffled buzzing filled the room and powerful shocks of pleasure ran through me as the toy started vibrating. The suction on my clit was enough to cause me to throw my head back, not even bothering to worry about if Ax would catch me or not. The vibration inside of me caused my whole body to tense and swear words filtered out of my mouth.

Her hand was strong on my back and her free hand came to pinch my nipples as I shuddered in her grasp. I struggled to open my eyes but was able to catch a glimpse of her cool and collected face. The only thing giving her away was the heat in her narrowed eyes just before a powerful orgasm ripped through my body.

I had gone too long and had been so turned on that it took mere minutes for the toy to turn me into a panting, moaning mess.

"There it is," Ax cooed. "Fuck, you are so beautiful."

Her words caused me to light up inside and had me squeezing around the toy so hard I was sure I was coming even before my last orgasm had left me.

"I've wanted you so bad, sir," I moaned and gripped her vest as pleasure coursed through me. "Please, please, I need more."

"Greedy," she hissed. Her hand rested on my inner thigh and pushed my legs farther apart. Her hands guided the leg that was against her so it was bent. She left fiery kisses on my knees and her hand stroked the sensitive flesh of my quivering inner thigh. "We'll get you there, in time. No need to rush."

"Please—"

"Tell me what you liked," she reminded me.

I struggled to find my words.

"Bondage, piercing, the—*fuck*—"

This time my mouth opened in a silent scream as my second orgasm flooded through me. I tried to close my legs, but she kept them pried open while whispering in my ear.

"God, you are so insatiable," she moaned. "I love it. So perfect. Tell me more."

I couldn't. My orgasm kept me from forming coherent words and I was stuck, frozen against her as wave after wave of heat rolled through me. My moans were so loud I was afraid people would come rushing in here at the sound.

"I liked watching," I admitted after my body regained control and I relaxed into her.

Her hands came to pluck at my nipples and I was about to beg her some more, but my eyes caught more movement in the doorframe.

*Sloan.*

She was there looking disheveled and exactly like how I thought she would after her scene was complete. There was a light sheen covering her face that shone in the dim light and her shirt had been almost torn open.

I should have been embarrassed. Should have wanted to close my legs and yell at her to leave.

But instead, I felt my body tensing in a different way.

# Ax

I couldn't be mad at Sloan for showing up. Not when Nyx had *that* reaction to her.

I was learning more and more about Nyx as the night unfolded and I had a feeling that she would very much like to try out what she had just seen on stage.

"I knew the show would get to her," Sloan said with a smirk as she entered my office.

Nyx was still lying on top of me with her filled pussy bared to the world as Sloan stalked forward. She gave no indication that she wanted her to stop.

"Safe word if you must," I reminded her.

She nodded. Sloan reached my desk and leaned over, her eyes trailing Nyx's body.

"Do you want us to share you tonight, Nyx?" Sloan asked.

Nyx's eyes widened before shooting toward me. I reached over and turned the toy off. She let out a whine.

"Why did you—"

"I want you alert," I said. "Now answer her question."

She hesitated, her eyes still watching me.

"Are you waiting for permission?" Sloan asked. She reached

forward and grabbed Nyx's chin so she was forced to look at her. "From who?"

Nyx's eyes darted toward me and there was a flash of satisfaction that shot through my chest. She wanted *me* to be the one to give her permission. She was looking to *me* to guide her through this. The boundaries that we hadn't yet established seemed to appear between us, and I couldn't have been more pleased with her.

"It's your choice," I said and placed another kiss on her knee.

I ran my hand down her inner thigh, taking in how beautiful she looked in the darkness with her clothing bunched around her waist. Her hair hung around her, shielding some of her body and creating a stark contrast between it and her skin. Her face was rosy, noticeable even in this dim lighting.

And let us not forget how she looked with her legs splayed open and that toy inside her. Her pussy was shining in the dim light with her own wetness and it had begun to drop onto my pants.

I continued to kiss her knee and rub meaningless patterns on her skin as she watched me.

"I want you to pierce me," she said, breaking the silence.

A delightful surprise played at my senses, and I shot a look at Sloan. She was already smiling.

"Let me go get my stuff," Sloan said and took a step back. "Prepare her for me, would you?"

I nodded and reached over to turn the toy back on. Nyx let out a surprised yelp before leaning back into me.

"One more," I whispered and placed my hand over hers, pushing the toy as far into her as it could go.

She turned to the side and captured my lips in hers. Her moans spilled into my mouth and echoed in the room as our tongues intertwined. It was sometime during this kiss that I began to lose the control I had. I was planning to have Nyx take it from here, but I couldn't help it with the way her moans turned me into an animal.

It started simply enough, taking the toy in hand and slowly pulling it out before thrusting it back into her. But when she broke our kiss and threw her head back to let out a loud moan, I found myself unable to hold back.

I lifted her just enough so I could place her on top of my desk, pushing off papers and decorations, and I forced her to lie flat on it. I leaned over her, my hand on the side of her head, taking in the way she looked under me, disheveled and panting. It was that moment, as she lay there looking like *that*, that I realized how much I didn't want to hold back anymore.

I took the toy in hand and began fucking her with it. Her hand clawed at my vest and she arched up toward me, but I kept the distance between us. I wasn't gentle as I pushed the toy into her. Over and over again, I thrust it into her, making her moan and writhe under me.

"Fuck, Ax," she nearly screamed as her back bowed, and she was coming again.

I grabbed her throat, her eyes widening as I pushed the toy into her and kept it there, making sure her needy clit was getting all the attention it deserved.

"This was not the ready I needed, but I will take it," Sloan said as she reentered the room.

I didn't even pay her any mind as she came and set the stuff by Nyx's head. I was too enamored by the way Nyx was looking at me.

Her eyebrows were pushed together and her eyes were wide. Her mouth was open as delicious sounds spilled out. I was ready to lean in and kiss her perfectly swollen lips until Sloan beat me to it.

I removed my hand from her throat and allowed her to cling to Sloan as they ravished each other.

It should have made me jealous, but instead, I found myself quickly enjoying the way that Nyx responded to Sloan.

I removed the toy from her and threw it across the room, not caring where it landed. Sloan pulled away at the same time, a trail of spit linking their mouths together.

"Where do you want it?" Sloan asked.

I leaned forward and took Nyx's right nipple into my mouth, biting on it gently.

"Here," I commanded before pulling it into my mouth and sucking on it lightly. "You'll take it here, won't you, kitten?"

Nyx's eyes shot to me and widened before looking back up at Sloan.

"My clit," she answered breathlessly. "My clit, please."

Sloan let out a chuckle, and I growled against her nipple.

"I don't think Ax will like—"

"Do it," I said and stood up straight. "But she has to earn it."

Before I gave them another answer, I fell to my knees and grabbed hold of Nyx's hips before descending on her pussy. Her hands flew to my hair and tugged at my locks, almost painfully so. I knew by now her clit was starting to become oversensitive, so I focused on the swollen nub, licking, biting, and sucking on it until I heard her sobbing.

Her sobs were quickly muffled, no doubt by Sloan's mouth.

"Two more," I said. "Two more and we can continue with the piercing."

It was an easy goal, not even a true punishment for her brattiness. But I couldn't bring myself to punish her for it. I wanted to see that piercing. I was just worried that it would have been too much for her too soon.

When her hips began bucking, I pushed down on her lower stomach and upped the intensity of my sucking. I was losing myself in her. I didn't care how much time I spent between her legs or how annoyed the patrons were now that all three of the hosts had now left. This place could be burned to the ground for all I'd care and I wouldn't have been able to budge from between her thighs.

Her skin was so soft. Her cries too beautiful. And that *cunt... God.*

Her sobs stopped as she came, tensing under my ministrations. She came hard against my mouth and continued to come as Sloan teased her.

"God, you're so needy," she said with a laugh. "How have you lasted this long without getting fucked by one of us, hmm? I bet you dreamed about it, didn't you?" I looked up to see Sloan standing over Nyx, her fingers plucking at her nipple, then without warning, she brought her hand back and slapped her breast. Hard enough for the smack to sound but not hard enough to cause any real pain. A test.

*How far was Nyx willing to go tonight?*

Nyx took a hand from my hair to cover her cries. I slowly licked the length of her cunt, enjoying the way she reacted to Sloan. Sloan leaned forward, their faces centimeters apart. She took Nyx's hand away from her mouth.

"Answer me," she commanded. "Did you dream about this moment? Wake up in soaked panties and forced to get yourself off before you came here?"

She slapped Nyx's breast again. I saw it coming just seconds before it landed and made sure to pull Nyx's clit inside my mouth.

"You think awfully high of yourself," Nyx answered with a choked sob.

Sloan pulled away, eyes gleaming. She leaned down and trailed kisses to Nyx's nipple, only to bite it. Hard. Hard enough that Nyx cried out. I pushed two fingers inside of her and continued to lick and suck on her clit as Sloan trailed bites along her breast and neck.

"Fuck," Nyx said as Sloan bit her neck.

"I think you're a liar," Sloan whispered in her ear, loud enough for me to hear over Nyx's pants.

"You wish," she spat. "Call this a moment of weakness."

I turned to place a bite of my own on Nyx's thigh before standing. They both turned to look at me and Sloan's smile swept her face when she realized what was next. With one last kiss to

Nyx's lips, Sloan whispered, "I am going to make you come so hard you'll regret that attitude of yours."

Nyx looked like she was about to bolt, so I quickly grabbed her hips and turned her over so that she was on her belly.

I grabbed her wrists and waited for Sloan to riffle through the side drawers, only to pull out a bright-red rope.

Sloan dragged the rope across Nyx's skin, teasing her with the sensation but also allowing her to understand what was coming next. She didn't fight as Sloan tied one wrist and then turned her over to tie the other one so they were both in front of her. She watched us with a curious stare, then when her eyes met mine, there was the slightest of smiles that ghosted her lips.

Her skin was already turning purple in the areas that Sloan had bitten and her makeup was already running down her face. There was trust in the way she bared her body to us. Even when she fought back or acted like a brat, you could tell that she was comfortable with us.

It made my heart soar.

Sloan had already reached into the drawers and handed me a wand while she began to fasten a strap-on to herself. A giddy sense of excitement filled me when I turned on the wand. I didn't bring it down to Nyx's clit first, instead, I glided it over her nipples and the sensitive skin of her breasts before traveling downward.

I took my free hand and lifted her bound hands and pushed them above her. I had never been happier to have a desk as big as the one I have more than this moment. Her legs were hanging off, but the rest of her body fit perfectly on the desk and I was able to push her wrists down on the wood beneath her.

When I reached her clit, I had to put more pressure on her wrists as she fought to move her hands.

"Not so tough now, huh?" Sloan asked.

Nyx glared at her before sending a pleading look to me.

"Please, Ax," she begged. "It's too much, I—"

She was cut off when I upped the vibrations on the toy.

"It's too much when I say it is," I warned in a low tone. "Do you understand me?"

When she nodded, I removed the toy and Sloan delivered a slap to her wet cunt.

"Use your words," Sloan sang.

I pushed the toy onto her clit once more and she let out a strangled moan.

"Fuck," she sobbed and looked toward me. "Do I have to? In front of—"

Another slap cut her off.

"Safe word if not," I reminded.

She threw her head back onto the desk.

I upped the vibrations once more and her entire body tensed.

"Do you understand me?" I asked. "I am not above denying you this orgasm, Nyx. Answer me."

She was writhing under me so hard it was difficult to keep her wrists bound.

"Yes," she sobbed. "Yes, *daddy.*"

She came seconds after, her back bowing and her screams cutting off.

"Fuck, that's hot," Sloan muttered and positioned the toy at her entrance. "One more. One more and I promise you that piercing."

Nyx's pleas had turned into choked sobs but we could make out the words well enough.

*Please. Yes. More.*

Sloan used the desk as leverage and began moving against her. Sloan didn't use any buildup like I had, she had no restraint. Instead, she began fucking her like an animal. My hold on Nyx's wrist was originally to stop her from moving but now it was used to stop Sloan from fucking her up the desk.

The force of her thrusts had begun to push the desk forward, screeches from the legs against the floor filled the air and intertwined with Nyx's moans. Sloan's hips hit the wand with each thrust, forcing it hard against Nyx's clit.

"Come on," I cooed to Nyx. "You got this, kitten. Just one more time."

She shook her head wildly, causing me to hit the toy up higher one more time, to its highest setting.

It was mere seconds before she was coming again.

I took the toy off her when she had stilled.

Sloan reached over while still inside her and began setting up, including the alcohol wipe and needle.

"Are you ready?" I asked, leaning over her. Her hair was stuck to her face and her chest was rising and falling rapidly. She swallowed thickly before leaning up to look at Sloan.

I knew it was a mistake instantly as her face lost all color and she threw her head back onto the desk.

"I'm scared of needles," she whispered.

I paused and looked at Sloan, who shrugged as if to say, *this is your problem, dude.*

I let up on her wrists and put her arms around my neck, bringing our faces so close her breath wafted across my face.

"Call the safe word if you want this to stop," I reminded. "It's there for a reason."

She shook her head and tightened her grip around me.

"Just be here, please," she said and took a deep breath of air as the package of the alcohol wipe ripping open sounded through the room.

I nodded.

"I'll be right here, kitten," I said and ran my fingers through her hair like I had been dying to do for weeks.

Nyx gasped as Sloan began wiping her down.

"This is going to be a bit sensitive, especially since we just finished," Sloan warned. "I am going to do a vertical hood since that will suit your shape the best. Are we good to proceed?"

Nyx nodded and I sent her a look.

"I'm ready," she said.

"Deep breath," Sloan commanded.

Nyx's face pinched and I took a deep breath in with her. She was watching me intently and fear was written across her face.

"It's okay," I whispered and placed a small kiss on her lips.

"Exhale," Sloan said.

Tears flowed freely down Nyx's face.

"Come on," I said and exhaled. She followed suit, and I saw right when the needle punctured her. She let out a strangled whine as tears descended faster. There was a shuffling behind me as Sloan put the piercing in.

"You did so good," I said and kissed her tears away. "So so good."

I placed a kiss to her lips and was taken aback when she deepened it. I felt Sloan disappear but didn't turn to her until she was back and pushing us apart.

"Cleaning," she said when I turned to her. "Our little plaything made quite a mess."

Nyx's face flamed.

I quickly stood up and began to untie her as Sloan cleaned between her legs with a wet cloth.

"Clean this a few times a day and try not to fuss with it until it's healed, okay?" she said.

"Okay," Nyx muttered.

I helped her sit up and was pushed away by Sloan, who took her face in her hands and kissed her deeply. When she pulled away, they were breathing hard.

Sloan leaned up to place a kiss on her forehead before taking her face in her hand and forcing their gazes to meet.

"You did so good, love," Sloan cooed. "I will have to go deal with the patrons downstairs, but I will leave you here with Ax for aftercare. Remember that this is nothing to feel weird or embarrassed about and my leaving does not reflect on the time we shared together. I enjoyed it very much and look forward to our next." She looked over to me and winked. "If Ax allows, of course."

I sent her a look and shooed her away before helping Nyx off the desk. I stripped her of her remaining clothes in silence and pulled her to my couch. I positioned us so that she was sitting on the couch with her legs over mine and as I held her, I pulled a blanket over us.

"Does it hurt?" I asked.

She nodded into my chest and let out a deep sigh.

"Tell me what you need," I said.

"Just this," she said, then paused. "Tell me more about how you got into this."

I paused and allowed myself to run my hands through her hair, reveling in the fact that we could exist in this space. Just the two of us. I tried to ignore the need to ask her about the life outside of this room and just focus on *this.*

"I had a... less than easy childhood," I said and continued to play with her hair. "I had immigrant parents who worked really hard to give us everything we needed and when I got old enough, I started to realize that I needed to work hard as well. But I didn't want to live a life full of struggle."

"You wanted to learn from their mistakes," she said, her voice muffled in my chest.

"Sort of," I admitted. "Though the only mistake my parents made was thinking that hard work could earn you a better life."

She moved to look at me but I pushed her head back down into my chest. She let out an annoyed huff.

"Hard work *can* earn you a better life," she insisted.

A genuine smile tugged at my lips.

"Hard work can work for some," I agreed. "Though you need lots of luck, smarts, and sometimes need to get your hands dirty to get to a certain place in life. I don't think I need to tell you that the richest people of this world were built on the backs of hard-working people, just like my parents, without a care in the world for their hardships."

She stayed silent.

"After working from an early age, I got into an... unsavory business," I said. "But that business allowed me to save for the future. To provide a life for my family. To retire my parents and allow them to pass peacefully. And then when I had enough, I decided to open this club. A place where people like us could come together and enjoy the things society shuns us for. Enjoy each other."

Nyx was so silent it caused me to regret spilling as much as I did.

"What type of unsavory business?" she asked in a small voice.

*Lie,* a voice in my head commanded.

The urge to lie to her and continue to spend these blissful few moments with her weighed over my conscience.

"Many things," I answered. Her hand reached out to grab my wrist. My throat swelled when she intertwined her fingers with mine. "The mob, a few gangs here and there. I would float around. Whoever would accept me and whoever had more power than from where I came."

Her thumb rubbed circles on the back of my hand.

"That must have been hard," she said.

I nodded, unable to speak.

She was comforting me. *She* was comforting *me.* This is her aftercare, and this was how it turned out.

"Did you kill people?" she asked.

"Would it scare you if I did?" I asked before I could stop the words. "Make you think less of me?"

There was a pause and the music from below us filtered through. I didn't know how long we had been gone, but I was sure by now we were in our final stretch and if I didn't show my face soon, many would be pissed.

"Yes," she answered and my heart dropped into my stomach. It was such a soft yet powerful word that had the ability to turn everything I had been feeling in that moment on its head. "Scare me, I mean. I wouldn't think less of you though. I understand what a hard life can do to people and that sometimes the only option available is the least savory one."

I gripped her tighter, relief flooding through me.

I shouldn't care what she thought. I shouldn't have these feelings for her, nor should I want to stay with her like this forever. I wanted to tell her everything. Tell her every painful little detail just so I could continue to feel the soothing motions of her thumb on the back of my hand and the high that shot through me as she accepted me as easily as if I told her something as simple as the time.

"I had a... rough childhood as well," she admitted, her hold on me tightening.

"You don't have to talk about it—"

"It's okay," she said. "It's not that hard anymore." She let out a sigh before continuing. "I grew up with a really religious family. I guess it's why it took me so long to come out and... get into the scene."

"Many people don't get into it until much later," I said, feeling the need to comfort her.

In reality, I knew most of what she was going to say and a part of it worried me. It would have been easy to pretend like I didn't know anything at all but I really didn't want to lie anymore.

"Ya, but that's not the main issue. I have had no contact with my extended family for years," she let out another sigh. "My mother had fallen in with a bad crowd when she was in between jobs and had gotten addicted to drugs. The family refused to help her and thought that if they *prayed* hard enough that it would get better. Then she got arrested."

"But it didn't," I finished for her.

She nodded into me. "So when I was forced to, I ventured out on my own, I had no contact with her as well," she said. "I know it may seem selfish but I just couldn't handle it."

I loved my family. They were what made me the person I am today. Every move I had made had been to ensure that *they* were taken care of... but I had been lucky. I had found a family that loved me and would have never shunned me like they had Nyx.

"I understand," I said and placed a kiss on her forehead. "Your own mental health is important. If they cannot accept you or help you when you're in need, they don't get the right to call you family."

She made a noise and settled deeper into me.

"My mom reached out again a few years after," she said, surprising me. "Though I don't call her anymore, she is the only person I could rely on. Which is why I was so stressed about losing my job."

"I remember when your boss called you," I muttered.

Even though I had been freaking out about my own attraction to Nyx when she was with my son, I had not been oblivious to how she had reacted to having to go back to work.

Looking back, it made my heart ache.

"I just really didn't want to contact her again," she sighed. "I didn't want to fall back into the pattern we once had."

"You were scared."

She nodded.

"You may want to call her at some point," I said.

She twisted to give me a look that caused my lips to twitch.

"I'm just saying she may regret her choices and feel bad. She could be just as afraid to reach out as you are."

She pouted.

"I guess you're right," she said with a sigh. "Maybe soon."

"Good girl," I said and kissed her lips. I paused before pulling back, unease eating at me.

"What is it?" she asked.

"I may or may not have used my contacts to get some information on you," I admitted.

I watched her face carefully and to my utter shock, there was an amused smile that pulled at her lips.

"Oh ya?" she asked. I nodded hesitantly.

"Just about your childhood," I said. "I got the gist of it, but you provided more color. Are you... mad?"

"Maybe I should be," she teased.

"You may be even madder when you hear that I visited the bakery every Saturday to catch a glimpse of you."

Her face positively lit up at my confession.

"You did not," she gasped.

My face heated unbearably.

"I did, though I promised myself I wouldn't cross a line," I said after clearing my throat. "You know I value the trust our patrons put in us."

"So you admit that I was a patron all along," she said with a laugh.

"Of course you were," I said with a sigh. "I was just being rude before. I didn't mean it."

A silence fell over us and there was a nagging question at the back of my mind that was begging to be let out.

I didn't want to push her into anything she wasn't ready for, but I wanted *more* between us. We had already made it clear that we couldn't stay away from each other, but that gave us no clarity on what we really *were.*

Maybe it was old-fashioned, but I wanted to be able to call her mine.

"What are we?" I asked, then backpedaled. "I mean, what do you want us to be?"

Her makeup was still smeared, but as soon as the question left my lips, there was a light to her eyes I hadn't seen before. Looking back, I would remember this moment as the one that changed everything.

"Are you saying you want us to be something?" she asked. "Last I checked, you were still worried about Asher."

A bitterness exploded in my mouth as I thought of what happened between her and Asher. Those fucking *pictures.*

"He's not an issue anymore," I said. "I will talk to him. This is between me and you."

She swallowed and looked toward our intertwined hands.

"I didn't want to come between you," she said. "I know that it has been tense since..."

When she trailed off, I cursed internally.

"My sister said something, didn't she?" I asked.

Nyx nodded.

"About Asher's birth mom," she said. "I just felt bad, and I didn't want to be the reason you guys fell out again. And I didn't know how to approach it with you. I know your business was dangerous, and I was worried that you weren't over her—"

I stopped her rambling by putting my mouth to hers.

When I pulled away, I grabbed at the hair at the base of her neck, forcing her eyes to me.

"What happens between me and Asher is not your fault," I said slowly. "And as far as his mother. I loved her—love her. That won't change. But that doesn't mean I will spend the rest of my life alone till I die. We had our time and as great as it was, it's over now."

She let out a breath.

"So we can... try *this*?" she asked.

I raised a brow.

"What is *this?*" I asked in return.

A smile pulled at her lips.

"Dating, I guess? I dunno, girlfriends?"

It was my turn to smile.

"Are you asking me out, kitten?" I said in a purr. "If so, you shouldn't half-ass it like that."

Her face flushed.

"Will you be my girlfriend?" she asked. "I know it's not really *dating* per se, but we can work up to it—"

I silenced her with another kiss.

"Girlfriends sounds nice," I said against her lips. "Though I am a bit old for that."

She let out a light laugh before returning my kiss.

"No such thing."

# Nyx

Three weeks.

It had been three weeks since the night of the event and everything had changed. Well… it was more like the world had shifted. Things like work and my routine had stayed the same for the most part, but there was something that had shifted between me and Ax.

Sloan was her same usual self and gave no indication that what had happened in Ax's office had changed our relationship. I was glad, for once.

I enjoyed what happened immensely and would find myself between the two of them on more than one occasion, but it was different with Ax.

Ax and I were… *serious.*

More serious than I had ever thought we would be.

"A date is a date," I said and shifted on the cool leather seats of Ax's limo.

I had worn the tight-fitting slip that she had gotten me just that morning and as beautiful as it was, it was uncomfortable as hell.

My shoulders were bare and the fabric was so thin that I

couldn't wear a bra, or panties... but by the look in Ax's eyes, that was exactly her plan.

She sat across from me in a pin-striped slacks-and-vest set with a white button-up shirt that had the sleeves rolled up, showing her dark tattoos. A request from me. I liked the primed yet sensual look the suit gave her but loved when she was able to show that extra bit of herself.

She shifted so that her arm was on top of the seat behind her and her head fell into her palm. She was staring at me with those expressive eyes yet kept her face blank except for the ghost of a smile on her lips.

"Coffee shops and walking to the bakery don't count," she said. "I told you I would give this *dating* thing a try and I intend to keep that promise."

I rolled my eyes at her.

Convincing her to give us being together a chance after that night hadn't been hard but aligning on what our expectations were was.

Ax was the type of person that loved planned dates and more than one time I had come to work with a bouquet of colorful flowers on my desk. She insisted that there was a correct way of doing things and that it was downright insulting to continue to treat me as some kind of toy to be used and abused whenever she wanted.

*Her words, not mine.*

"I told you it doesn't have to be like this," I said with a sigh and ran my hands through my hair. I hadn't had much time to get ready as we had left directly from the office so I was forced to wear it down in waves. "I just like to spend time with you, wherever that may be."

She leaned forward and took my hand in hers, electricity buzzing under my skin where hers touched. She brought my hand up to her lips before pressing a scorching kiss on the back of my hand.

"I want it to be," she said. "I want to bring you out. Show you off. Are you ashamed, kitten?"

Heat flushed inside me.

"Ashamed?" I choked out.

Her lips quirked and she leaned back against her seat.

"I am much older than you," she said. "I wouldn't take offense if you're not ready to be seen with me in public yet."

Shock and guilt rose in me so wildly that it felt like a punch to the gut.

"No," I said quickly. Too quickly. Her face fell.

I hadn't given it much thought, to be honest. Ax was older, that much was obvious, but I hadn't ever felt the difference in our age. Whether that be in work or pleasure. I saw Ax as Ax. The person who ignited such a hidden desire in me. The person who made me feel warmth and security that I had never felt before.

I had never once thought about the age difference *or* what people thought about us.

Maybe one time, before I had gone to the club. Before I had come out and before I was shunned by my parents... but not now. Not anymore.

I had gotten a taste of the freedom that Ax had given me with the club and in our relationship and it was so intoxicating that there was no way I could give it up now.

No matter what the others said.

"I don't care what people think," I clarified after a moment. "And before you mentioned it just now, I never gave it much thought."

She raised a brow.

"Even when my son was on your arm?" she asked.

I *hated* talking about Asher. Usually, she wouldn't push, but there was something about this question that felt different. More serious.

"Not even then," I admitted. "Though I must admit at some point, I longed to tell him his mom had been the best lay I'd ever had."

*That* got a real smile out of her. Her breathy chuckle filled the air.

"I shouldn't find that amusing," she said, then turned serious. "But I almost wish you had."

Shock washed through me. She noticed.

"It's exciting, isn't it?" she asked. "A taste of the forbidden?"

I squeezed my thighs together, heat coiling in my belly.

"I thought about him, or anyone really, walking in on us while you had me pushed up against the window," I admitted in one breath.

The confession sucked the air out of the car, lighting an electrifying tension between us.

"Would you have asked me to stop?" she asked. "If they walked in?"

I shook my head and averted my gaze as shame coursed through me.

"Look at me," she snapped.

The intensity in her voice caused my gaze to snap back to hers. There was a small frown on her face.

"Don't feel shame for what you want, love."

That nickname was one I rarely heard and it was enough to send my heart into a frenzy. She patted her lap, but instead, I dropped down to my knees and slid my head on her lap. I looked up at her from under my lashes and caught sight of that ever-powerful look of satisfaction that crossed her face.

It had been a while since we had played *this* game, but it was one that I missed.

We fell into our roles quickly and found an easy rhythm for the two of us to follow, but she had never required me to kneel, call her sir or daddy outside the bedroom, or really anything else.

She let me decide when and where I wanted our dynamic to change and being able to have that choice alone turned me on to no end. Because it was a way that I could have control even if I preferred for her to control me.

"Is this how you want our dinner to go?" she asked, her hand brushing across my cheek.

I leaned into it and sighed as the warmth of her skin heated my own. With just that single touch, I was melting against her.

"Yes," I breathed. "I am not afraid of what they think. I want to be fully yours tonight. No exceptions."

A smirk spread across her lips.

"No exceptions?" she asked in a teasing tone. "So if I told you to get up on the table and spread your legs for me so I could feast on that delectable pussy of yours until you screamed, you would do as you're told?"

A buzz of excitement traveled my body and left goose bumps on my skin.

"I may make it a bit difficult for you," I admitted.

Her lips quirked and her hand trailed from my cheek to my hair, where she grabbed a fistful of it and forced my head back. She leaned forward, exhaling a hot breath against my bare neck and pulling a whimper from me.

"I wouldn't have it any other way," she breathed with a chuckle. Her lips traveled up to my ear before nipping at my lobe. "Edge yourself for me. Bring yourself to the brink over and over again until we arrive. Don't try to pull something. I promise you will not like the outcome."

I swallowed the knot in my throat and leaned back against the seat. I trailed my hand down my stomach and between my legs, gasping as my fingers came into contact with my swollen, pierced clit. The piercing had already healed and to my surprise, it made everything much more sensitive than before.

She leaned forward, hands on her elbows and eyes trained on my spread legs.

"Show me," she growled. "Spread your pussy lips and show me how wet you are."

I whimpered at her command but moved my dress so that she could see how swollen and wet I was. I paused the motion on my clit to spread my folds for her. I was rewarded with a groan from her.

"Do you like it?" I asked and began to circle my clit. Her eyes flashed to mine.

"Like it?" she asked. "Baby, you spreading your beautiful cunt like that for me is downright intoxicating. It's so hard for me to sit back here and watch you fuck yourself when my mouth is fucking watering at the thought of tasting you."

I picked up the pace on my clit, her words sending a bolt of pleasure through me.

"Watch yourself," she commanded when my eyes fluttered closed. My orgasm was already cresting and I had a hard time focusing on anything but the feeling of the heat coiling in my belly.

She leaned forward even more and made direct eye contact with me as she *spat* directly on my pussy.

"Two fingers. Inside. *Now.*"

I didn't even think about disobeying her. Not when I was so close to orgasm and the sight of her spitting on me was still in my mind.

I had never thought that spitting would have aroused me as much as it did, but I was beginning to lose myself as I used it to fuck myself.

"You're not supposed to come, baby," she reminded me.

I let out a whine but slowed my thrusts, my orgasm slipping away.

"Let me taste."

I scrambled to push myself up and force my two fingers into her mouth. She sucked on them and used her tongue to lap up every bit. My clit pulsed at the action and I moaned when she bit down on my fingers. When she pulled back, a trail of spit followed her.

"Again," she commanded.

And I did. I listened to her and fucked myself with my fingers still covered in her spit. I did exactly as she said the rest of the ride to the restaurant and by the time we had arrived, I was begging for release.

But Ax didn't give in.

She pulled me out of the car with her, probably looking like a sweaty, panting mess, and brought me straight into the restaurant. My pussy was throbbing, and with each step, the piercing created delightful friction, causing pleasure to soar through me. My clit was aching and I felt hot all over. If I wasn't careful, one touch would be all that it took to set me off.

The restaurant she had brought us to looked to be high class, with a formal dress code, dim lighting, and private seating, though I had never been to something so fancy or seen anything like it outside of movies and TV shows.

The drapes, floors, and booths were all the same shade of black, with the only color being the bloodred roses that decorated the tables and bar.

To my delight, we were brought to a private room on the far side of the restaurant and up a floor. There was only enough room for a table, chairs, and a tray, but the view was spectacular.

We had driven more than fifty minutes away and there was nothing around besides trees and a small garden which our room overlooked. Off in the distance, you could get just a glimpse of Manhattan.

I met Ax's gaze with an excited smile.

"This is so beautiful," I said.

She smiled back and ushered me to my chair, pulling it out for me. I flushed at her actions.

"I know you said you didn't mind being in public with me," she said and moved the chair across from me so that she was sitting next to me instead. "But I have to admit, I would be a little jealous if anyone got to see how beautiful you look right now."

Heat exploded on my face and I looked down to avoid her hungry gaze, but she grabbed my chin and forced me to look at her.

"Don't look away from me when I am complimenting you," she said, her tone low.

I swallowed thickly.

"Yes, sir," I whispered.

Her eyes flashed and there was a small look of satisfaction that spread across her face.

"Good girl," she murmured. Her words sent butterflies off in my stomach.

The door opened and in came a waiter, already holding two drinks in his hand.

"I ordered ahead of time," she said. "I hope you don't mind."

I shook my head and smiled at the waiter as he placed the drink in front of me. It was a mojito.

I took a sip and squirmed in my chair as the waiter left Ax and me alone. The ache between my legs was killing me and it took all my restraint to not finish the job myself.

"Ax—"

She shot me a look. *That's right. I asked for this tonight.*

"Please, sir," I whispered. "I was good like you said."

Her face remained expressionless as she lifted her drink and took a long sip of the amber liquid.

"What are you asking me, Nyx?"

I swallowed thickly, embarrassment creeping along the back of my neck.

"Please make me come, sir," I begged.

When a small smirk spread across her face, I felt the urge to spread my legs and finish it right there, but I held off. Ax, so far, had been true to her word and I didn't want to think of what my punishment would be. In a crowded restaurant, no less.

"Are you asking me to slip my hand under the table and fuck you right here?" she asked. "Don't you realize anyone could walk in on us and see?"

I couldn't meet her gaze, shame washing over me.

She lifted my chin so our eyes met once more.

"Or is that what you want, kitten?" she asked. "Does it excite you that they could walk in on us any moment while I'm pounding into that needy cunt of yours?"

I held her gaze even as heat traveled across my face.

Her eyes lit up.

"So it *does*," she said with a laugh. "You are a little whore, aren't you?"

Feeling a bit of confidence, I leaned forward and dropped my voice into a whisper.

"Your whore," I said.

She clicked her tongue and gave me a hard look.

"Here I was trying to treat you like a nice respectable date," she said. "I took you to a nice restaurant, had a whole night planned for us, including sightseeing and maybe a club if you were interested... but the first stop and you're already begging for me to bed you."

I leaned back in my chair, my own smile spreading across my face.

"Well, if you won't," I said and dipped my hand under my dress. I made a show of gasping as my fingers came in contact with my clit. "Then I will and you'll just have to sit there and watch."

It would be a lie if I said I didn't get aroused by the thought of someone walking in on us. Combined with the look that Ax was giving me, I was ready to combust.

She let out a sigh and reached over to my drink, bringing out an ice cube before forcing it past my lips. It was cold as it lay on my tongue and I didn't really understand where she was going with it.

"Keep going," she said and leaned forward to kiss me. She pushed my mouth open with her tongue and took the ice from my mouth.

She pulled away with a smile before pressing her lips to my neck, her tongue coming out to tease me. I shivered at the coldness of it.

Her hand moved to tug down the top of my dress and expose my breast. I let out a whimper before she moved to latch on to my nipple. The sudden coldness of the ice made me let out a hiss, but when she began to suck, I couldn't help but moan and move my fingers faster against my clit.

She used her other hand to tease my entrance before pushing two fingers inside of me.

A gargled moan escaped my mouth. She bit down on my nipple before moving to the other one.

"Fuck," I moaned. "I'm going to come."

The teasing in the car had prepared me for this moment. All the tension in my body rose together and just as she began thrusting into me, I found myself falling over the edge. This time my orgasm was so powerful I couldn't even let out a noise other than a choked sob as I came on her fingers.

She continued to fuck me as I rode out wave after wave of my orgasm. All the previous denied ones came back to hit me like a truck.

Her mouth crashed into mine. I tried to deepen it but she pulled away with a laugh.

"I should have punished you for that," she said and helped me fix my dress. "But I couldn't help myself."

Then to prove her point, she leaned back and popped her fingers right into her mouth. Heat flared inside me as she kept my gaze and cleaned my arousal off her fingers.

"I really did want to treat you tonight," she said, her voice turning serious. "I didn't want you to think that everything between us is just sexual."

I shifted in my seat and sat up straight.

"I know that," I said with a small pout.

"Do you?" she asked with a raised brow. "I mean, I haven't really given you reason to think otherwise. I have to admit, I am a little embarrassed with how crazy you make me sometimes."

A burst of pride warmed my chest.

"I could say the same about you," I said with a small smile. "After all, you were the one that found me masturbating in *your* office."

Her lips twisted into a smile.

"You make me crazy, Nyx," she admitted and leaned over to thread her fingers through mine. "I haven't felt this way in years. But I like it. You make me feel renewed. Energized... with you, I don't feel like the world is out to get me. I feel like anything is possible."

My throat tightened and I had to clear it in order to speak.

"You know it's the same for me, right?" I asked. "Sure, the sex is amazing, but I've been drawn to you from the start."

It was her turn for her face to flush. I decided in the moment I quite liked how Ax looked when she was embarrassed.

"You make me feel safe," I explained. "Wanted in a way other than just sex. I feel *seen* with you. I don't feel like anyone has ever read me as well as you do."

"You don't mind the age difference?" she asked. "Truly? It's okay, it won't hurt my feelings."

I let out a laugh and shook my head.

"If anything, it makes it hotter," I admitted. "I do kind of like it when you make me call you *daddy*."

She gave me a smile. This was the first time I was able to have a conversation with someone so easily about our relationship. Sexual or not. The words came out easy with her. Even when I got embarrassed, I never had to worry about her judging me for what I wanted or thought.

It was comforting in a way I had not yet experienced. *Secure.*

The door opened, startling me, and I jumped in my chair, much to Ax's delight.

"Let's enjoy our evening, hmm?" Ax asked as soon as the waiter left. "I promise you we will have time for *daddy* later."

I let out another laugh and dug in, loving the way her words and smile caused my insides to flutter.

*Maybe... maybe this would work out for real this time.*

# Ax

"Are you sure it's him?" I asked as we pulled up to the café.

It had been over a month since the last time I had spoken to Asher and now I was about to do something that would change the course of our relationship for the rest of my life.

Sloan nodded and let out a sigh.

"We traced it back to him," she said and leaned forward to look out the windows of the SUV. From our spot, we could see Asher sitting at the back of the café through their large windows. He had a coffee in his hand and a computer on his table. On the outside, it looked as though he was just another worker or even a student, but it was only Sloan and I that knew that he was currently riffling through all of Club Pétale's files.

There had been no rhyme or reason to his search anymore. At this point, he was just trying to get anything and everything he could get his hands on. It was almost like he had been goading us. Showing us just how easy it would have been to get access to everything.

All because he had been using my own account.

"Did he leak them on the social sites as well?" I asked.

Sloan made a noise.

"We think so, but he could have had someone else do it as well," she explained. "There were a few devices associated with the accounts that posted, one of which we are still trying to locate."

I nodded.

"I don't want to do this," I whispered.

"Do you want me to come with you?" Sloan asked, her hand brushing across mine.

I shook my head.

This wasn't supposed to be an ambush. No matter how angry I was at him for trying to ruin me, I wanted to do this the right way.

Asher was not my enemy, and I shouldn't treat him that way.

"I got it," I said, then looked in the rearview mirror.

Yvon had taken off this week and so I had used a backup. Sven was just as proficient and knew how to keep a secret. His brown eyes watched me carefully in the mirror.

"Stay near, I'll call you when it's done," I said.

He nodded. I turned back to Sloan.

"Go back to the club," I said. "I don't want to leave Nyx alone too long."

She gave me a look.

"She is a big girl, Ax," Sloan said with a snort. "I think catching your blackmailing son would be more of a priority now than a prett—"

"*Please,*" I said. "I don't know how this will go over and I want to make sure she isn't worried if I disappear for half a day."

She paused.

"Are you prepared for the fallout?" she asked.

"No," I answered honestly. "Which is why if I go off the rails, I need someone there with her."

"And who will be there for you?" she asked without hesitation.

There was silence because I had no answer and instead said, "Just do what I say."

Without letting her respond, I climbed out of the car.

Sounds of honking cars and chattering hit me as I exited and felt the heat of the summer sun through my clothing, threatening to burn my skin. The city was bustling on a Monday, and I hated it.

Hated the sounds.

Hated the smells.

And most of all, I hated what I was going to do.

I had thought long and hard night after night about it. I should have faced him as soon as Nyx told me about the pictures. I don't know how I could have been so stupid... but waiting for Sloan to confirm that it was Asher all along was important. No matter how much I trusted Nyx, I needed to wait for the confirmation and even after I had it... I couldn't come to terms with what was happening.

He was my son. Regardless of what happened between all of us. Regardless if I had messed up, or he had messed up.

He was the son that I raised.

He was the son that someone I loved dearly had given me. And even though it was under horrible, heart-wrenching circumstances... I still loved him.

I had learned to love him. And I know that I was a shitty parent. I always knew that I was never good enough, but how could he do this to me?

I let out a deep sigh, my body sagging with it. My legs felt heavy and my body didn't want to cooperate. It took me a few moments just staring at my son through the window until I finally pushed myself forward and stepped into the café that was somewhat busy. And I knew that if I wasn't careful, we'd make a bigger scene than I wanted.

We were in Ryder's territory.

So it was dangerous for me to even be here. It was dangerous for him to be here. I wouldn't put it past Ryder to come and ambush him. I was surprised that he had let him stay here for so long. Ryder had to have known about him, about Nyx, about everyone involved with me.

So just being here was like having a target on my back and Asher's.

Asher didn't even look up at me as I sat down at the table, the metal chair screeching as I dragged it across the café's linoleum floor. The sound of the baristas making coffees and orders being called out swirled around us, but the silence between us seemed more potent than all of that and drowned out everything except my own heartbeat.

Even though he didn't look up and was still typing on his keyboard, I knew that he was aware of me sitting across from him. He was ignoring me on purpose.

"Asher," I said in a tone much cooler than I had wanted.

His eyes drifted up until they locked on mine. I saw so much of his mother in front of me right now, until a slimy smirk spread across his face.

"Mom," he said, his tone much lighter than my own, though it didn't match his expression. "Fancy seeing you here."

"Asher," I said again. "You know why I'm here? Don't you?"

He sat up finally, stopped typing, and looked at me. His eyes narrowed and he let out a sigh before looking around the café.

"Yes," he said, not looking at me. "Surprised it actually took you so long."

I straightened and grabbed the edge of my seat, making sure that I stayed planted. It had been hard keeping my impulses at bay, and now, sitting in front of the person who was single-handedly trying to destroy my career and admitted to it so easily was making it harder and harder to stay in my seat and be the person I wanted to be.

"Am I to assume that you were waiting for me?" I asked.

He let out a huff of a laugh. "I don't come here for fun, Mother. I never have. You know I'm not into whatever it is that people do here. I'm not like you. I'm not like your little slut. Speaking of Nyx, I have to ask. How is she? Did I keep her warm enough for you?"

Red.

All I saw was red.

Anger so strong flashed through me that it caused my head to spin. My heart started pounding in my chest and I could feel the heat flush across my entire being.

I stood up abruptly. The seat fell to the floor behind me and the café turned silent. Asher just looked up as if I wasn't fuming in front of him and ready to pounce. If anything, he looked downright amused.

"I'm not here to fight with you about Nyx," I growled. "But if I hear you utter something so disrespectful like that ever again, son or not, I won't hold back."

He let out a little whistle, closed his computer, and stood as well.

"You and your women," he muttered. "I didn't know that you would let someone like her come between us like this. I always knew that you held some sort of resentment toward me for not being the perfect little protégé you wanted, but I didn't know you hated me this much. I didn't know you'd cast aside your own son for a whore."

I leaned over the table and grabbed a fistful of his shirt, pulling him to me.

"What has gotten into you, Asher?" I growled at him. "This is not you. You don't get to call her my *whore*. You don't get to insult her like that, and you don't get to insult *me* like that. Why are you doing this?"

Even though our faces were inches apart, and my fist was still tangled in his shirt, he let out a laugh, a slow smile spreading across his face.

"Don't get so butt hurt abou—"

"It's not just about her," I interrupted. "My club, the files, blackmailing her. Blackmailing all of my patrons. Where do you get off?"

We were locked in a glaring contest when a soft-spoken voice interrupted us.

"Excuse me," a voice called out.

I glared toward the interruption and saw a small barista looking at us with a fearful expression.

"Excuse me, but you need to take this outside," she said, her voice trembling slightly.

"Perfect timing," Asher said and slapped my hand away. If the whole café wasn't looking at us right now, I would have done much worse.

I didn't like this line of thinking. I didn't like that I wanted to hurt my own son. But all of the feelings of anger and pain and betrayal swirled through me and it was as though I was no longer looking at the son that I once loved. I was looking at someone who had hurt me so deeply that I could no longer stand to be in their presence.

*This person was a stranger.*

He knew what the club meant to me. He knew that for my entire life. I'd been working for this moment. He knew that I put my life and everyone else's in danger so he could have a good education. And so, finally, I could build the club of my dreams and do something that was more than hurting people and hurting myself. Didn't he know that I was trying so hard to get my life straight?

*Why?*

"Asher," I said in a hushed tone. "We have to talk about this."

He grabbed his backpack and put his computer in it before swinging it over his shoulder and motioning for me to leave out back with the tilt of his head.

"There's an exit out there," he said. "You're right about one thing though, I've been waiting for you. Not just today, but for days or weeks to catch on. And now that you finally have, I think it's time that we have a talk."

He walked out back without me being able to reply. I headed after him after sending a forced smile to the barista. Even as we exited out the back into a small, damp alleyway, he didn't stop. I followed him down the alleyway, turned around the corner onto a busy street, and wound around buildings until we came to a stop at a dead end.

I couldn't keep the nagging thoughts out of my head. The ones that urged me to call for Sloan. The ones that begged me to stop this while I still could.

But I didn't listen to any of the warnings still in my head.

"What were you going to do with those files, Asher?" I asked as he came to a stop. The alleyway we had ended up in was damp, and there was a sweet but pungent smell that burned my nose. In the distance, I could hear voices from above us, no doubt the residents of the buildings next to us peeking out of their windows, watching excitedly to see what would happen. "Why did you leak those images on the internet?"

He turned to me with a frown on his face

"Why do you think, *Mother*?" he asked.

"I don't know," I admitted, my voice on the verge of hysterics. "Maybe you wanted to ruin the club. I understand that you don't like it. I understand that. But Asher, this isn't—"

"You're so self-absorbed," he spat. "Can't you think of anything other than your stupid club?"

His words were so cold they felt like a knife straight to the chest. There was so much venom and rage laced into them that it caused my heart to ache.

"Yes, I leaked the photos," he said. "*Yes*, I went through all of the files on all of your platinum clients and have them stashed away, but all you can think about is *your club.* Do you not realize that in *my* hand, I hold all of the dark and dirty secrets of some of the most prominent people out there?"

"But why, Asher?" I asked. "Why would you do that? None of this makes sense. You gain nothing from this game you're playing."

His lips quirked.

"I have nothing to gain from the files. You're right," he said, his eyes turning to slits. "But someone else does, and that someone has promised to help me with a little *something*."

*Sirens.*

Sirens erupted around us, and at first, I ignored it because it was New York and sirens could be heard at all hours every single day... but then they got closer.

"Asher," I breathed. "What did you do?"

He let out a laugh.

"I helped a friend so I could get what I want."

The sound of the tires screeching as they turned into the dead end filled the air. They were so close their sirens were hurting my ears.

"And what is it that you want after?" I asked.

"I want you gone," he said, but his voice was barely a whisper over the loud sirens and the shouts of the officers piling out of their cars.

Loud, angry voices yelled at me to turn around and put my hands up.

Everything slowed down in that moment. Asher slowly put his hands up and dropped his bag to the ground, his face morphing from malice and resentment into one that was fearful. To the officers, he looked like nothing more than a scared boy, cornered by me.

*He was playing a part*, I realized.

This *entire* time. He had gotten me right where he wanted. He never wanted to talk. This was all a setup.

*But why? Why did he want me gone?*

I funded everything for him. I gave him *everything* he wanted. He didn't even have to ask most of the time and he got whatever he wanted.

This wasn't about Nyx. This had to be about something else.

*But what?*

"Asher," I gasped as hard bodies slammed into me, and I was forced to the wet ground.

Pain erupted across my face and in the back of my head as I was hit with something that felt like the butt of the gun combined with the solid concrete below me. Bodies upon bodies toppled over me, gripping my arms and forcing them behind me. Hands twisted my wrist so painfully that I couldn't help but cry out. Cold metal handcuffs were slapped onto my wrists, I was hoisted up, forcing me to look at Asher....

He smiled as they took me away.

As much anger as I was feeling, it was no comparison to the feeling of my heart shattering as I watched the person I loved change completely.

I don't know what Asher had planned. I don't know what he had said to the police to get them here, but I knew it wasn't good.

The reality of the situation slapped me hard in the face and knocked the breath from my lungs.

*He* was the person I should have been watching all along. I let everything else in the world blind me to his real motives. Blind me to his real actions. I should have seen it.

*How could I have been so blind?*

*How could I have been so distracted?*

# Nyx

"Sloan," I called as I stared out the windows of Ax's office.

She groaned and slammed her phone on the desk.

"Why the *fuck* isn't she answering?" she growled. "I knew this was a bad idea. I knew I should have stayed with her. Especially when that little—"

"Sloan," I called again, louder this time. "Please come look."

Fear raced up my spine and left goose bumps on my skin as I watched car after car pull onto our front lawn, not caring that they were tearing up the grass.

About half of them were police cars but there were no sirens on. The other half were unmarked vehicles and caused my hackles to rise. It took them mere seconds to step out of their cars. The police uniforms and badges stood out against the grass like a beacon, but the ones that caused unease to claw at me were the ones in suits.

They stood together and held an authority that caused the air to shift.

I have never seen so many police congregated in one area in my life.

Sloan grumbled under her breath and came to stand by me, looking out the window as well.

"Fuck," she muttered under her breath.

"Please tell me this was you," I begged.

"Unfortunately, I can't take credit this time," she answered. More cars pulled up, and this time when they stepped out of the cars, they were already armed.

"*Fuck,*" she said even louder. "Marissa! Cas! Lock everything down."

I heard the rustle of Sloan's workers working in the background, but I couldn't take my eyes off of the police swarming the property below. They hadn't yet approached our door, but I knew it'd only be a matter of time.

"What do we do?" I asked, panicking.

Sloan grabbed her phone before pushing it into my hand.

"Call Jonson," she said. "Tell him who you work for and tell him what's happening."

"But Sloan—"

"Just do it," she said, interrupting me. "I have to go face them. Stay in here, don't come out."

She left me in the room, slamming the door behind her. I turned back to stare at the police in our yard when multiple eyes shot up to look at me. I inhaled sharply and took a step back., fumbling with Sloan's phone and trying to find Jonson's contact.

I had heard about him once, though admittedly not at the best time, as Ax was threatening him and now I had no faith that he would be able to help with anything. Or be willing to.

Ax had been gone since this morning and now it was already four o'clock. No one had heard from her since.

With shaky fingers, I found Jonson's contact and hit the call button. The phone rang twice before it was picked up.

"Sloan?" a gruff voice came from the other line. "I told Ax to stop—"

"I'm not Sloan," I said quickly. There was a pause from the other line.

"Who is this?" he asked.

"My name is Nyx. I work for Ax. We haven't seen her all day, and now there are police at our door—"

"Hold up," he interrupted. "The police? What do you expect me to do about them?"

My heart froze and ice-cold fear was injected straight into my veins.

"Please," I said. "Sloan said that you would help. There's so many of them, and this doesn't seem right—"

"Listen, Nyx," he said. "Ax has been bleeding me dry. I can't keep—"

"You listen here, Jonson," I growled, my anger growing as sounds of yelling reached my ears. "Ax is missing, and from what I have gathered, she has a ton of shit on you. And don't you dare try to deny it. Now do whatever it is that you do and find out what is going on—"

I was cut off by a commotion from beyond the office doors. There was a loud crash followed by a shattering of glass and screams.

Jonson laughed even though the crashes and screams from the other room got louder.

"Do you know who I am?" he asked. "You're threatening an FBI agent, sweetheart. This isn't a good look for you—"

He was cut off by the sound of the door being kicked open.

"Hands in the air!" the police yelled. Guns were drawn and pointed toward me, and there were screams coming from beyond.

I dropped the phone and kicked it under Ax's desk before raising my hands.

"Look, I don't know what's going on," I said, my voice shaking. "But all of this has to be a mist—"

"*Stop,*" commanded one of the policemen, though this one was in a suit and pushed through the ones holding guns. He was the one in charge in this situation. You could tell by the way the policemen around him moved with him. They were tuned into him, their eyes darting toward him and back to me.

I peered to the side and could just make out Sloane being pushed against a wall and her hands being pulled behind her back.

"Don't make this worse for yourself," he said. "Now lie on the floor with your hands behind your back, or else I'll have to add resisting arrest on top of the money laundering, fraud, and drug trafficking."

"What are you talking about?" I asked and shakily got to my knees.

"Hands behind your back, face down on the floor!" the police commanded.

I did what they said and tried to stay still as they came toward me. I could see the phone lying facedown under the desk and I hoped that Jonson had heard all of this and found a heart.

*A fucking FBI agent. I had threatened an FBI agent.*

If I survived this, my name was going to be on a list somewhere.

The police descended on me. Multiple pairs of knees dig into my back, pulling a whine from my lips. Hands grasped at my wrists and twisted my arms so hard I thought I heard a crack.

When they forced me to a standing position, the man in the suit walked up to me with a smile.

"Aren't you going to read my *Miranda* rights?" I spat.

He let out a laugh.

"You aren't going to need those where you're going," he said and motioned for the men to take me.

That's when I started to kick and scream. My fight-or-flight response kicked in, and as badly as I wanted to flee, I could not if these fuckers had me in their grasp. I flailed in their arms. They struggled to keep me still, and when one got too close, I reared my head back into his face. There was a sickening crack that echoed through the room.

The others were fighting with their captors as well, causing all of the police to scramble. Many of them were on Sloan as she cursed and fought them, so that gave me a small chance to get out of here while they were distracted.

The cop who continued to hold me flew back, letting go of me. There was another one to my right, who cursed as I bucked wildly in his arms. He wrapped his arms around my waist and tried to lift me up but I kicked wildly until he was forced to put me down and then as we were bent over, I reared my head back up to him as well.

When his hands let go of me, I saw my chance. Now it was time to flee.

I ran past the others, trying to get to the door at the end of the room. The others were yelling and screaming for me, but it was no use. I was one person and I could not stay back and fight them or free them. I'd have to bide my time until I was ready.

My hands were still cuffed behind my back, so when I came to the door, I was relieved to find It halfway open. I pushed out into the hallway that led to the stairs.

A glimmer of hope spread in my chest.

I didn't know how I was going to get out of here or how I was going to get these handcuffs off. But I knew that as soon as I got down those stairs, I would at least have a chance because whoever it was that was taking us... they weren't real cops. Or at least if they were, they were dirty as hell.

As soon as my sneaker-clad foot reached the first step, pain erupted in the back of my head and the world went black.

When I came to the next time, there was a dull throbbing in my head, and the room had dropped at least thirty degrees.

I tried not to make a sound as I came to because the first thing I heard was hushed voices and one of them was familiar.

"I got what you wanted," Asher said. "I got the files. She's in jail. You could easily off her if you wanted to. Nyx has nothing to do with this. She was merely a pawn, you know this. You've known this from the star—"

There was a slap that echoed through the room, and Asher's voice was cut short.

"It sounds like you found a favorite," a voice spoke and it took me a while to connect the dots that this was the same man that Asher had introduced me to the night of his party. Ryder.

It quickly became clear that I was in way over my head. I was bound to a chair or something and my hands were still cuffed behind my back, but now I could feel that my ankles were as well.

"Your *mother* has people that work for her that are hiding some of the most important things that I need to know," Ryder growled. "Her files on these people are only the beginning. Do you know how much money she has stashed in that club? Do you know how many deals she has brokered with the police? With the mob? I need that information, and I cannot get it unless someone spills."

"But Nyx doesn't know that," Asher said. "She's merely a fuck toy, a *whore*. My mother said so herself. She is not important and never was."

Pain radiated through my chest.

*What the fuck was Asher doing?*

"I'm not using her for information, you fucking idiot," he said. "Can you use your brain for one minute? You're lucky this plan even worked out." There was a deep sigh. "God, you're so fucking disappointing. Your mother was so bright, but it would seem none of that transferred."

There was a rustle, and then suddenly, warm hands squeezed my shoulders. "I know you're awake," Asher said, whispering in my ear. "Stay this way. Don't move."

There has never once been a time in my life where I have ever trusted Asher. But in this moment, I didn't know what to believe. So I did what he said and shut up and stayed still.

There was the squeak of metal doors opening and closing, and then I heard the fighting. There was something that sounded much like a punch, then silence.

"How'd you like the cell?" Ryder asked. "I asked that our

friends at the precinct be extra nice to you. Though I don't know how you managed to shell out so much fucking money for them. Do you know how much I had to give them to just have them do their job?"

"What do you want?" Ax's voice cut through the room.

My heart stopped, and my breath caught in my throat. Asher's hand gripped my shoulder tighter.

*A warning.*

His words from earlier flooded through my mind.

*What has he done?*

"I want *everything,*" Ryder said. "First up was your club. Security was pitiful. Then I want your accounts, and then I need you to tell me every single thing about the people you are working with. I need your dealers. I need your government contacts. I need every slimy little person that you have on your payroll."

The sound of Ax spitting hit me, and I couldn't help but open my eyes. Right in front of me, Ax was on her knees, her hands tied behind her back. Her face was looking up toward Ryder, who now had spit dripping off of his face. He glared at Ax.

"Such a dumb fuck," Ax said. "You know, even if I gave you the information, that doesn't mean that you'll be half the person I am. You and your pitiful little gang don't even understand the game you are—"

She was cut off by a slap. Ryder had slapped her so hard that she fell to the ground and let out a groan.

I swallowed my gasp, but Ryder was already looking at me.

"Well, look who's awake," Ryder cooed. He walked over to me, his footsteps echoing in the space. Now that I had opened my eyes, I realized that we were in an empty warehouse. The sun had set long ago, and it was not just me, Asher, Ryder, and Ax that were in here. There were multiple men guarding the exits as well.

In other words, we were fucked.

There was no way out, and I definitely didn't want to be stuck in here with these people.

Ax's eyes drifted toward me, and then when our gazes met,

she looked away to the ground. The act broke my heart more than whatever her son had said. I should have known that getting involved with her was a bad idea. Once I saw a little bit into Asher's world and then heard about Ax's from her own mouth... I should have left.

I thought that I would be able to handle whatever it was that she was into. Because for some weird reason, I thought that she'd keep me out of it. She would protect me from whatever it was that she was doing. But here I am. Mere weeks later, tied to a chair while a psychopath looked down on me. I was angry. Infuriated... but I was also scared. Scared of how I'd ended up this way. Scared that Ax and I were at the whim of these crazy people.

*And what the fuck did Asher do to get us into this?*

"I remember you," I told him.

"And I remember you," he said. "For once, Asher proved to me that he could do something right."

"Care to explain what's going on here?" I asked.

Asher's hand gripped me so tight I couldn't help but wince.

"Not particularly," Ryder said. "Though, I'm surprised to see that a grown woman with a reputation such as Ax's fell for such a weak little distraction."

His words hit me like a punch to the gut.

My mind whirled. *This couldn't have all been because of me, could it?*

"Shut up," Ax growled.

Ryder let out a laugh.

"Aren't you a protective one? Can't do much over there though," he said and walked over to me until he was right in front of me, and then he leaned down, his hands clasping my jean-covered legs. A smile spread across his face.

"There's a couple of ways this could go," he said. "You can either help persuade her to give me the information that I need, or I'll do it for you."

"I don't know what kind of power you think I hold," I said. I was very tempted to spit in his face just like Ax did, but instead, I leaned forward and ran my eyes down his disgustingly satisfied face.

"Pussy holds power," he said. "Don't you realize that?"

Ax and I hadn't been together long, but that didn't stop me from wanting to protect her. Whatever I tried to do here would have drastic consequences on both of our futures.

And so, with that, I smirked and asked, "What's your idea of persuasion?"

I didn't let my eyes shift toward Ax as she fought against her restraints.

"Aren't you full of surprises," he said. His voice was but a whisper as his hands trailed farther up my thighs.

"I think I learned what you like at that party," I said.

"Oh yeah?" he asked.

"Yeah," I whispered. He leaned closer to me, our faces inches apart.

"You want to prey on my weaknesses, hmm?" he asked. "I don't particularly like traitors."

I smiled.

"No," I answered. "I'm not."

And then I reared back and headbutted him right in the nose.

His screams echoed in the room.

Asher held me back as I tried to lunge at the man screaming and clutching his nose.

"Let me go," I growled to Asher and tried again to throw myself at the man on the floor, but Asher's grip was too tight. I could hear Ax struggling from beyond, but I was too focused on trying to get to Ryder that I couldn't even glance up to look at her.

"That was stupid," Asher hissed in my ear, then he hoisted me up, put his arms around my waist and held me to his chest. I flailed and kicked in his grasp, but nothing weakened his hold.

Ryder collected himself and slowly stood. Blood was smeared all over his face and the look that he gave me was bone chilling.

From the moment I walked into that hotel room, I knew that

Ryder was not the type of person to take these actions from a woman, nor was he the type of person to let a woman rule over him. It made sense why he was going after Ax. With what little knowledge I had, I could clearly see how the relationship between these two parties developed, and now I was stuck.

Right in the middle.

"You're just threatened that a woman could get the upper hand," I growled. "You're pathetic."

"There is so much more than that," Ryder said and wiped his hand across his nose, inhaling deeply. "How disappointing."

He motioned for the guards at the door to come toward him and held his hand out. Without hesitation, one of them reached into the back of their jeans and pulled out a gun, giving it straight to Ryder.

My heart dropped when Ryder looked at me next. There was a gleam in his eye.

"I'm going to kill you, Ax," I threatened. Ryder let out a snort.

"Step aside, Asher."

"I told you," Asher said. "She doesn't have any of that information—"

"I *know*," Ryder groaned, interrupting Asher. "Do what I say, boy."

Asher reluctantly set me on my feet and took a step away from me. Ryder pointed the gun at me. Directly at my head.

Staring into the barrel of a presumably loaded gun may have been one of the most terrifying experiences I've ever had. It wasn't even as bad as the actual gunshot. The terror of looking death in the face, behind it the man that was smiling as he fingered the trigger.

My mind was a tsunami of memories of everything I *wished* I had done and everything I regretted. I wish I had never met Asher, or at least if I had, I would have known better than to let him back into my life.

I cursed myself the most in those few seconds.

It was my fault this all happened.

I saw the warning signs all around me. I knew that there was no good reason to get involved with Asher or Ax, and yet I *still* did.

Panic and fear swelled in my throat and caused tears to prick my eyes.

I didn't want to die here.

I didn't want it to end.

I still had so much of my life to live.

I still had so many things to experience, so many things to love... and yet, staring down the barrel of his gun, I knew that I would not make it out of this.

He didn't want me for information.

I look toward Ax. Her eyes were wide, and she was frozen, just like I was. Unmoving.

"It's not what you think," I rushed out. "I don't hold power here."

Ryder lowered the gun just enough so he could look me in my eyes.

"If you're trying to sav—"

"I'm not," I interrupted. "Asher's right. I was nothing more than a toy. *A whore*. She said so herself. This is not the way you get information from her."

Ryder looked toward Ax, lowering his gun.

"Is that true?"

"Yes," Ax answered, her voice hoarse.

"Is it true that you don't care about her?" Ryder asked. "See her as nothing more than a piece of ass?"

He was testing her. That much was obvious. I prayed that this last-ditch effort worked.

Hesitation flashed across her features but her words came out cold.

"Always has been," she said. "I'm surprised she's even here. I'm more pissed that you brought me here like this, that you're hurting my employees. But if you're looking to get information out of me, shooting her isn't going to do that."

Ryder let out a laugh.

"Are you sure about that?" he asked. "So if I just shot her right here right now in the head, you wouldn't spare so much as a second glance at her?"

"*No.*"

"Pity. I don't believe you," he said.

I heard the shot before I felt it. The sound was so loud it caused the walls of the concrete fortress around us to rattle.

The wind was knocked out of me, and suddenly the ground was coming closer.

Asher's hands caught me before I fell to the ground, and slowly he lowered us. When I looked down, I saw bright red. It was almost fake looking. The way my blood covered my shirt and began spilling out of me.

It was so *fast,* and it was so *bright.*

And then the pain came.

"Fuck," I groaned and tried to hold in my scream, but it was no use. Sobs rack my body, causing more pain to shoot through me.

My whole body was on fire.

White-hot pain ripped through my abdomen, and I clutched Asher to me. His hands wrapped around me and tried to put pressure on my wound, causing me to cry out.

"Stop, please," I begged.

"W-we have to stop the bl-bleeding," Asher stuttered, his voice panicked.

"I told you *enough,*" Ryder yelled and rushed forward, pointing the gun at my head. "Spill."

He was staring at Ax now.

The barrel burned my skin as it touched my temple. Asher's breathing had paused behind me, and I could feel wet droplets fall onto my face, leaving a cool trail on my overly heated skin.

*Rain?*

"*Please,*" Asher begged. "My mom doesn't care about her, but I do. If you want to keep me—"

"I don't want to keep you, boy," Ryder hissed. "I could shoot you right here and not give two fucks. The only reason you're still here is that if I kill her next, you're the only one that can help me. Bloodline be damned."

As the pain ripped through me, I found that I could no longer feel my fingers or toes. An icy coldness was sweeping up my body, chasing away the heat from the pain.

I longed to close my eyes and rest in Asher's warm hold. I sighed into him.

"Ash," I whispered.

His tearstained face came into view, and now I realized that I wished the rain had come sooner. Maybe I wouldn't have been stuck here if that was the case. Maybe I would have more time with them.

I tried to lift myself up to look at Ax, but my body wasn't cooperating. My vision was failing me. Asher was speaking, but I couldn't hear the words.

All I could hear was a cold voice. The voice I had grown so comfortable with, the one I had grown to look for. The one I dreamed about.

"Do it."

# Ax

Not again.

Please, *please,* not again.

I couldn't bear to sit here and watch this happen *again.*

Ryder was the devil incarnate. I had been too lenient on him, too distracted with life. As soon as I heard of him, I should have taken him out...

But now it was too late.

Ryder looked over to me with an almost offended expression, then clicked his tongue.

"Your son thought he could distract you enough to get what we needed," he said and pushed Nyx's head with the barrel of the gun. "But it turns out he didn't know you well enough, did he?"

"Do it," I said again.

Each word felt like it was being carved into my skin. Nyx was lifeless in his arms, and I prayed Sloan was out there somewhere trying to save us from this mess.

"But you know what they say," Ryder said with a sigh. "Know thy enemy better than thyself? Or some shit like that." He paused and grabbed a handful of Nyx's hair. She didn't make a noise as he tore her from Asher's arms and held her up by her hair, gun dancing dangerously close to her head. "How does it feel to see your girlfriend full of holes? Maybe I will drop this one off at your doorstep too when I am done with her."

The anger boiling up inside me exploded, and my vision went white.

Images of a mangled, bloody body right outside of my door flashed through my mind. Images of Asher's tear-stricken face and the sound of his cries echoed through my mind.

Hannah... she had been running away from a bad situation when we met under less-than-ideal circumstances. I hadn't thought twice about accepting her. It didn't matter that she was pregnant, and I never wanted to bring up what happened. I wanted her and Asher to have a happy life with me...

It all made too much sense.

"What did you say?" Asher's voice echoed through the room.

Ryder made a show of rolling his eyes.

"Don't act stupid," he growled. "You know that I had to teach that bitch a lesson. After all, not only did she run away while pregnant, but she decided to whore herself out to Ax. She was meant to be mine, meant to carry on our an—"

I didn't register that I had moved until I was right in front of Ryder. My hands were tied behind my back, but that didn't stop me from ramming into Ryder.

We fell to the ground in a heap, and I heard the guards near the exit shout at us, but they made no move to stop me. That was until Asher pushed me off and started pummeling his fists into Ryder's unsuspecting face.

Ryder flailed his arms out to try and protect himself from Asher's blows, but it was no use. Blow after blow hit Ryder's face, even when his body had become slack. His face was so bloody it became unrecognizable.

Footsteps from the guards sounded, but Asher was too fast. He took the discarded gun from Ryder's hand, stood, and shot Ryder point blank.

Blood splattered onto Asher's face, and in that moment, I saw what I had really done to my son.

I had made him into the same monster I was.

His head whipped to look at the guards, and he held his gun up to them.

I turned to watch them slowly put their guns on the ground and their hands up.

"Leave if you want to live and spread the word," Asher commanded. "I'm taking over."

The guards didn't need to be told twice and left. As soon as they did, I lunged for Nyx. Asher worked to remove my cuffs while I took in the lifeless, pale body of Nyx.

Her black hair had fallen around her like a wave and the faded-pink ends were now bright red from the blood pooling beneath her. Her skin was pale and her lips had lost their color. As soon as my hands were free, I put pressure on her wound with one hand while checking for a pulse with the other.

I couldn't breathe. I couldn't think. My entire world had begun to spin, and a coldness started to spread through me.

"Please," I begged her, my voice sounding unrecognizable to my ears. It was hoarse and grief-stricken. "Please don't do this. Not again."

I didn't know what would have become of Nyx and me if this had never happened, but I would have liked to think that she would have stayed by my side. That we would have built the life that I had always envisioned together and when we were tired of the hustle, we would leave for the property.

I would like to think that the next wedding I held in the backyard would have been my own. I would have liked to see her in a white dress and her cheeks red from drinking and dancing.

I would have liked to see her live a full and happy life. One that would have made her childhood self weep with joy.

I wanted to do that with her. I wanted to watch as she became the happiest version of herself.

But now everything that awaited us would be snuffed out.

"Mo—"

"Please," I begged again, cutting Asher off. My hand cupped her cheek and my thumb brushed across her cold lips. "I'm sorry. I didn't mean for any of this to happen. *Please—* "

My pleading was cut off by my own sobs.

"Mom, we have to—"

Sirens filled the air. The sound of boots on the dirt and then on concrete hit my ears, and I gripped Nyx, cradling her as close to my body as I could. With my free hand, I slapped the gun out of Asher's hand and hooked my arm over his neck, pulling him to me.

When the yelling came, I was prepared.

"Help!" I yelled. "She's been shot!"

I looked over to the doorway to see uniformed men with guns entering. There were dozens and dozens of them, and all of them had "FBI" stamped across their vests in big yellow letters.

The leader of the group was the first to spot us and called for backup.

They swarmed us, hands everywhere. They pulled at me, trying to get me to my feet. They pulled Asher away from me, and then they pulled Nyx.

Asher and I both fought them as they tried to take her away. Not until I heard a familiar voice yelling my name did I pause.

I turned in the arms of the many men holding me back to see Jonson. His black hair, once slicked back, had strands falling into his face. He had a bulletproof vest on that matched the others, and he was panting. Sweat covered his face and when he reached us, I noticed that he only had a T-shirt on.

I had never been so glad to see him.

"She's dying, Jonson," I said and reached for his vest. "You have to get her—"

"I heard the shots," he said quickly and motioned for the men around us to let us go. "They have already called for a helicopter. She will be brought to the closest surgical center."

To prove his point, I heard the powerful bursts of a helicopter coming closer. But it wasn't fast enough.

"She's bleeding out," I rushed. "She won't make it. You have to—"

The sound of the helicopter landing outside the warehouse washed out my cries.

"Let me go with her!" Asher yelled. He tried to make a break for the exit, but the men around him lunged for him.

"No," Jonson said, his eyes narrowing at Asher. "She needs medical attention. You will just slow everyone down and get in the way. Besides, I need to hear everything that happened, starting from when black-and-whites showed up at your club, pretended to arrest your employees, then end with why an innocent party has a gunshot wound to her torso."

"Please," I begged and tugged at his vest. "Please, I know I've been an ass to you, but please let me go with her."

Jonson let out a sigh. My heart dropped when I heard the helicopter take off.

"Both of you are riding with me," he said. "In the *car.* And I need an explanation on the way."

"Deal," Asher and I said at the same time. If I wasn't rapidly losing my mind, I may have even laughed.

Twelve hours.

Nyx had spent twelve hours in surgery while Asher, Jonson, and I waited in the hospital waiting room. When we were called into her room, my heart broke in two.

She had made it. *Thank God.*

But her injuries had taken a toll on her body. She had bled out a lot, and during surgery, they had to reconstruct part of her bowels. When they found the bullet, it was only three centimeters away from her spine.

She barely survived this and would need to be in recovery for months.

I sat at her side in the uncomfortable hospital chair. Her slim, cold hand was in mine, and every few moments, I would bring it to my mouth and huff hot air into it.

Jonson was standing in the corner of the room, watching it all, and Asher was sitting in a seat near the foot of her bed, his head in his hands.

"This is a fucked-up family dynamic," Jonson said, his gaze slipping to Asher. "You know I can't hide all of this." His eyes traveled to mine. "Your part in this especially."

"I know," Asher groaned into his hands.

"There were real arrest warrants," he continued. "Even if they didn't execute them. I may be able to get the fraud charge thrown out, but the money laundering?"

"That was your guy. Your money," I reminded him and placed a kiss on Nyx's knuckles.

Her heart monitor was steady in the background, it was the only thing keeping me grounded.

I didn't want to blame Asher. I didn't want to hate him as much as I did right now. I knew inside that I still loved him, but the betrayal of it all was not something I would get over soon.

"That you were supposed to plant in *Ryder's* territory," Jonson huffed. "Ryder was new to this game. He shouldn't have been able to—"

"It was my fault," Asher said, cutting him off. "I got the information from Yvon, and I was so sure that you had murder—"

"Don't," I commanded.

The room fell silent.

I took a deep, calming breath and closed my eyes.

*Stay cool. For Nyx. For Jonson. For Asher. Stay cool.*

"How long are we looking at?" I asked and opened my eyes again to look at Nyx.

"For Asher?" Jonson asked. "Probably house arrest for a few months, then probation. He was far removed from most crimes, but he was still there and there was no doubt he helped Ryder carry out his plans."

"I can do that," Asher said, then froze.

I looked over to him just in time to catch his head lifting and our eyes locking.

"I'm probably looking at prison time, hmm?" I asked.

Jonson was quiet for a moment.

"Some of your patrons in the department of treasury are not happy about the leak," he said. "They made their sentiments pretty well known, and once they find out about the money... I can try, but there is no guarant—"

"I know," I said with a sigh. "I know."

I locked my eyes on Nyx. It had been heart wrenching when I thought I was going to lose her. I had thought that there was no way that I would ever go through something more painful than losing Asher's mom... but my entire world crashed and burned when I saw her bleeding out.

But now, as I sat here after it all... I realized that this couldn't go on any longer.

I had gotten attached to Nyx in a way I shouldn't have. In a way that almost caused her death.

Nyx wasn't supposed to be in this world. She was too good for it and last night was a reminder that no matter how hard I tried to redeem myself... I never could.

My past would always come back to haunt me, and as long as I was alive, there would be people out there that would want to do me harm.

Ryder was but a small pawn in a bigger game played by far more powerful people. As soon as it got out to my patrons and enemies that I was going to spend time in jail, I would be at my weakest.

And so would everyone around me.

I stood and leaned over Nyx, planting a kiss on her forehead. I inhaled her scent deeply, committing it to memory. Then I stood and turned to Jonson.

"You can get her off, right?" I asked.

He gave me a long look.

"Only through witness protection," he answered and let out a sigh. "She had worked for you and been seen with you *in public.* It doesn't look good unless—"

"Do what you have to. I don't care how you paint it. Just make sure she doesn't go down with us," I said and looked toward Asher. "We are leaving."

He shot up.

"We can't, Nyx hasn't—"

"We are leaving," I said, this time harder. I walked toward the door, not looking back at the woman in the bed because I knew that if I did, I wouldn't have been able to keep going. "Come, Asher. We have things to prepare for. We need to get home, clean up everything. I have a few lawyers that we can contact. They will have their hands full with everyone, but we should be able to get some time off regardless."

As soon as Asher and I were both out of the room, Nyx's heart monitor jumped. Asher grabbed my wrist and forced me to stop walking.

"Mom, I'm sorr—"

"Stop," I whispered. "Please, stop."

I heard Nyx's groan from the hallway.

"Hello, Nyx," Jonson said. I heard the sound of his shoes squeak against the linoleum floor. "We spoke on the phone, I am—"

"Fuck you," she grumbled. Her voice was hoarse and there was no power behind it. "I know who you are. Fucking bitch almost got me—"

"I'll have you know I saved your life, young lady," he said, his tone light. Almost as if he wanted to laugh.

"Where are they?" she asked. "Ax? Asher? God, what about Sloa—"

She was cut off by heavy coughing. It was painful to hear

because I knew just how much it had to hurt with a fresh gunshot wound.

I heard Jonson give her a cup of water from her bedside table.

"You are the only person that sustained injuries," he said. "Unless you count Ryder's death. Shot to the head."

There was a pause.

"Good," she said. I looked toward Asher, noticing right away that his shoulders had deflated.

"Where are they?" she asked. "Can I see—"

"Nyx," Jonson said in a harsh tone. "There have been some... developments."

There was another pause.

"You're going into witness protection," Jonson added.

"Like hell I am," Nyx growled.

My heart swelled when I heard her talk back to him. I wanted so badly to peek back into the room and take in her angry face and hopefully flushed skin.

"That or jail," he countered. "There is no going back from that, Nyx. You can have a normal life, a normal job. Once this stains your record, you can never—"

"What happens to the rest?" she asked. "I can already tell this will be unfair."

Asher's hand gripped my wrist tighter.

"Let's go," he whispered. The fight from before lost. "I don't think I can stay here any longer."

I nodded, grateful that he was the one to push me because as soon as I heard her voice, I had lost myself in it.

# Nyx

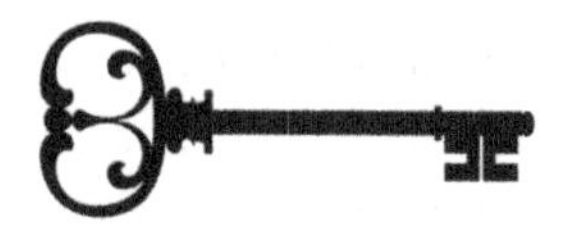

Four years later.

Cheers echoed all around me. The sound of champagne popping filled the air and arms enveloped me.

I let out a laugh and hugged Sabrina back as she jumped up and down excitedly in the air.

"To Blom Design Studios!"

More arms enveloped me, and I was swung from person to person. It seemed like hundreds even though I knew that we had only invited twenty to our celebration ceremony.

It was all the new office could fit anyway.

After three years of hustling for clients and expanding, my team and I were finally able to open a *real* office. And right smack-dab in the middle of Portland.

It had taken some digging to find a high-rise that allowed us to take an entire floor, but man, was I glad I persevered. The new space was perfect for Blom Design Studios.

The floor-to-ceiling windows overlooked the city and gave us the perfect view of the sunset. The interior had been bare enough that it allowed us to bring in our own interior designer and make it the space we had always dreamed of.

Beige, white, and a bit of black were splashed around the

office. Desks, kitchens, and meeting rooms had a homey yet minimalistic style, and there were plants on almost every surface.

We even had a VIP lounge where we could finally take our clients, as opposed to keeping everything online.

I had invited all ten of my employees, their partners, and some of our VIP clients to this event. We had stocked up on champagne, hired caterers, and decorated the office with streamers.

"I'm so proud of you!" Anne exclaimed as she threw her arms around me.

"I couldn't have done it without you," I said and hugged her back.

It was true. After all, Anne was the marketing head at Anneu. She had been my first client when I built this design agency.

It *technically* broke all the rules of my witness protection, but it's not like I was actually trying to hide anyway. I needed to make a living, after all.

"Eat!" I yelled as I pulled away from her. "I don't want to see anything left!"

It wasn't hard to convince people. I stood back and watched as the team and makeshift family I built laughed and conversed in front of me.

I chose to hang back near the windows, just taking it all in.

It had been hard to build myself up after... everything.

I had struggled for a bit. I was in a city I didn't know anything about. I had no job. No friends.

They had given me an apartment and some money every month, but it was only just enough to make sure I didn't starve.

I tried many things at first. Went back to being a barista. Tried being an assistant. None of it worked out great, and that was when I decided to try my hand at brand designing again, but this time I didn't want to work for someone else.

So, I started freelancing. And now, here I am. With my very own company.

I should have felt ecstatic as I watched everyone. I should have been overjoyed... and for the most part, I was, but there was something missing.

"Congrats," a deep voice said from my right.

My heart skipped a beat.

"I didn't think you'd show," I said and turned to look up at Jonson.

He hadn't changed much since I last saw him, though there was a noticeable amount of facial hair. He had bags under his eyes and there was an overall tiredness about him, but his eyes shined under the dim lights.

He was the only person I was able to keep in contact with from my old life and the only reminder that I hadn't dreamed up everything. Sometimes it felt like his visits, no matter how few and far between, were the only thing keeping me from spiraling.

"I made things happen," he said and took a sip from his champagne flute.

"You shouldn't drink on the job," I chided.

"And you shouldn't be trying to contact people from your old life," he said, his eyes locked on Anne.

"Touché," I said, a smile pulling at my lips.

There was a pause, and I was tempted to ask him if any of the others had asked about me, but I chose to leave it.

"You did good," he said. "Really. I mean it."

My throat tightened, and my eyes stung.

"Thank you," I choked out.

He sighed and straightened his back before sending me a hesitant smile.

"She's been paroled," he said. "Good behavior and everything. The bureau is reconsidering your witness protection."

I swallowed thickly.

"I heard," I answered.

I had been watching the jail like a hawk and stalking every and all social media around Ax for the last three years, hoping that if she ever got a parole hearing, I would know.

She had gotten out five weeks ago. *Five.*

And I hadn't heard anything.

When I woke up in the hospital room alone with Jonson, I couldn't get over my own feelings of betrayal. I was angry—*pissed*—at her and Asher. They had torn my life apart. Got me shot and almost killed, for fuck's sake, and they didn't even have the balls to look me in the face.

But most of all, I was hurt. I had been cast aside. No matter how it was painted, that was what happened.

*Do it.*

I had nightmares about her words. I had woken up crying because I had to watch her face twist into a smile as she said those words.

They were the last thing I heard her say to me.

I tried to hold on to the Ax in my memories. The one that was sweet and caring. The one that was more than what she was charged with... but after being separated for so long, it made it harder and harder to remember the good times.

"Just thought I would deliver the news in person. After all, it's a cause for celebration and means that you are no longer my ward," he said. "... and also to let you know the nightclub is back up."

I took a step forward, trying to ignore the feelings that ripped through me.

"I hope I never have to see you again," I murmured bitterly.

He let out a laugh.

"I'll be over for Christmas."

There was a sharp gasp, followed by a scream that caused both Jonson and me to jerk upright. The room fell silent as Anne stopped at the food table. Her plate had been dropped to the ground, food spilling everywhere. Her eyes were wide, and slowly, a beaming smile spread across her lips.

"John Bennett, CEO of Bennett Design Studios, has been charged with fraud and embezzlement after it came to light that he had used company money to fuel his lavish lifestyle. In the wake of this, five employees had taken a stand to report other misconducts, including sexual harassment, retaliation, and abuse," she announced, her voice excited and her face bright.

Each word felt like it was carved into my skin and it took a few moments before the shock could wear off and giddiness filled me.

There were hushed voices of excitement as they talked over the article. Anne's gaze never wavered on mine, and she gave me a smile. We had talked about the horrors of my old job on many occasions, and I even slipped and told her a bit about how I was fired. She had been there right beside me, stating that we had to fight this, had to fight *him* and now...

I should be happy. I am happy. Elated that that bastard got what was coming to him, but...

Jonson cleared his throat, causing me to look back up at him.

"I guess I am not the only person who wants to say congratulations," he teased.

My throat tightened, and I found myself unable to breathe.

There was only one person that I could think of that would have gone this far.

I groaned as I kicked off my heels. My apartment was dark, with only the moonlight coming through the windows.

"Naya?" I called, looking for the white ball of fluff that should have been meowing at my feet.

Naya, my cat, had been my sole company for the last few years and was always waiting for me when I came home, begging to be fed.

I waited a moment, and when she didn't respond, I walked into the kitchen.

"Naya, please tell me you didn—"

My words were cut off with a scream as a shadowy figure stood in the middle of my kitchen. I scrambled for something to use as a weapon and after finding my cutting board, I used it to hit the intruder right in the face.

"Ow *fuck,* Nyx, it's me!" The intruder lunges for the wall, and the kitchen lit up, showing me Asher. His hair had grown longer in the four years we had been separated and his face had filled out. He had a healthy glow to him that made him look far younger and happier than when I had seen him last.

I dropped the cutting board, the wood plank clanging to the ground and shattering the silence of my apartment.

"Sorry it took me so long to—"

I didn't hesitate to ram my fist right into his face. He let out a groan and reared his head back, his hands flying to his nose. I used his shock to send another punch to the gut.

He bent over, one hand on his stomach, the other flying out to try and stop me.

"Nyx, please let me—"

"What?" I asked and pushed him against the counter. "Explain how you fucked us all over? Got me shot? I may not have been there, but I listened to the sentencing, Asher. I heard *everything.*"

And whatever I didn't get, Jonson sent me obscure messages in the mail in the form of newspaper clippings. I didn't spend months in a fucking hospital and having to do physical therapy to just *forget* everything that this bastard has done to me.

"Apologize," he said and looked up at me. Blood was dripping down his face and staining his white button-down.

Naya meowed, causing me to jump. Only now did I notice her on the island, eating a whole can of wet food.

I turned to Asher and slapped him one more time across the face.

"That's for breaking into my apartment and scaring the shit out of me, you asshole."

He rubbed his cheek with a groan.

"Language," he chided. "Jeez, you can pack a punch. What have you been eating?"

I raised my hand again, ready to show him what years of self-defense lessons have taught me. A burst of satisfaction ran through me when he flinched.

"I don't accept it," I said and moved to grab Naya before she had a chance to finish the entire can.

He let out a sigh and leaned against the table.

"I'm sorry," he said. "I truly am."

"Then why did it take you four years?" I asked. "If you were truly sorry, you would have said so sooner. On top of that, this is not just something you can move on from, Asher."

"Mom asked me not to," he said.

My heart skipped a beat when Ax was mentioned. Even after all this time and all the shit we went through, I still had feelings for her.

"You got me shot, Asher," I growled, trying to ignore the feeling in my chest. "I deserve some type of explanation."

During the sentencing, they shared how Asher had been manipulated by his biological father into turning on Ax. They used that to get a shorter sentence, and Asher gave a tearful plea, saying that he really didn't mean to hurt his mom.

*I call bullshit.*

He let out a sigh and ran his hand through his hair. My eyes fell to a scar that lined the right side of his jaw.

"Growing up, I loved her," he said and leaned against the counter. "With all my heart, truly. But I was..."

"Spoiled," I supplied.

He gave me a sheepish smile.

"Yes," he admitted. "I got too comfortable being handed things. Too comfortable knowing that my mom would give me whatever I wanted... but it wasn't enough. I wanted some type of... connection to her. She was always working and—"

"You are seriously not trying to blame Ax's making a life for you as the reason you shot me?" I asked.

He cleared his throat.

"I am *not*," he said. "But it made me start to act out to get her attention, and when it didn't work, I... began to resent her. I started to look at our life under a microscope and I began to look at the death of my biological mother differently."

"Asher," I sighed. "Please don't tell me—"

"It just... looking back now, I see how stupid this all was, but then, all I could think about was how her shady businesses had led us to my mother's death. I blamed her wholeheartedly, so when Ryder showed up on my doorstep... I couldn't push him away."

I could see it unfolding in my mind. I didn't want to empathize with Asher, but I couldn't help it. After going through what I went through with my mother firsthand, I knew how heart wrenching it could be and how desperate he must have felt to believe anything and everything.

"Her opening the club," he continued. "It was the last straw."

Confusion clouded my brain.

"Why?" I asked.

He shook his head.

"I didn't want my mother to move on," he admitted. "I didn't think she deserved it."

Pain shot through my chest and I raised my hand, ready to hit him again, but he stepped back and held up his hands.

"Imagine my surprise when I saw you there," he said. "With an appointment with my mother, no less."

Sourness exploded across my tongue.

"You shouldn't have—"

"I know," he interrupted. "I *know.* I was pissed but didn't think anything of it... until I found out that she had gotten *distracted* by you. So I proposed to Ryder that we work together to destroy the club and take down her other businesses, all while her mind was... elsewhere."

Tears pricked my eyes.

"You're horrible," I whispered.

His shoulders slumped, and a frown marred his face.

"I need you to understand that it was all a stupid mistake," he pleaded. "I didn't want anyone to get hurt. I was stupid and didn't see it until the very end. I'm sorry, Nyx. I truly am. But I have seen how my mother was with you. I wouldn't be here if I didn't need your help. I wanted to leave you to have the happy life you deserve, but Mom—"

"But what?" I asked, bitterness filling my tone. "Now, all of a sudden, you want to turn your life around? Be a decent son? You are pathetic."

He swallowed and leaned against the island, nodding.

"I deserve that," he said and looked out my windows. "Though I am serious. I fucked up, I know. But Mom is not doing well. Ever since she got out, I have had to watch her slowly deteriorate and I don't know what to do anymore."

I couldn't help but laugh.

"You're something else," I said with a headshake.

"Believe me," he said quickly. "I wouldn't come here unless I needed to. I was going to leave you alone. She was right. You don't belong in that world. It will bring you nothing—"

"I don't *belong*?" I asked incredulously.

Asher's eyes widened, and he took a step back while holding his hands up. He knew he'd fucked up.

"Just that it's a dangerous life and even though we are out, doesn't mean—"

"So, you came here just to insult me?" I asked, anger rising in me and all the pity I had for him disappearing into the night air. "Then I hope you and your mom both suffer. Good fucking riddance."

"Nyx, please," he begged and leaned forward, his hands clasping around my wrist. "She's in real bad shape."

I didn't want to admit what those words did to me.

"You realize you are asking *me,* your ex-girlfriend, to go and fuck your mom?" I asked. "Are you a masochist or just stupid? You have a stepmom fetish or something?"

He groaned and dropped his head into his hands.

"So, stupid then," I said with a huff when he didn't respond.

"I'm serious, Nyx!" he yelled and slammed his hand on the

table. "She wasn't even this bad with my mom. She doesn't care about anything. Barely eats. She works all the time and has been more reckless than ever."

"She's been out for *five wee—*"

"And she has already opened the club, taken over Ryder's territory *and* men, and has started washing money," he said. "Do you know how many dangerous people she has been meeting recently?"

I shook my head and let out a bitter laugh.

"Am I always just a distraction to you? A tool for you to use whenever convenient?" I asked. "What about me? My life? I have my own company, an apartment, a cat! I am living the life I only dreamed of, and as soon as it gets good, you come back in and fuck it up again!"

He was silent at my outburst.

"I knew this was a mistake," he said and stood straight. "She won't come to you, Nyx. So if you were hoping that she would come groveling at your feet, she won't. She is content just punishing the both of you. You know how she is."

"I don't," I spat out. "I don't know how she is, and I never did. It was all a fucking lie. I knew her for less than a year, Asher."

He sighed and walked past me and out of the kitchen.

"Your ears get red when you lie!" he yelled and shut the door behind him.

I scrambled to pull my phone out and turn on the front-facing camera.

My ears were bright red.

*Fuck.*

# Ax

I let out a sigh of frustration as I accidentally stepped in the sticky wet blood that coated the floor of the basement of a new bar I had taken over.

Ryder's territory had been a mess to clean up after taking it over from Asher, but I assured myself it would all be worth it in the end. Asher had done almost nothing when I was locked up, proving that he wasn't as cut out for this life as he tried to make everyone believe.

I should have been relieved that he had come to that realization on his own, but instead, I was furious.

"Clean this up," I ordered Yvon.

He gave me a look and motioned for our guys to take care of the mangled body that now lay on the ground, bleeding out.

Number thirty-two on my list of suspects involved in both Nyx's and Hannah's murder.

I knew from the start that Ryder was in over his head and somewhat incompetent. By the time I had heard of him, he had taken over several smaller gangs to build up his own, but his real accomplice had stayed in the shadows like the coward he was.

So it was up to me to find him.

Luckily I had spent the last four years of my life trying to find every bit of information on Ryder and his partner as I could. By the time I had been released, I had a list of fifty names of those who either had a hand in what happened or had been directly involved.

There was only one name left. And he was right here in this room with me.

I sighed and looked over at Yvon. He hadn't left me since I had been locked up and even then, he had made no move to try and take over the empire I had left and when I got back, everything was in working order.

All the men he had hired were vetted. There was not a cent missing in any of the accounts. And most importantly, he had worked with the team that wasn't locked away to save the reputation of Club Pétale.

*So what was his motive for working with Ryder? What did he get out of it?*

"You should rest after this," he told me, his eyes still on the corpse in front of us. "It has been almost twenty hours since you last rested."

I paused a moment and looked at Yvon. When I saw his name on the list, I had felt like it was the ultimate betrayal. I had helped this man escape the life that held us in a choke hold, and all I asked was for his loyalty.

I could be a pain in the ass at times, I knew that... but what had I done to make him run to Ryder? And why, all this time, did he stay by my side? Had he always known of Ryder's fate?

"Is there something you want to tell me, Yvon?" I asked him.

His eyes shifted to me, the single icy-blue one feeling as though it was burning into my soul.

"Maybe I am just trying to make a break for it," he teased, then his voice took a serious tone. "After all, my boss has been killing people left and right. One might worry if they will be next."

I shifted and tightened my grip on the gun in my hand.

"The only people I kill are those who betray me," I said.

Yvon's lips twitched.

"Like I said, one might worry," he said. "After all, Asher's still alive and look what he did to you."

I gritted my teeth, trying to control the anger rising inside me. At times, I felt that prison had helped me rein in my rage. Ignoring the outside world and solely focusing on containing it inside me while I planned for the downfall of the people who betrayed me.

But now, all I could think of was the way the prisoners egged me on. The times that I spent in the corners of the cafeteria pounding into the face of the person who dared to test me that day.

I watched as the men started to dismember his body and place them into bags. They were professionals at this by now, though I would have to be careful from now on. Our hiding spots were beginning to fill up.

"I don't trust you," I growled.

"You don't need to," he said. "After all, a job well done is just that."

"Give me one good reason why I shouldn't shoot you in the head," I demanded, though I already had a million in my head. If anything, I was begging him to stop me from killing him.

"I think you already have your answer," he said.

I let out a loud sigh and put the safety on my gun before putting it back into my jeans.

"Maybe I'll change my mind one day," I said and walked past him and up the rickety stairs. My client was waiting for me, and I had spent too long down here with them.

"I'll be waiting," he called as I entered the bar above.

It was far better off than its basement. The entire room was dark, with only the neon lights and a few dim overhead lights to brighten the space. There was a stage with a few poles, a DJ booth, and tables toward the back of the room, while the front was left for the actual bar and booths. It was cozy and in a part of the city that would accrue a lot of wealthy clients who would want a night to blow off some steam.

Ryder's men had taken care of it well and when I peeked at the last few months' financial records, I was also pleasantly surprised to find that it was clean and steadily growing its revenue.

Too bad the owner would never be seen again.

There was a lone bartender at the counter, pouring my client a glass of whiskey. The man sitting at the barstool sent me a smile when he noticed me. I returned it even as his bodyguard was standing mere feet away, armed, and glaring at me.

"Anton," I greeted and moved to sit by him, making sure to keep a seat between us. "It is nice to see you."

"And you as well, Ax," he said, his voice thick with a Russian accent. His hair was almost all gray, save for a few sprinkles of dark strands. His icy-blue eyes were sharp and there was an air about him that put me on edge.

I met Anton when I was working at the restaurant as a server, the same one Yvon had been at previously as well. He had been a powerful man back then, and I had seen him put more than a few people in their place for talking back to him.

If anything, he had only grown in power since then. But unlike people like Ryder, Anton liked to stay in the dark and had... higher standards than most.

Which is why I brought him to this club.

The bartender gave me a whiskey as well, but I waved him off.

"It's clean," I told him. "No washing. No drugs. The clientele is legit, and business is booming."

He nodded, his eyes transfixed on the swirling amber liquid in his glass as he tilted it.

"I have my doubts, you know," he said, still not looking at me. "After all, not only were you just jailed for the very crimes you stated did not happen here, but you have lost a considerable amount of trust from your clientele. Please, tell me this isn't a last-ditch effort to save yourself, is it?"

When his eyes met mine, my heart all but stopped in my chest.

"I don't plan to do this for free," I answered honestly. "And yes, it would help to continue doing business with you and your resources, but this is not to save me or my reputation. I am doing that on my own."

"And the money?" he asked.

I swallowed thickly.

"I am not doing this for the money," I said.

He clicked his tongue.

"I feel that's a lie," he said. His bodyguard shifted, and my hand twitched, wanting to grasp the gun I kept tucked into my pants.

"I will make money if this works," I said. "But I don't want money from you."

He made a noise and threw back his whiskey before slamming it on the table.

"You want clients," he said.

"Yes," I answered. "I want to use this club to funnel clients into my other businesses, but this club is all yours. I don't want any of the profits, nor do I expect you to refer me to your other contacts. All I want are the clients."

He hummed and stood.

"You really want that club of yours to work, hmm?" he asked. "What was it? A lesbian sex dungeon?"

A smile pulled at my lips as I stood as well.

"All women," I corrected. "Though we allow genderqueer, nonbinary, and transgender clients in as well."

He let out a light laugh.

"Pity there is nothing for the male clients," he said.

"There are already many clubs like that for men," I said. "It's time to break out a little."

Anton fixed his suit jacket before sending me a smile.

"You know, if you had never worked for me as a little runt, there would be no way I would take this club from you," he said.

An unnamed emotion clawed at my throat. Maybe not directly, but I would run for him on occasion and whenever he had come into the shop, I would be his main hand. Without him, I wouldn't be where I was today.

"I never worked for you," I said in a weak voice.

He shook his head.

"I wonder what other lies you tell yourself," he said and turned to leave.

*Too fucking many.*

"Damn, it feels good to be back," Sloan said as she sat down in the love seat next to me. "These rooms are nice."

I made a noise of agreement as I sank farther into my chair and took a sip of the old-fashioned in my hand. The bitterness of the alcohol grounded me, and the flush of warmth that spread throughout my body was a welcome distraction.

The rooms in question were the newest addition to the house. It had taken some work, but I had already sketched the whole thing out a month before I was due to be released and started construction right when I got out. The back of the house that had already been gutted for a stage show left enough room for a crowd to join and people to sit in the audience, but it was missing something.

I wanted a private place where people could have a good view but also have enough room to act out whatever fantasies that pleased them. These rooms were easy enough to construct. We had made the stage room smaller by a quarter, still letting people sit in the seats but only left a few places for people to stand on watch.

We erected black glass one-way mirrors that were divided into four separate rooms, all with an elevated height so that the people in them could see the ongoings of the show. Each room was fitted with something different. The smallest one, the one we were in now, was just a view room with a few seats, a table, and not much else.

The others had beds, some just a chassis, but it was enough to enjoy the room without feeling too squished.

The mirrors were a hit with the performers because now they had a full unobstructed view of themselves as they were fucked.

"I took the inspiration from one of Jenny's clubs," I said. "Though they had much more space than we did and a lot fewer mirrors."

Sloan made a noise and sipped on her drink. I think it was a glass of champagne, though I couldn't be sure. I had kept my eyes on the performers.

Blake had returned, much to my surprise and delight. She was currently being tied up. It was an erotic display, though this one was much more gentle than her last ones had been. It made me wonder what had changed.

"Membership is up almost twenty percent with the recent changes," she said. "They like the mirrors, and the outdoor addition is nice. Though they are asking for more locations, I was thinking about other ways to get clients."

I let out a sigh.

"I am not sure we will be able to expand," I said and lifted my ankle. The heavy bracelet sat on it, a green light flickering on and off every few seconds. "They got me this morning."

Sloan let out a laugh.

"How'd you get them to hold off for so long?" she asked. "You should have just gotten it over with like I did."

"You had thirty days, Sloan," I grumbled. "They gave me three months."

There was a silence that passed between us as the show on stage got more intense. I knew the words that Sloan wanted to say, she had been trying to get them out since we had shared a cell together. Though she had gotten a lot less time than I had, so I didn't have to hear her lecturing for the majority of the time I was imprisoned.

"Nyx opened—"

"I don't want to talk about it," I said quickly, cutting her off.

I knew about the company. I knew fucking everything about Nyx, whether I wanted to or not. My obsession with her got worse as I rotted in prison.

I had some of my men on the outside following her and reporting back on every move she had made. My heart swelled when I heard about her company. She had been working tirelessly for years. The reports had said that on most nights, she would be up until one or two in the morning just working nonstop.

I rejoiced seeing her live the life she had always wanted.

A part of me felt hurt and maybe even a bit envious... but I refused to cross the line again.

Watching her like this was my own form of punishment. One that I would take readily. I had fucked up, bad. Not just with her but with Asher as well. I didn't deserve her, and it would have been selfish of me to even try.

Sloan let out a sigh and stood.

"You know, I wanted to come here and have a good time—"

"You *can,* Sloan," I said. "I just don't want to—"

"Face reality," she said and threw her hands in the air with a loud groan. "Fine. If you don't want to talk about Nyx, then how about Asher?"

"There is nothing wrong with Asher and me—"

"Except that you cut him out of literally every business deal," she said. "He had to run Ryder's territory when you were gone and now that you are back, you just pushed him out of it—"

"He was horrible at it," I defended. "He was losing us money."

"You know that's a damn lie," she hissed. "He may not have been the best, but without him, you wouldn't have had anything when you came back."

"It's better this way," I said. "He can focus on his relationship—"

Sloan let out a loud groan.

"Then what about you? Are you eating? Sleeping? The bags under your eyes are so dark I thought your mascara had smudged, Ax," she said, her tone had turned pleading.

"I don't wear mascara," I grumbled under my breath and took a sip of my drink, only for it to be smacked out of my hand and sent crashing to the floor.

"I am *tired* of you acting this way," Sloan said and stalked over to me. She gripped the sides of my chair and leaned forward, invading my space. "You went to jail for *years,* Ax. This should be the time that you are trying to build the perfect life for yourself. When will you stop lying to yourself?"

Anger coursed through me, and I stood up, pushing Sloan back.

"Everyone is accusing me of *lying,* but I have been nothing but truthful since I got out," I growled. "I am trying my *best* to create a life for myself and my family. Just because I don't want to sit here and talk about the past and idiotic things, like my eating and sleeping habits, doesn't mean that I am lying about anything. When will you get off my back?"

Sloan looked at me with a mixture of pity and anger before shaking her head.

"I am trying to help you as a friend, Ax."

"I don't need it, and I don't need you," I growled.

Hurt twisted her face, and I regretted my words almost instantly.

"I will pretend I didn't hear that," she said with a sigh and turned to leave. "I'll see you on Monday."

# Nyx

This time, when I stepped out of the taxi in front of Club Pétale, I was already wearing my mask.

It was warmer this time of year, but there was still a small chill in the wind that caused me to shiver and regret not bringing a jacket for the *second* time.

I thought it would be fitting to wear the same dress as *that* night, but I had decided on something a bit different this time around. I wore the same mask as last time, complete with a sparkly sapphire in the middle of my forehead, but that was the only thing that was the same.

This time, the tips of my hair had been dyed a deep blue to match my dress. It was a two-piece dark-blue set that shined in the light. The top was thin straps with a deep neck that showed off my cleavage. The skirt was barely midthigh and was held together by a loose strap around my waist.

I clutched my phone for dear life and shifted on my aching feet. The heels were a far cry from what I usually wore. But they were perfect for the occasion.

After three weeks of indecision, two missed calls from Asher and two hour-long conversations with Sloan… I had decided that I needed to face Ax.

It would have been a lie if I said that I was here solely for my own closure. Jonson had officially kicked me out of witness protection, as the threat against my life was deemed "not severe enough for the government to step in."

I wondered if he had done it for Ax or for me, or maybe we had just covered our tracks for long enough so that everyone had forgotten what happened here.

I was worried about Ax.

I hated to admit it, but I was. I had spent night after night awake with my phone in my hand, looking for whatever info I could find on her.

And so I found myself here, staring at the house that looked so innocent in comparison to what had happened inside.

The grass under my feet was neatly trimmed and held no indication that it had been torn up by the police cars that ran through the yard. The porch was empty save for the two bodyguards by the doors, looking nothing like it did during the sentencing, where boxes upon boxes of evidence had been gathered.

It looked like the time I had spent here all those years ago was nothing but a dream. Like that *too* had been forgotten.

*Just like me.*

I took a deep breath and walked up the winding walkway and stopped at the stairs to smile at the men that waited for me. They opened the door for me without a word.

The inside was so similar to four years ago that it gave me whiplash.

I stepped in, taking in the number of people that were gathering behind the doors. It was at least twice what I had seen on a busy night at the club. People were chatting excitedly and partaking in various lewd activities that made heat stir inside me.

*You are not here for that,* I chided myself. But I couldn't help it when my eyes lingered on a pair of women on the couch just beyond the foyer. The one on the bottom was splayed out, her gasps and moans mixing in with the dull thrum of music throughout the house. The one on top was ramming into her with a strap-on that looked far larger than any I had ever tried and held a vibrator to her clit.

Memories of my time with Ax and Sloan on the office desk filled my mind, and I felt my face heat.

My gaze was interrupted by a young woman stepping out in front of me. She didn't wear a mask, but the rest of her body was covered in a sheer type of bodysuit that left little to the imagination.

"Nyx, right?" she asked and looked down at her iPad. "Sloan said to be expecting you. Do you need a tour?"

I swallowed thickly. A flurry of emotions had begun to unravel inside me, and I didn't know how much I would be able to handle tonight. Especially if I was treated like a stranger.

It had hurt so badly to hear Ax discard me like she had in the warehouse with Ryder. A part of me knew that it was what had to happen... but having *those* as her last words to me left a scar on me, no matter what Asher had tried to convince me was said afterward.

"I do not need a tour," I said with a forced smile. "And please don't signal her that I am here yet. I would like to look around before then."

Her face twisted, showing just how much she disliked the idea of lying to Sloan.

I gave her another small smile.

"Just a five-minute head start?" I asked.

She looked around before she motioned me in.

"Five minutes," she agreed.

I let out a sigh of relief.

"Just enough time to get a drink," I said with a smile and hurried past her.

My first stop was to the kitchen to act on my promise. I had to pass room after room of activities that I would have rather watched, but the thought of facing Ax stone-cold sober scared me shitless.

The kitchen was a thrum of activity, but I pushed past the

people and beelined to the bartender that was on duty that night. The kitchen was industrial-like and was used before opening to make a variety of snacks and finger foods, but my favorite part was when the extra-long metal table used for prepping food was made into a bar.

"Two shots of vodka and a Long Island, please." I placed my order with the woman behind the bar.

She gave me a look but placed two shots in front of me anyway and filled them with vodka.

"This isn't a place where you can get sloppy," she said in warning, though she didn't stop making exactly what I had ordered.

"I know," I said. "I used to work here."

She paused before setting the drink in front of me and nodding.

"Well, good luck with whatever you have to face out there," she said. "Make good decisions."

"Always," I said and turned straight back the way I came.

It took me longer than usual to make my way to the stage. I had gotten distracted multiple times on my way over. I had forgotten just how it felt to be in Club Pétale.

The sights, the sounds, it was like I had never left. I lost myself in watching people enjoy themselves and felt a familiar ache between my legs not long after. I had ditched my Long Island, feeling buzzed already, but not just from the alcohol.

I hadn't joined the BDSM club scene in Portland, I didn't have the time. Even coming back to New York for these next few days would be a hit to my busy schedule. But that didn't mean that I hadn't *missed* this place.

Before the incident, I had been yearning for something more. A place where I could have fun and be accepted. This was that place for me, or at least it had been.

Being around the people here just reminded me how much I had missed out on in the years I had been gone... but there was still something off about the entire thing.

It wasn't the place or the people, but more like I had been

expecting something—*or someone*—to fill the hole that this place had left behind.

Tonight was a dominatrix special, though I paid no attention to the couple on stage even though I recognized the sub as Blake. I was too entranced by the floor-to-ceiling mirrors that had taken over the back wall.

Just as I was about to pull my gaze away, a portion of the mirror swung out, showing Sloan.

My mouth dropped when I saw her, not expecting the mirror to open like it had. When her eyes scanned the crowd and finally landed on me, my throat constricted.

She was frozen as I began to push through the crowd to her. When I reached her, her arms were already out for me. She pulled me into a hug, one arm around my back, the other pushing my head into her chest.

"I'm sorry I didn't make it out to the hospital," she said above me. "I've missed you, Nyx. I can't thank you enough—"

I shook my head and held her tighter.

"You were in jail, stupid," I said with a laugh, though my eyes were already beginning to sting with unshed tears.

She placed a soft kiss on the top of my head.

"That's no excuse," she said and then slowly pushed me away.

I couldn't help but smile as I took her in. She hadn't worn a mask. There was a new eyebrow piercing above her right eye, and her silver hair had grown out to show dark roots.

"I kept it," I whispered to her in a devious tone.

She gave me a forced smile before looking back into the room she came from.

"We can talk about that later," she said and pushed me into the room behind her. "I am sorry, and thank you in advance."

She shut the door behind her, and I watched through the one-way mirror as she held the door closed. Even through the pane of glass, she gave me a stern look.

I was about to try and open the door when a noise from behind me startled me.

I turned to see the ghost of my nightmares dressed in a loose button-down and black slacks. Her hair fell limp around her face and her honey eyes had deep-set dark circles under them. Normally I would have begun to drool when I saw her open shirt and rolled-up sleeves combo, but the change in her stature had caused my heart to twist.

She had lost weight, just like Asher had warned. But there was an air about her, one that I distinctly remember from when we had first met.

She seemed to have sunken into herself. Her eyes no longer had the gleam that they once did. Before, when she walked into a room, your eyes would be drawn to her, but her whole aura screamed, "back off."

This wasn't the Ax I knew. This one was in pain.

"Ax," I breathed and clenched my chest.

"You shouldn't be here," she growled and stared at the floor. Only now did I realize that there was broken glass on the ground and the sound that had called me to her presence was the act of her stepping on it.

The room was small, only fitting a few chairs, and it caused the tension to spike.

"I am a patron," I said. Though I wanted to say much more.

She straightened and rolled her neck.

"Then I will let you be," she said and brushed past me.

I reached out to grab her wrist, but she jerked away and turned to glare at me.

"Don't," she growled with the same tone she did *that* night.

I was too stunned to chase after her, and Sloan was no match as she pushed open the door and stalked out of the room. The two of us were stuck there, staring at each other with varying levels of shock written across our faces.

"It's worse than I thought," I admitted after I had some time to digest.

"I told you," Sloan said with a sigh. "I don't know what to do. You were my last idea."

I swallowed thickly.

"Three days," I said and gave her a look. "I leave on Monday morning, a red-eye."

Sloan nodded and motioned for me to leave.

"We have some planning to do."

I shifted on the soft covers of the somewhat familiar bed underneath me.

It was Sloan's idea to sneak into Ax's room while she was distracted by the club for the night. After last night, I was hesitant to ever show my face in front of Ax again... but the way she had caved in on herself had caused my heart to break.

I had spent the day preparing for this. Rehearsing what I wanted to say, but now that I was sitting on her bed, with her due to come up any moment, the nerves started to consume me.

I doubted if this was the right way to do this. I thought of my home, my cat, my job. I had left that, at least temporarily, to try and get Ax to talk to me.

And who's to say this would be the end of it all?

What if she wasn't willing to listen? What then?

I had an entire life across the country. This place had forgotten about me, but as much as I tried, I couldn't forget about it. This place had changed me, and I prayed it was for the better.

With that thought, I took a deep breath and sat up straight, my eyes focused on the door.

It was another thirty minutes before Ax stumbled in.

She didn't even see me at first. She headed straight for the bathroom. I waited with bated breath as she showered and when she opened the door again, light splashing into my eyes, I let out a small gasp.

She definitely saw me then. Her eyes had narrowed right on

me. And worst of all, she wasn't even wearing her towel. It was being used to dry her hair.

"You are trespassing," she said in a cold tone. Her eyes never left mine as she continued to dry her hair. I tried to keep my gaze on hers, but when I caught a stray water droplet, I couldn't help but follow it.

I had never seen her fully naked. All of her tattoos were showing, and the light from the bathroom behind her had cast a glow onto her skin. My mouth was watering by the time the water droplet had reached her navel. I had to press my thighs together when I caught a glimpse of the soft brown curls between her legs.

"I wanted to talk," I said, though my voice came out husky and it was obvious that I wanted to do much more than talk.

It was easy to forget all about the outside world with Ax. That was how it always had been. I could fall into her easily and it became harder and harder to pull myself away from the thoughts of her the longer I was in her presence.

Day one, I was already a wreck after seeing her. Images and old wounds were slashed open, and I was forced to relive every little painful thing that had happened between us.

Day two was a different story. I saw different images when I woke and when I got ready for tonight. I was wearing nothing but a dark-green slip and images of her mouth trailing my skin easily came to mind. Those thoughts began to overpower the important ones.

"I told you—"

"I'm sorry," I blurted out.

Her eyes widened before they looked at the ground.

"I am sorry for not coming sooner," I said. "I am sorry for not visiting you in prison. I am so—"

"You were in witness protection," she muttered. "You wouldn't have been able to anyway."

A smile played on my lips.

"Thank you for that, by the way," I said. "Jonson told me."

She shook her head.

"Why are you here, Nyx?" she asked and walked to her dresser, ignoring me completely.

"I was worried about you," I admitted. "I had plans, you know. To yell at you. Hit you. I was so mad that you got me into that shit, then *abandoned* me... but when I saw you yesterday—" I had to clear the lump in my throat to continue. "But when I saw you yesterday, I realized that I should have been more considerate of your feelings."

She rounded on me so fast I didn't even have time to blink before she pushed me to the bed. Droplets of water fell onto my face as she leaned over me. Her eyes were narrowed and her jaw tight.

"Just because a few years have passed doesn't mean that you are safe here," she spat. "*Nothing* has changed since then. You come here because you see a pitiful puppy that you want to take in. Maybe try and turn their fucked-up life upside down, but I am here to tell you I am *not* a project. I am exactly the person you thought I was and if you knew what was good for you, you would turn back to Portland and get on with your life."

Her words stuck me straight in the chest, but I forced a smirk on my face.

"So you *have* been paying attention," I teased.

Her hand fastened around my throat, and she got so close to my face that her hot breath wafted across my lips. I licked my lips and shifted so that my legs were spread wider for her.

"Ask me how many people I have killed with this hand since I have been out," she demanded.

A shiver ran through me.

"I don't care about that," I said. "All I care about is that you are healthy and happ—"

"Stop it," she commanded. "You did not come here because you were concerned for me."

Her hand tightened on my neck, making it harder to breathe.

"Then tell me," I said, dropping my voice to a whisper. "Why did I come here?"

The tension between us was electrifying and grew tenfold when her eyes trailed down my face. Her free hand brushed so lightly against the outside of my thigh, I almost didn't catch it.

"You came here because you're a needy *whore* that was just looking to get fucked," she said. "You probably haven't been able to make yourself come as hard as I could in the last four years, so as soon as you heard that I was out, you came here to spread your legs for me."

Her hands trailed from my outer thighs to my inner. My heart pounded in my chest and the lack of oxygen was causing my head to swim. Desire built up inside me and the heat that started as a low fire was now roaring inside me. Her touch had caused shivers to run through me, and my pussy was positively aching at the promise of her hand between my legs once more.

"I'm your *needy* whore," I whispered.

Her eyes snapped back to me, and rage contorted her face. She let go of my neck to grab a handful of my hair and pull it back.

"You don't want to test me right now, Nyx," she said. "You think you saw my worst? You haven't even scratched the surface. I am not the person you once knew."

I let out a whimper as her hand teased my wet folds.

"Are you going to talk all night, or are you going to fuck me?" I growled.

My words snapped something in her, and her lips crashed to mine in a bruising kiss.

This wasn't like before. She was right. This time it was desperate, if not a bit feral. Our tongues fought for dominance and our teeth clashed together more than once. She pulled away to bite down hard on my lip, pulling a pained moan from me.

"You're so fucking wet already," she growled against my throat and bit into my neck.

I cried out again and arched into her. Her hand was running through my folds, but it wasn't enough to relieve the throbbing ache. I spread my legs farther for her and bucked my hips to meet her hand, but she refused to take it any further.

"Fuck, Ax," I cried as she brushed across my clit. She delivered a stinging slap to my pussy in combination with a bite right on my nipple, not bothering to take off my slip.

"Have you forgotten?" she asked.

"No, sir—"

I let out another whine when she slapped my wet pussy again. This time, I jerked as a burst of pleasure ran through me. She had aimed for my clit that time.

"Please, please, *daddy*," I gasped out as she delivered bite after bite to my neck and chest while massaging my folds. She was purposefully harsh and had given zero attention to my clit except when she slapped it.

"Please what?" she asked and circled her thumb over my clit while teasingly pushing two fingers against my entrance.

"Please fuck me, *daddy*," I begged. My cries paused as she slowly pushed two fingers into me and began to circle my clit in earnest.

"God, I fucking love it when you call me that," she moaned before placing her arm on the left side of my head and leaning over me. The pounding of her fingers into me was just as harsh as her slaps had been and caused me to have to remain as still as possible in hopes of avoiding an accident. My legs had stiffened and moans came out grumbled as each timed thrust caused me to choke on my own cries.

"Again," she commanded.

Her demands, on top of her ruthlessness, had me barreling toward an orgasm so fast that I couldn't answer her. All the tension from the last four years seemed to build and build until, *finally,* I was coming on her fingers. My pussy convulsed violently and I couldn't hold back my sobs as I came.

"Fuck, *fuck, fuck,*" I moaned in time with her thrusts. I tried to reach up to her and pull her mouth to mine, but she stayed above me, continuing to circle my clit as she helped me ride out my orgasm.

"Say it again," she growled. "Whose whore are you?"

"Yours, *daddy*," I cried and was rewarded with a light kiss to my lips.

"And whose pussy is this?" she asked, circling her fingers inside me.

"*Yours, daddy*—oh god—" My cries were cut off by a second orgasm. I had no warning this time as it exploded inside me.

"That's right," Ax cooed. "Fuck, I missed this. You're so fucking beautiful, Nyx. I dreamed about this moment. About you. Fuck, I can't believe you're here with me."

Before I could speak, she flipped us on the bed so that I was straddling her. I placed my hand on either side of her head and rolled my hips into her hands.

"That's right, baby," she moaned, her eyes drilling into mine. "Ride my hand. Show me how much you missed me taking care of this needy cunt."

Her words alone were enough to spur another orgasm, but I worked toward it like I meant it. I ground on her hand, bursts of pleasure coursing through me each time her hand brushed across my clit.

When I met her eyes again, I was brought back to the time in the limo. We were in a similar position, and the look in her eyes... it was nothing like it was now.

Back then, it was cold, guarded. *That* Ax wanted nothing to do with me.

But this one... her eyes were light with an emotion that made my throat clog. *This* was the Ax that I had been missing. *This* was the person that made me feel the security of a warm blanket on a cold night. She was the one I had asked for more that night.

And *she* was the one I came for tonight.

Tears leaked from my eyes and fell onto her. She lunged forward, taking my mouth with hers. I kissed her back as I fucked her hand.

"I missed you," I whispered against her lips.

She grabbed my hips with her free hand, stopping my movement before taking over for me completely.

"I missed you too, kitten," she said. Just as my next orgasm came coursing through me, she leaned back to look at me as I came undone. Her expression was hungry and only heightened the exoticness of it all.

"I'm sorry," I cried as I came down from my orgasm.

She shook her head and flipped us again on the bed before littering kisses on my swollen and bruised skin.

"I'm the one that's sorry," she said against my skin. "Please forgive me. I never meant to bring you into any of this."

She yanked down my dress and latched on to my nipple. I cried out as she began sucking hard on the sensitive nub.

"It was my choice," I said with a moan. "I knew who you were—"

I was cut off by her trailing kisses down my stomach and landing between my legs.

"No matter what you say," she said and leaned forward to place a light kiss on my swollen clit. "I will spend the rest of my existence apologizing. Starting with feasting on this cunt like it deserves."

I cried out when she latched on to my clit and sucked it into her mouth.

My legs were already trembling, but her action had caused them to start to shake violently. I had long since lost control of my body and reactions, but that sinfully talented mouth on my pussy pushed me further into the warm pool of pleasure she was creating for me.

"Please," I cried. "Please, no more."

She pulled back and slapped my pussy before kissing away the sharp burst of pain it left.

"You're done when I say you are," she growled. "Do you understand?"

I nodded and was punished with another slap.

"Say it."

"Yes, *daddy.*"

# EPILOGUE

## TWO YEARS LATER

"Hurry," I whispered as Ax pushed me against the wall of our mudroom.

The air in the cramped space had turned hot as we collided. Sounds of light music and guests were muffled just beyond the walls, causing an excited tremor to shoot up my spine.

"This dress has so many goddamn layers," she growled as she grabbed hold of the hem of my underskirt and forced it up to my waist. She let out a sharp exhale as my bare ass was exposed.

I squirmed as the toy inside me continued to vibrate, sending shocks of pleasure coursing through me.

"Don't mess up my hair," I ordered.

"Hold the dress," she commanded and dropped to her knees. I obeyed and let out a gasp when her hot tongue licked my inner thigh and her teeth grabbed hold of the lace garter.

"That's for later," I hissed.

She let out a chuckle before her hands found my hips and pulled me back to her. I tried to swallow my moan as she attacked my clit. The toy was still vibrating inside me, and I was so close to an orgasm I was about to lose my mind.

"Count them for me, baby," she reminded, her words muffled by my folds.

I let out a cry as heat unfurled in my belly and my pussy squeezed around the toy.

"Five," I choked out. "Please take out the toy. I don't know how much I can take. Especially when they are watching."

By *they,* I meant the over one hundred wedding guests we had invited to our ceremony. It had been hard enough to get away with this little game while Ax had been brutally teasing me since the ceremony, but now that the reception had started and people were busy drinking and music was playing, she had taken it up a notch.

I had barely gotten her to this room before I came again. And thank god I did because this one had been so powerful that there was no way I would have been able to keep in my noises.

A lot of the people we had invited were a part of the club or had at least visited so it wouldn't have been as embarrassing in front of them, but there was also family here and there was no way I was going to let Ax make me come in front of my *mother.*

I was surprised she had even shown up. After the news of my engagement to a *woman* older than myself, she had kind of freaked. With our background, I wasn't surprised that it had affected her in some way. After all, I had been the same once upon a time.

It had taken over a year for her to talk to me again, and each time she had to remind me just how wrong she thought this marriage would be. It *almost* made me lose hope for our relationship, but she showed up anyway and I was grateful.

Ax stood and helped me fix my dress before turning me and delivering a bruising kiss to my mouth. When she pulled away, I was still panting and still coming off the high of my orgasm.

She gave me a wicked smile. Her hair, which had been slicked back, now had a few strands in her face, and her cheeks were flushed. She was panting just as I was, and a light sheen of sweat was covering her face. Her tux was slightly askew but thankfully, there were no makeup stains.

She took out her phone with smooth movements and turned

off the vibrator, allowing me to relax against her. Her musky cologne invaded my scent and caused a comforting warmth to spread through me.

"Keep it on," she said. "I have some plans for later."

The dark tone in her voice caused excited shivers to shoot up my spine.

There was a knock on the pool house door and not a second later, a silver-haired, grinning Sloan peeked her head in.

"Are you done?" she asked. "People have already begun to notice, and I have been waiting impatiently for a dance with the bride."

"Which one?" I asked with a laugh and pulled Ax out of the pool house.

"Obviously, the pretty one in the white dress," she said and took my hand as soon as I got close enough, stealing me away from Ax.

I gave Ax a look full of mock pity and let Sloan pull me to the dance floor.

"Your sister has been asking for you!" Sloan yelled back.

Ax shook her head and searched the crowd only to be whisked away by said sister mere moments later. She gave me a wink as she pulled Ax to the dance floor.

I sighed and leaned into Sloan as she led us through a slow dance, enjoying the fresh air and the light scent of apple blossoms. The air had a slight chill to it as the evening winded down, and I used it as an excuse to cuddle into Sloan.

Just like we dreamed, we were finally having our own wedding in the backyard of the house that started it all. The fresh doors to the house were open, allowing people to come and go as they pleased. Food had been served, and we had a full-function bar that had taken over our kitchen.

The dance floor had been polished, the grass had been trimmed, chairs set, and white blossoms fell around us during and after the ceremony. It had been the most perfect and awe-inspiring wedding I could have ever dreamed of.

"I'm happy for you, Nyx," Sloan said against my hair. Her hand came up to clasp my left hand, her thumb brushing against the gold and sapphire ring Ax had used to propose. "And I don't know how to thank you enough for taking care of her."

I let out a small laugh and shook my head. I leaned back to peer up at her and couldn't help but smile.

Sloan, even after everything, had been integral to our life and the club's business. I couldn't have imagined the last few years without her, and for once, I knew that we had truly found a friend that would be there with us until the end.

"She's the one taking care of me," I said and looked over to Ax, who was in deep conversation with her sister. By the twisted look on her face, I had a sneaking suspicion that the conversation wasn't going well.

"If you say so," she said and motioned for Ax to come over. "I'll stop hogging you now and try to find someone else to pester. Maybe I'll steal Wendy from Asher."

I followed Sloan's line of sight to Asher, his girlfriend, and his newest baby still at the tables, eating and chatting happily. Wendy was just over a year old and had curly brownish-red hair and green eyes that matched her mother's, she was the life of the party.

Next to them was a cheerful Mrs. Pruitt. She had been just as enamored with Wendy as everyone else, so much so that she had resigned herself to sitting by Asher. Even after all these years, she still hated him.

Her laughs and jabs could be heard across the dance floor, and it caused my chest to warm.

"I didn't know you even liked kids," I teased.

"Of course I do," she said, then her face twisted. "Though I am not sure about having any of my own someday."

I patted her on the back.

"You need a girlfriend before that can happen," I said.

She rolled her eyes.

"That's very old-timey thinking, Nyx," she teased. "Now go. Ax is glaring at me."

I sent her a smile and crossed the floor to Ax, who was waiting for me with her hand out. Her sister had left off to the side and sent me a wink before turning back to the rest of the party, no doubt trying to find one of her children to pester.

She had been the least surprised of the family and cited that she always knew this would happen. She had also been our strongest advocate. Besides Asher and Sloan, that was. I never thought that I would have been able to stand near Asher and not want to throttle him, but he had made some big changes in his life.

Ax watched me with a heated gaze and flexed her fingers. Her gaze told me she'd better not be kept waiting.

As soon as my fingers intertwined with hers, sirens echoed through the air.

My heart dropped, and I looked to Ax for an answer, but she merely shook her head.

Mere minutes later, uniformed men were walking into our backyard. Ax pushed me behind her and began to walk toward the officers, but they pushed past her and went straight to Sloan.

The whole party had crashed to a halt and everyone turned to watch as they trampled through the area. Their black uniforms stood out like a beacon against the dance floor and white flowers.

My mother was the first to catch my eyes. She was standing in the far corner with her date. Her black hair pulled up into a ponytail and her brown eyes widened. She had gone pale as a ghost.

I motioned for her to calm and did to a few others as well. We watched in silence as they approached.

"Goddammit," Sloan groaned. "Really, guys, at a wedding? You couldn't have waited until after?"

A few cops made some noises, and the one in front smiled down at Sloan. His grin was one full of ill intent.

"Hands behind your back, you know the drill," the cop in charge said. I squinted and realized that I had seen him before.

I sent Ax a look.

"He's on the payroll," I whispered.

Her face was hard as she watched them cuff Sloan.

"I can't do anything here," she whispered back. "People are watching."

Unease unfurled inside me, and I reached out for Sloan as she passed with the officers on either side of her, but Ax pulled me back.

"Sorry to ruin your wedding," Sloan said with a sheepish smile. "I'll make it up to you!"

"Give me some time," Ax said, but Sloan was already being taken back inside the house. I was stuck trying to figure out what the hell just happened as whispers erupted.

I cleared my throat, forced a smile on my face, and clapped my hands together to get everyone's attention.

"Alright!" I yelled. "Party's not over. Eat, relax, enjoy! This is the norm for her."

There were a few laughs here and there, and just as quickly as the party stopped, it started again. The music was bumped up, and a handful of people dove back into the kitchen to get a drink refill.

I let out a sigh and looked toward Ax.

"This is something that's going to happen for the rest of our lives, huh?" I asked. "Do we even know what she got arrested for this time?"

She shook her head and leaned down to place a chaste kiss on my lips.

"No clue, but as long as Sloan is single and without a care, we can expect to be visited by the cops often," she said, a hint of amusement in her tone. "Are you ready to sneak away, love?"

I let out a light laugh.

"What about Sloan?" I asked.

"She can handle herself for a moment," she said. "It'll give her time to think about what she has done."

I shook my head.

"You cruel, *cruel* woman," I teased and pulled her closer.

"But never to you," she said.

"I love you," I said against her lips.

She smiled.

"I love you too, Nyx."

**THE END**

**Sloan's love story is coming next...**

I am a professional liar.

But not because I like to lie... because people **don't like the truth.**

I did what I had to survive, but I made a promise once.

There was a single person on this earth that I could never lie to.

***My step sister, Lillian.***

The problem is that along the way I begun to lie to myself. I'm a good person. I am happy with my life.

And lastly... I am ***not*** in love with Lilian. It has been nine years since I last saw her and twelve since I confessed my love.

***This time will she finally believe me?***

**Preorder here:** Don't Leave Me

# If you liked this, please review!

Reviews really help indie authors get their books out there so, please make sure to share your thoughts!

# Want more smutty books?

Check out my pen name Elle Mae, for more paranormal spicy wlw books!

You can find me on instagram, Facebook, and tiktok @ellemaebooks

Check out my newest release here! Or search Contract Bound by Elle Mae!

You may also find free shorts and ebooks on my Patreon: ellemaebooks

# Acknowledgments

Thank you to everyone who has found my books! Without your I would not be able to continue publishing as I have been!

Also to my writer friends who kept encouraging me through it all, thank you!

# About the Author

Eden Emory is a contemporary spicy pen name for Elle Mae. This pen name will mostly focus on spicy dark wlw romance that pushes the boundaries and incorporates troupes normally seen in f/m romance.

Eden Emory was born out of a want for more. More spice, more wlw, and even more smutty vibes with little to no plot.

Loved this book? Please leave a review!

For more behind the scene content, sign up for my newsletter at https://view.flodesk.com/pages/61722d0874d564fa09f4021b